BLACK LIGHT EXPRESS

★ "Hop aboard and prepare for the ride of your life."
—*Kirkus Reviews*, starred review

★ "As the narrative unfurls, the tangle of truth about the origin and control of the rails and K-gates is just as exciting as the hunt itself."
—*School Library Journal*, starred review

PRAISE FOR RAILHEAD

★ "Reeve has crafted something at once weirdly familiar and marvelously original. Thank the stars there's at least one sequel planned already."
—*Kirkus Reviews*, starred review

★ "This thrilling and imaginative escapade will captivate the Carnegie Medal–winner's many fans."
—*Publishers Weekly*, starred review

★ "With adept and thoughtful hands, Reeve constructs a big, sprawling, and thrilling universe . . . Sci-fi fans will delight in this lightning-paced and satisfying read."
—*School Library Journal*, starred review

"Reeve (*Fever Crumb*, 2010) carefully builds his world, balancing the plot's action with politics, history, and inventive technologies . . ."
—*Booklist*

"[*Railhead*] rattles along like an interstellar express, leaving you eager for the next thrilling ride."
—*The Guardian*

Black Light Express is published in the United States
by Switch Press
a Capstone imprint
1710 Roe Crest Drive
North Mankato, Minnesota 56003
www.switchpress.com

"Black Light Express" was originally published in English in 2016.
This edition is published by arrangement with Oxford University Press.

Library of Congress Cataloging-in-Publication Data is available on
the Library of Congress website.

ISBN: 978-1-63079-096-7 (hardcover)
ISBN: 978-1-63079-097-4 (paperback)

Book design by Kay Fraser

Image Credits:
Shutterstock: Guliveris, NASA images, warin keawchookul

For my excellent friend Sarah McIntyre

Printed in the United States of America.
000367

BLACK LIGHT EXPRESS

PHILIP REEVE

SWITCH
PRESS
a capstone imprint

PART ONE
WEB OF WORLDS

Trainsong and engine-roar rolled ahead of it along the tunnel. In the first carriage a lean, brown boy named Zen Starling and a girl named Nova, who wasn't really a girl at all, pressed their faces to the windows.

At first they saw only the seared, glassy rock of the tunnel walls rushing past. Then they shot out of the tunnel mouth; the walls were gone and the train was running across an open plain. Looming shapes flashed by, weird hammerhead things rearing up on either side of the train, scaring even Nova until she realized they were only rocks. Wide lagoons like fallen mirrors reflected a dusty blue sky, several suns, and a lot of daytime stars.

This was not the first time Zen and Nova had ridden a train from one world to another. They came from the Network Empire, whose stations were scattered across half the galaxy, linked by K-gates through which trains sped from one planet to the next in a heartbeat. But the gate through which they had just passed was a new one; it was not supposed to exist at all, and they had come through it not knowing where it led.

"A new world," said Nova. "A new planet, under a new sun. A place that no one but us has ever seen . . ."

"But there's nothing here!" said Zen, half disappointed, half relieved. He was not sure what he had expected. Mystic cities? Towers of light? A million Station Angels doing dances of welcome? There were just lagoons, and low islands of grass and reddish rock, and here or there a cluster of pale flaglike things standing in the shallows.

The train spoke. The old red loco *Damask Rose* had a mind of her own, like all the locos of the Network Empire. "The air is breathable," she said. "No communications that I can detect— I'm getting no messages from signaling systems or rail traffic control . . ."

Nova was a Motorik: a humanoid machine. She scanned the wavelengths with her wireless mind, looking for this world's Datasea. There was nothing. Just static rolling like surf and the mindless warble of a quasar a million light-years away.

"Maybe this world is empty," she said.

"But there are rails here," said the *Damask Rose*.

"Real rails?" asked Zen. "Ordinary ones? The right gauge and everything?"

"Hmmm," said the train. "There's a simple test we can do that will tell us that. Are we crashing? No. So I'd say the rails are just fine. Just like the rails at home."

"But where did they come from?"

"It's the Worm," said Nova. "The Worm is laying them . . ."

The Worm was the alien machine that had pried open the fabric of reality to form the new gate and melted that tunnel out of the mountains' heart. As it sped away from the mountains it let out its sleek new rails like spider silk. Soon Zen and Nova could see it on the *Rose's* cameras, a cloud of dust moving steadily ahead of them. Inside that cloud, sometimes the waving spines and colorless lightning crackle of the Worm showed, and the hunched mass of it, like an immense half-mechanical maggot, a rolling cathedral of hi-biotech, spewing vapor and weird shears of light. Within it and beneath it, huge industrial processes were happening at dizzying speed. It wasn't just a matter of laying the ceramic crossties like eggs and running the rails over them and bolting the rails down. There were ridges that needed cuttings or short tunnels melted through them. And there had to be some foundation for the tracks to lie on, so something was being done to the ground beneath the Worm, leaving it harder and shinier than the ground around, and fizzing with odd motes of light that danced awhile then faded, and were mostly gone by the time the *Rose* reached them.

"It is slowing," said the train at last, and she slowed too. "It's moving off the line. It's making a siding for itself . . ."

They went past the Worm at walking pace. It had lost its iridescent sheen, that restless movement. It seemed burned out: a black hill, cooling like clinker. Somewhere inside it lay the dead body of Raven, the man who had built it, entombed on this new world.

The sound of the wheels changed.

"Are there still tracks?" asked Zen.

"Let's see," said the *Damask Rose*. "Again we must ask ourselves, 'Are we crashing?' Ooh, and again, no . . ."

"I mean, *how* are there tracks?"

The Worm had fallen behind, lost in the hazy light that hung above the alien lagoons, but on the *Rose*'s screens the rails still stretched ahead, not quite so shiny now. They ran all the way to the horizon, where perspective pinched them together like an arrowhead.

"These rails were here before," said Nova. "The Worm made a spur to join the new gate to a line that was here already."

With a rattle of dry wings a big insect launched itself sleepily from a luggage rack and started battering at the glass in front of Zen's face, as if it were eager to get outside and explore this new world. A Monk bug. Zen flinched. He had been through some bad stuff recently, and some of the worst had involved those insects. If enough of them got together they formed a hive-intelligence, and one of those hives had attacked him back in Desdemor. This bug must be a survivor from it. Mindless without its million friends, it had blundered aboard the train.

Nova caught it gently between her cupped hands. Zen

thought she should kill it, but she said, "That's mean. Poor thing. We can let it out when we find somewhere suitable . . ."

So he went to find a box to put the bug in.

The train's three carriages had been prepared by Raven. Zen and Nova had not yet had time to explore them. The front carriage was a grand old state car with a bedroom and bathroom on the upper deck, living quarters downstairs, a small medical bay at the rear. The middle one was a dining car, its freezers packed with food. In the rear car was a store of things Raven must have thought he'd need: an industrial 3-D printer, a small flatbed truck with off-road tires, two shielded compartments stacked with spare fuel cells. There was a locker full of spacesuits, a dock where flashlights and butterfly drones were charging. There were racks of guns, and ice axes, and coils of rope, and box upon box of other supplies.

Just glancing at all that heaped-up stuff was enough to make Zen feel a warm glow of ownership. He'd done it, made himself rich, the way he'd always dreamed of. He had *his own train* now. Except that there was no one he could show it off to. The Guardians, the wise artificial intelligences who watched over humanity, had not wanted a new K-gate opened. Raven had done terrible things in order to open it, and Zen and Nova had been his pawns. They had wrecked the Emperor's train, and the Emperor himself had been killed. They could never go back to the Network Empire. Zen's mother, his sister, and the people he'd called his friends were all cut off from him as surely as if he'd died. Running his fingertips over the smooth surfaces of Raven's livewood cabinets, he sensed the first sharp twinge of homesickness.

He tipped some packets of Railforce emergency rations out of their plastic box and went back with it to the state car.

Nova was standing where he had left her. The trapped bug made rattly, rustly sounds inside her cupped hands. She had tipped her head to one side.

"What is it?" Zen asked.

"Voices," she said. "Way down around seventy-five kilohertz. Very primitive radio transmissions. I *think* they're voices . . ."

The *Damask Rose* cut in. "I hear them too. And there seems to be a station ahead . . ."

She opened a holoscreen and showed them the view from a forward-pointing camera on her hull. A low hill rose from the mirror-lagoons. The line ran toward it, and Zen could see other lines converging there, curving across the lagoons on low embankments, one crossing a long white bridge that looked like fish bones. There were more white things all around the edges of the hill—maybe trees, or maybe buildings. And up on the hill's top were larger structures, strange angles shining.

"Raven was right," said Nova quietly. For her, saying "Raven was" instead of "Raven is" seemed stranger than anything this world could show her. Motorik did not have parents, but she thought that she felt about Raven the way a human being might feel about their father, if their father was brilliant, secretive, and rather dangerous. She had not exactly loved him, but she had never imagined herself outliving him. She wished he could have seen all this.

The insect fluttered impatiently between her hands. Zen held out the box and tried not to look as she bundled the bug inside and sealed the lid. It gave him a nasty thought about the approaching station. The Station Angels, those mysterious light-forms that appeared sometimes near the K-gates of home and had told Raven how to open his new gate, had looked a bit like insects themselves: giant mantis shapes made out of light.

Perhaps they would be waiting here to welcome the *Damask Rose*. But Raven had said they were just projections—so what if the real Station Angels were actual giant bugs? Insects as big as jungle gyms?

Nova had put the box with the bug in it into her jacket pocket. Now she was standing at the window, gazing out. Zen went to join her. She did not take her eyes away from the sights sliding past outside, but her hand found Zen's, and he twined his fingers through hers. Back on Tristesse, in the desperate hours before the new gate opened, he had told her that he loved her, and they had kissed. He wasn't sure how he felt about that now. It was a strange thing, wanting to kiss a Motorik. It was probably just as strange for a Moto to want to kiss a human, and he wondered if she would want to do it again. He had always hidden his emotions, even from himself. In the type of places he came from you never showed that you cared about anything, because other people might take it from you, or smash it just to hurt you. He felt almost frightened by his feelings for Nova. But he was very glad that she was there.

Outside the window he saw pale, spindly trees with plate-shaped leaves spinning in the breeze, and between them . . . were those *buildings*? Were those *people*? Apart from the trees there was nothing that looked like anything Zen had seen before. And then a long shape moving . . .

"Is that a *train*?"

"It's a Worm," said Nova.

"Not quite," said the *Damask Rose*. "It's smaller, and simpler."

It had the same half-built, half-grown look as Raven's Worm. A silvery shell through which long spines stuck up, waving back and forth as if they were feeling the air. There were patterns on its flanks like the markings on cowrie shells, and a horny plate

The mass of beings drew back a little, as if shocked by the strangeness of the travelers. Then some things that Zen had thought were old, bleached tents came suddenly to life. They were the same creatures he had seen standing in colonies out in the lagoons, only he hadn't realized that they were creatures then. They crowded around him, making buzzing, rattling sounds by quivering the papery swags of skin that stretched between their bean-pole limbs. They reached out little starfish hands to feel his clothes and face. He shrank back from them, wondering if he should be afraid. It was like being a tiny child, new to everything. Except even a tiny child had instincts, and Zen's instincts were useless here. Were the tent things attacking him or just being friendly? He wondered if he should bow, or smile, or say, "We come in peace." But with no mouths of their own, how would they understand a smile? Bowing might be a deadly insult, and his words would be no more than noise to them.

Then Nova opened her mouth, and the same buzzings and rattlings that the tents were making came pouring out of her.

The aliens went still, quivering, opening and closing their little hands. Dark eye-spots that lay like seeds inside the outer layers of their skin slid to focus on her. The crowd fell silent, listening. Nova turned and let out hooting, whinnying sounds that seemed to please the three-legged antelopes; they raised their triangular heads, and dim lights flickered behind their masks.

She glanced quickly at Zen and smiled, pleased with herself. "They say we're welcome."

"How did you do that?"

She tapped the side of her head. "Decryption software. I'm already starting to translate some simple phrases. I've recorded their sounds so that I can speak back to them . . ."

The antelope things hooted and whinnied, dipping their heads.

"They say welcome to . . . to Yaarm. That's the name of this place: 'Yaarm in the Jeweled Garden.' Pretty! They are glad to meet us. They say it has been a long time since a new race found its way onto the Web of Worlds."

The conversation continued. The see-through newts had voices that sounded like someone farting in the bath. The things with tentacles used a complicated sign language, and when Nova tried to talk to them by waving both arms and one leg they rippled with oily rainbow colors that Zen guessed was their way of laughing. Sometimes she would send a message to his headset, explaining something she had just been told: *It sounds very big, this Web of Worlds—thousands of stations . . . They call those living locomotives* morvah . . . But mostly she was too busy trying to keep up with the talk, editing and playing back her own responses.

anything after us. And it's not all a lie; we *will* be trading. The *Rose*'s third car is full of Raven's stuff, and it's all unique here. Unique is valuable."

Nova laughed. She had been worried about Zen. She was glad to see he was still scheming. "But one day we'll have to admit that we can't go back."

"We'll be far away by then."

Nova thought about that for a microsecond, then turned and told the crowd. They seemed pleased. They understood why the humans would want to see the Web before trade was opened. The Herastec themselves (she thought that meant the antelope-y ones) had kept the gateway to their homeworlds closed for many years after they first made contact. A barrier would be erected, so that no trains could pass onto the humans' homelines without permission. And they would be welcome at all the stations of the Web: among the Herastec, the Deeka, the Chmoii . . .

Nova found the box in her pocket. The Monk bug seemed to have woven a cocoon for itself in there; she could just make out the dark cigar shape of its body through the silken strands. She held it up to ask if it would be all right to release an insect like this on Yaarm, but some of the Herastec misunderstood and thought she was trying to sell it. Yes, yes, they would buy! They had no use for insects themselves, but they traded sometimes with the Neem, and the Neem liked insects, or ate insects, or collected insects, or perhaps were insects themselves (Nova's translation software had not yet learned to cope with all the inflections of their whinnying language). She gave them the bug box, and they gave her in return three little rods of metal. She had made her first trade on the Web of Worlds.

*

another nine years and six months—a prospect that suddenly seemed so frightening to Chandni that she started shaking, almost started crying like a little girl.

She held it together, though. "Okay," she said, and strolled toward the lobby doors, telling herself there would be a moment's confusion when the lady outside saw they'd defrosted the wrong person, and in that moment she would take her chance and run. Her legs felt weak from the freezers, but if she could make it to the K-bahn station, maybe she could get aboard a kindly train that would take her to another planet.

The doors slid open. The woman in the lobby turned. She was older than Chandni and a total stranger. But when she saw Chandni, her plain, yellowish face split suddenly into a lovely smile. "Chandni!" she said too loudly and came forward to wrap Chandni in the first actual hug Chandni had been given since she was a kid.

"Well, this is odd," said Chandni, muffled in the fake-fur collar of her fake sister's coat.

"I have so much to tell you, little sis," the stranger said, still too loud, taking Chandni's hand and more or less dragging her outside into the misty sunlight. "I'll explain once we're on the train. Come on! If we hurry we can catch the twenty-six thirty-two . . ."

*

The 26:32 to Grand Central was waiting at the platform: a big Ngyuen 60 loco with a line of double-decker silver cars. Chandni started to relax when she saw it. She liked trains. No matter how strange it was coming out of cold-prison, no matter how much things had changed while you'd been frozen, the trains were always there, threading their patient way through the K-gates from world to world. You knew where you were with trains.

Plus, there were lots of people on them, so if the strange woman who had just collected you from cold storage pretending to be your long-lost sister turned out to be some kind of psycho who wanted to murder you and use your skin to cover throw pillows, a train journey would offer plenty of chances to give her the slip.

To Chandni's surprise, the woman had first-class tickets, which didn't seem to go with her cheap coat. She led her to the front car and into a classy private compartment. As the doors slid softly shut, she took her coat off. Underneath she was wearing black clothes that looked both very simple and very expensive and made Chandni feel a bit overdressed.

"My name is Kala Tanaka," said the woman. "I work for the Noon family."

"You mean the people who got me frozen for ten years because their son said I took some of his spare money?" asked Chandni.

"The Noons are a corporate family," said Kala Tanaka patiently. "That means they have many branches, many different interests . . ."

"I don't need a history lesson about the Noon family . . ."

"Yes, you do," said Kala Tanaka. "Sit down." She said it quietly, but so firmly that Chandni fell silent and sat down. As she sank into the soft seat cushions, the train began to move. "I am *L'Esprit de l'Escalier*," it said, through speakers set in the tortoiseshell ceiling. "I will be stopping at Przedwiosnie, Glorieta, Bhose Harbor, and Grand Central . . ."

"You do need a history lesson," said Kala Tanaka. "You may only have been in the freezers for six months this time, but a lot has changed." She pointed out through the window, where the buildings of Karavina's small station city were sliding by at gathering speed. Like all the station cities Chandni had ever seen, it had found wall space for a holographic portrait of the Emperor as high as a couple of houses. Only, for some reason, this one didn't show the Emperor. It showed a young woman of about Chandni's age with blue hair and a kind of ordinary face.

"A few days after you were frozen," said Kala Tanaka, "there was a train crash on the Spindlebridge. The Emperor Mahalaxmi was killed. There was some debate as to who would succeed him, but eventually Railforce decided to support his younger daughter, Threnody Noon. She is the new Empress of the Great Network. She is the person I work for. And she is the person who arranged for you to be released early from the freezers, though if you tell anyone that, you will find that there is absolutely no proof of it, and we will deny everything. The Empress Threnody wishes to talk with you, and she wishes to do so in absolute confidence. You know what that means?"

"I'm not stupid," said Chandni. "It means secret."

Kala Tanaka smiled at her. "Good. I'm glad you're not stupid. It is a long haul to Grand Central and it might have been boring, but I can see we're going to get along very well. Are you hungry yet? I'll order us something from the dining car. But we'll eat here, I think. Best if you are seen by as few people as possible."

They were outside the city by then. The famous vapor lakes of Karavina went past, and then the mountains. The train was gathering speed, heading toward the K-gate that would take it to Przedwiosnie, thirty thousand light-years away. Chandni thought about food and decided that she liked the idea. She was still confused, though.

"What does this new Empress want to talk to me about?" she asked.

"She will tell you that herself," said Kala Tanaka.

At the center of the Network lay the planet called Grand Central, a hub-world whose K-gates gave access to all the major lines of the galaxy. A sprawling city had grown up there: a green city, more like a beautifully managed forest with tall buildings rising here and there above the trees. A broad river, dotted with the sails of pleasure boats, wound through it to the ocean. Along the river's banks were some of the great buildings of the Empire: the K-bahn Timetable Authority, Railforce Tower, the pyramids that housed the shrines of the Guardians. In the hills farther north, where the river began, stood the imperial palace, the greatest of them all.

Its proper name was the Durga, but that just meant fortress or stronghold or something in one of the Old Earth languages and didn't really suit it. It had probably started out as a fortress, thousands of years ago, but after so many generations of peace it had grown distinctly palace-y. It was built on, and in, a flat-topped granite mountain. The first humans to arrive on Grand

Central, before it even had a breathable atmosphere, had made their homes in the caverns inside it. Later, when things were more stable, they had started to build on the sides and top too, extending it upward in spires of biotech ivory and specially grown bone. Broad decks jutted out, planted with elaborate gardens. On one of the highest of them, the Empress herself sat looking out across her capital.

No one had ever intended for Threnody Noon to become Empress. Her mother's marriage to the late Emperor had only been a temporary one, designed to seal some business contract between her mother's family and the House of Noon. Threnody had grown up knowing that the heir to the throne was her half-sister Priya, who had been destined to rule since before she was born, and who the family geneticists had ensured would look the part: glossy, exquisite Priya, the Empress-to-be. But somehow, in the confusion that had followed her father's death, Priya had failed to convince Rail Marshal Lyssa Delius that she would be a good Empress. Since Lyssa Delius commanded Railforce, with all its troops and wartrains, her opinion tended to be listened to, and she had decided that she would rather see Threnody rule the rails. Priya had vanished, and Threnody had taken her place upon the Flatcar Throne of the Empire.

Even now, six months after her coronation, she still felt numb with the strangeness of it all. There were so many parties and functions to attend, so many visiting dignitaries who needed to pay their respects to her, so many official portraits to pose for and new clothes to be fitted for. That was why, whenever she could, she liked to escape from her ladies-in-waiting and hairdressers and makeup advisors and social media strategists and security people and come up here, to the most overgrown and least fashionable of the palace's many gardens. She was still

27

not technically alone—her cloud of personal security drones, disguised as hummingbirds, hovered around her at all times, while bigger machines cruised above the garden, ready to put a warning laser-bolt across the bows of any paparazzi drone that tried to snatch a photo of her for the gossip sites. But she could *feel* alone, and that was important. At home on Malapet she'd had whole days to herself, walking on the beach of black sand below the house while her mother worked on paintings of the icebergs that the currents stranded there. She had found solitude boring then; she had longed for something to happen to her. Now it had, and these quiet times in the high garden were one of the few things that kept her sane.

So she was annoyed at first when Kala Tanaka messaged her headset to say that she was on her way up. And then she wasn't, because Kala said, "I am bringing the girl."

Kala Tanaka was another of the things that kept her sane. Everybody seemed to think it must be wonderful to live in the palace, and go out every night to dinners and balls. The rest of her vast family envied Threnody, wishing that Lyssa Delius had picked them for the job. Only her uncle Nilesh seemed to understand that the new Empress might feel frightened and alone. He was Threnody's favorite uncle—a mild, lazy, completely unambitious man who seemed quite content as Stationmaster on the little end-of-the-line tourist moon Khoorsandi. "And even that would be too much for me," he had told Threnody at her coronation ball, "if I didn't have my assistant to take care of me. You should borrow her for a while. Kala has been with me for years and years, and Khoorsandi isn't to everyone's taste. I expect she'd enjoy a stay at the palace."

Kala Tanaka had come to Grand Central with him, and she stayed on after he left. She was plain and kind and smart and extremely efficient. She was not afraid to tell the highest-ranking members of the family to leave Threnody alone if she thought the Empress was too tired to listen to their latest schemes and proposals. She would even stand up to Rail Marshal Delius when the schedule of official duties grew too frantic. She was the sort of person who could clear time in a busy Empress's day for a walk in the gardens. She was also the sort of person you could send secretly to Karavina to arrange the early release of petty criminals from freezer prisons.

Threnody felt a little nervous as she watched Kala and the girl come toward her along the overgrown paths. She'd not had much experience with lower-class people, except for smiling politely at them from the observation car of the imperial train while they stood on station platforms waving tiny flags at her. She had only really ever known one, and that had not turned out too well. This girl, this Chandni Hansa, looked pretty frightening. She was short and wiry. Kala had made her wear a headscarf to hide her shaved head, but her clothes were alarming, all video-fabric and cultured diamonds, the sort of thing you'd see . . . well, Threnody wasn't sure *where* you'd have to go to see clothes like those. And although her face was pretty, it lost its prettiness when she looked at you; her eyes seemed too old for her—bitter and suspicious.

"Bow," said Kala Tanaka, bowing herself, and the girl gave a sullen little nod, glaring at Threnody.

Threnody inclined her own head slightly in response, and said, "Welcome to Grand Central, Miss Hansa. I hope your journey was comfortable?"

"It would have been more comfortable if she'd told me what you want me here for," said Chandni Hansa, with a quick, sharp look at Kala Tanaka. "I haven't done anything."

Threnody's cloud of drones sensed the hostility in the girl's voice and adopted a defensive formation. Threnody reminded herself that she was the Network Empress and could not be intimidated by people like Chandni Hansa.

"That's not true, is it?" she said. "Six months ago you made friends with a young man named Tallis Noon, whom you met on a train at Przedwiosnie. You took him with you to Karavina, and while you were there you robbed him."

Chandni Hansa glared past her into the blue parkland beyond the palace, where gene-teched dinosaurs were calling.

"It's all right," said Threnody. "I met Tallis Noon at my coronation. He is very boring, and he probably deserved to be robbed. You probably taught him a valuable lesson. It was wrong of him to demand that you were frozen for such a minor crime."

Chandni Hansa looked at her again. She wasn't used to people in power talking to her like that. She was suspicious. "That why you let me out?"

"Partly," said Threnody.

There was a stone bench overlooking a chess garden: a checkerboard lawn with topiary chess pieces clipped out of yew. The yew had been spliced with crustacean DNA, and the pieces moved slowly back and forth on crablike roots, laboriously playing out a game of chess. Threnody sat down on the bench and gestured for Chandni to sit beside her. Chandni looked back at Kala Tanaka as if she suspected a trick. Then, reluctantly, she sat down.

"While you were on Karavina with Tallis Noon," Threnody said, "a young man came aboard the Noon train. He said he was Tallis Noon, and he looked enough like the real Tallis that we believed him. But he turned out to be an imposter. His real name was Zen Starling. He sabotaged the train somehow, on Spindlebridge, killing my father and a lot of other people. Later on, he showed up on Sundarban and caused more trouble there, before he vanished down the derelict Dog Star Line on an old train. And I've never been able to find out what it was about or why any of it happened. An actual, living, breathing interface of the Guardian Anais Six took charge of things on Sundarban and went off after Zen Starling down the dead line with a Railforce officer named Malik, and nothing has been heard of either of them since. There's no mention of any of it in the Datasea, Rail Marshal Delius claims to know nothing about it, and I'm the Empress—you'd think I'd be able to find out the truth about something like that!"

She realized that her voice had been growing louder and louder, more and more angry. Chandni Hansa looked scared of *her* now. She calmed herself, and said, "The only thing I was able to find out is that the real Tallis Noon was on Karavina when it all happened, with a girl he'd met on a train, who ended up robbing him. And I thought that seemed like a bit too much of a coincidence. So I thought I'd bring you here, and ask you if you had anything to do with it, and I'm not even going to punish you if you say you did, I just want to *know*."

"I didn't know anything about sabotaging the Noon train," said Chandni Hansa.

"So you just started talking to Tallis Noon because you had a crush on him?" asked Kala Tanaka, who was standing guard a little way off, watching the slow movements of the chess pieces.

Chandni made a scornful sound. "A crush? On that stuck-up Noon boy? No. I'm not interested in boys. I'm not interested in girls, either, in case you're getting any ideas. A man paid me to make friends with Tallis Noon and take him to Karavina, that's all. Said I was to keep him there for a week, but after a few days I was sick of him, so I stole his headset and his cash and took off."

"This man who paid you," Threnody said. "Was it Zen Starling?"

"I've never heard of any Zen Starling," said Chandni. "He sure didn't look anything like Tallis Noon. He was old."

"How old?"

"Hard to say. Old and weird. White. With white hair. And skinny. Like someone out of a history show, some duke or something from the Old Earth times. Said his name was Raven."

"Do you know where I can find him?"

Chandni shook her head. "I'd seen him a couple of times on Glorieta. The night he talked to me I ran into him down near the old station, the boarded-up one . . ."

"The Dog Star Line station?" asked Threnody.

"Yes . . ." said Chandni. "He said he had a job for me. Said he thought I might like to earn a cool thousand and really stick it to the Noon family, and I was up for both of those. He paid in advance too. Said if I didn't do the job like he told me, he'd know about it and come and find me, but I don't see how, and I wasn't scared of him anyway." She shrugged. "I guess your Zen Starling must have been working for him too."

"Anything more you can tell me about this Raven?"

Chandni thought. Six months in the freezers left holes in your memories. "The night he hired me he was on his own, but once before I saw him with a wire dolly. She was a funny-looking one. Dressed like a real girl, and had, like, freckles on her face, but she was Motorik all right."

"Nova," said Threnody.

"I never heard him call her anything. They just went past me one night and I thought, 'they're an odd pair.'"

Out on the chessboard lawn, the red queen made a surprisingly quick move and landed on a black pawn, crushing the smaller bush to the ground, tearing at it with her crab-claw roots. Threnody would have liked to tear at Zen Starling like that—at him, and this Raven, and the Motorik named Nova. Those three had caused all this, she was sure of it. But they were gone, and talking to Chandni Hansa had given her no answers, only more questions.

"Why were you so eager to hurt the Noons?" she asked.

Chandni shrugged again. She was surprised at how much she had told the stuck-up little Empress. It was a change of pace to talk to someone. She didn't see how it would do much harm to talk some more, before they threw her back onto the streets.

"My family used to be all right," she said. "My dad was Stationmaster on a place called Shelan Junction that you've probably never heard of. But Shelan Junction was a Noon world, and the Noon Emperor decided to get rid of him so some useless, stuck-up Noon boy could have his job. My dad went downhill after that. Things fell apart pretty fast."

Threnody was shocked. "I'm sure my father would never have thrown someone out of a post in that way!"

"Not your father, Empress," said Kala Tanaka. "This would have been the Emperor before him: your great uncle. He was notoriously corrupt."

"But Chandni Hansa can't be old enough to have been alive when he was on the throne!"

"You don't age in the freezers," said Chandni Hansa, with a kind of bleak pride. She pulled her headscarf back and Threnody saw the prison barcodes tattooed on her scalp.

"Chandni has been in the freezers a lot," said Kala Tanaka. "The first spell was the longest—fifty years for burning down the

Stationmaster's villa at Shelan Junction. Since then it's been five years for this, ten years for that. She's about nineteen years old if you just count actual life, but she was born ninety-six years ago."

Chandni shrugged again, an odd, somehow aggressive little movement. "It's hard to fit back in once you've been in the freezers," she said. "I got out the first time and everything was different, everybody I knew had moved on. I couldn't even talk right; people who used the slang I used were all grandparents. So I got in trouble again, because that's the only thing I'm any good at. After a few tries, it's kind of a relief to go back in the fridge."

On the chessboard, the red queen had almost finished destroying the pawn. Torn leaves blew across the garden. The first of Grand Central's twin suns was sinking into the bank of low cloud that lay along the horizon. Chandni Hansa stood up, and Threnody's drones buzzed angrily, tracking her movements. "So do I make my own way out?" she asked.

"No!" said Threnody. She wasn't sure what she was doing, only that she could not let this damaged girl go back out into the world, back to her life of crime and another spell on ice. She turned to Kala Tanaka. "How did you get her into the palace without anyone knowing?"

"If anyone inquires," said Kala, "they will find that Miss Hansa is a friend of a friend whom you were considering for a job here, Empress. An act of charity."

"I don't need Noon charity!" said Chandni angrily.

"Quiet," Kala told her. "You didn't say that when I bought you dinner on the train."

"Then I shall offer her a job," said Threnody, quite softly, but loud enough to silence them both. She smiled to herself. When she became Empress she had acquired ladies-in-waiting: a lot of daughters of distant Noon cousins and other minor families, whose job it was to help her dress and keep her company. Most of them were much more posh and sophisticated than Threnody. They scared and annoyed her, but she was pretty sure that Chandni Hansa could cope with them, just as Kala Tanaka could cope with Chandni Hansa.

"Chandni will be my new lady-in-waiting," she said. "Madhur Noon can go home to Golden Junction; she is always bragging about that boyfriend she has there, and how she misses him. Chandni will take her place." She felt quite commanding for a moment, then spoiled it by looking at Kala Tanaka. "I can do that, can't I?"

Kala Tanaka bowed. "You are the Empress of the Galaxy, Empress. You can do whatever you want."

So Chandni became a kind of glorified servant. The palace staff
and the Motorik and the security guards all called her "Lady
Chandni," but a servant was what she was. "Bring the Empress's
coat, Lady Chandni," "Wake the Empress for her breakfast with
the Stationmaster of Vagh, Lady Chandni," "You will accompany
the Empress on her pilgrimage to Mars, Lady Chandni." The
other ladies-in-waiting were all horrified by her—she had known
they would be, and she thought Threnody had known it too.
She didn't know what to say to them and they didn't know what
to say to her, so they quickly reached an arrangement where she
didn't speak to them at all, and that was fine by her.

She wasn't planning to stay long, anyway. The imperial
palace was no place for a girl who'd run with zip gangs in the
submarine slums on Ayaguz. She didn't like being Threnody
Noon's little charity project. As she followed the Empress
through the bewildering maze of the palace—the Jade Room,
the Mirrored Ballroom, the Waterfall Room—she sized up

the valuables. Pretty much everything here was valuable; even the stuff that looked like junk turned out to be priceless antiques from Old Earth. Chandni hoped that if she took a few good pieces with her when she left, Threnody might be too kind or too embarrassed to send Railforce after her.

But somehow she kept on finding reasons to stay. The food was good, and free, and she told herself she needed fattening up before she hit the streets again. She had a room of her own that was about the size of the house she had grown up in, the one she'd wound up burning. The room was next to Kala Tanaka's suite, on the floor below the Empress's quarters. All the things in it were bigger or better or just nicer than anything Chandni had been around before. Even the light looked expensive, filtering through the decorative screen that walled her bed space off from the living area. The bed was circular and as soft as cartoon clouds. She sprawled out in it and slept on her back, snoring. She could have spent all day in that bed, but Kala Tanaka made sure she was always up early and ready to go and do whatever stupid duties needed doing.

Every time Kala Tanaka woke her up, or ordered her around, Chandni told herself that this was it, she wasn't a slave, she was going to load up with some portable wealth and slip out of a back entrance that very night. But somehow when Kala came banging on her door the next morning before first sunrise, there she still was. Well, it would be a shame to skip town before the K-bahn Timetable Authority's banquet; she had never been to an actual banquet before. And if she was staying till then, it would be a shame not to go along for the ride when Threnody made her pilgrimage to Mars . . .

Mars was a pointless kind of desert-y planet way off down at the end of the Hydrogen Line, but it had been the first station on the Network, where the Guardians had opened the very first K-gate. So for some reason each new Empress or Emperor had to go there, and be photographed looking thoughtful while they peered through the pressure-dome at Earth itself, which you could see sometimes if there wasn't a sandstorm raging. Other things you could see from the pressure dome included the remains of some of the spaceships that human beings had ridden in to Mars so they could board the first trains and go through the Mars gate to explore and settle all the other worlds. Threnody stood on the viewing platform and pointed out the sand-covered hulk of the *Varanasi*, the ship on which the ancestors of the Noons had made the crossing. It gave Chandni a strange feeling, kind of shivery, like she used to get in history lessons when she was little, thinking about how far human beings had come. And there wasn't a sandstorm blowing, and there was Old Earth, hanging in the Martian sky like a tiny blue star. Chandni thought it would be nice to go there, but there wasn't time—for some reason the Guardians had never opened a K-gate on Earth itself, and it took months and months to get there by spaceship. The Empress needed to be back on Grand Central in time for her summer party.

*

It was on the way back from Mars that Chandni had her first chance to talk to Threnody since that day in the chess garden. Actually, that wasn't quite true: on most days since then Threnody had said, "How are you settling in, Chandni?" or "Are you happy, Chandni?" but this was the first time that Chandni had felt she wanted a real answer.

They were riding on the new Noon train. Everybody said it didn't compare to the old Noon train, but it still seemed pretty fancy to Chandni: sixty carriages, pulled by an enormous old loco called the *Crystal Horizon*. Threnody's quarters were in the middle of the train: a carriage for her clothes, and two for herself and her staff, with war drones buzzing along outside the windows and then nipping quickly into hangars in the carriage roofs whenever the train approached a K-gate, since nothing could go through a K-gate unless it was on a train. One night Chandni was trying to sleep, and finding it difficult because the train kept passing across worlds where it was daytime, so she went from her cabin downstairs into the lounge part of the car and found that Threnody was having the same problem. The Empress of the Network, with her halo of little drones, was standing at a window with a glass of hot chocolate in her hand and a little chocolate moustache where she'd been drinking it.

"So what do you think of this life, Chandni Hansa?" she asked.

Chandni, who had been about to make an excuse and go back to her cabin, stayed where she was and shrugged. She wanted to say something about the way she'd felt when she stood on Mars and looked up at Old Earth, but she couldn't find the right sort of words. "It's like living in an ad," she said at last.

Threnody laughed. "You're right! It is! We *are* living in an ad. My whole life is just a great, big-budget advertisement, designed to show the people of the Network that everything is under control and all's well with the worlds. And we're just actresses, playing our parts."

Chandni frowned. "But you're the Empress . . ."

Threnody laughed some more. "Have you not noticed Lyssa Delius?"

"The tall black lady with the tall white hair? The Rail Marshal?" Chandni had noticed the Rail Marshal all right. And she had only been in the Empress's service for a few days before the Rail Marshal had noticed her. Chandni had heard her ask Kala Tanaka who the new girl was. Kala Tanaka, who had just magicked Chandni through all the palace employee security checks and had her tracker bracelet removed, had trotted out her friend-of-the-family-charity-job story, but Chandni could tell the Rail Marshal didn't buy it. She had narrowed her wise old eyes and said, "I trust you know what you're doing, Kala . . ."

"She's the real ruler of the rails," said Threnody. "I'm just her puppet. That's why she chose me. I'm young and I don't know how things work and I don't have any ideas of my own. I'm just a Noon doll she can prop up on the Flatcar Throne while she tries to get the senate to pass new laws in my name. If I tried to argue she'd probably do with me whatever she did with my sister Priya, and no one knows what's become of Priya. Lyssa Delius comes from some horrible industrial world; she grew up poor, and she wants laws that will help other poor people. Banning Motorik labor, and raising wages, and stuff like that. But you can imagine how that goes down with my family and all the other corporate families. They say I'm bringing in dangerous laws and risking instability because I'm young and foolish. But it's not my fault! I'm just her puppet!"

Chandni thought she liked the sound of Lyssa Delius and her laws. She wondered if it would be worth asking her to bring in another, so that people couldn't be frozen for years at a time and end up skipping across the surface of the decades like a skimmed stone. But all she said was, "It's the Guardians who really run things, isn't it? Even I know that."

Threnody peered into her hot chocolate as if there might be answers there. "The Guardians haven't said anything about what Lyssa Delius is up to. They stay in the Datasea and don't share their thoughts with anyone. If they approve, they ought to say so, so everyone would know."

"If they don't approve, they could burn you and Lyssa Delius up with a lightning bolt or something," said Chandni. She'd never really given a lot of thought to those all-wise AIs who were supposed to watch and guide everybody. It was pretty obvious they didn't care about her, so why should she care about them? Still, she had a vague idea that if they didn't like you they would say it with lightning bolts.

"I met a Guardian once," said Threnody. "It was an interface of Anais Six. On Sundarban. The night Zen Starling and his Moto girl escaped. The night Lyssa Delius woke me up to tell me I was going to be Empress. That was the last time I saw Kobi."

Chandni sat down, sensing that this was going to be a long talk. Her father used to get in this mood at the end, although he'd done it on rice wine, not hot chocolate. The train passed through a K-gate and ran out across a plain of what looked like ice beneath two red suns that appeared to be eating each other. Chandni and Threnody, experienced rail travelers, barely bothered glancing at the view.

Chandni said, "Who's Kobi?"

"He and I were supposed to get married, before I was Empress," said Threnody. "It was just a business marriage, meant to link the Noons to a Sundarban spacer clan, the Chen-Tulsis. Kobi was an oaf. Well, he used to be an oaf . . . but just at the end he was quite brave. You know how, when things get bad, you see people as they really are? And Kobi was all right, really. I think he truly cared about me. But once I was Empress it was all off. The Empress can't go marrying into some little family nobody's ever heard of. I'll have to marry an Albayek or a Ngyuen or somebody . . ."

41

Chandni sat there in the glow of the dying suns and watched tears run down the face of the Empress of the Galaxy, and thought what a strange turn of events this was for a popsicle girl.

"I wasn't in love with him or anything," said Threnody. "I don't know why I'm crying. I haven't thought about him much, until tonight. I'm just tired. Kobi Chen-Tulsi! I'm lucky to be rid of him, really. I wonder what he's doing now?"

PART THREE
BROKEN MOON

Kobi Chen-Tulsi saw the images from Mars on his headset while a train called *Heavy Weather* carried him across a series of dull and mostly snowbound industrial worlds way out on the Trans-Chiba branch lines. These were the strongholds of the Prell family, with whom his own family was hoping to do an important business deal. He supposed it would be some sort of consolation after the collapse of the merger with the Noons, but he didn't like the Prells, he didn't like their cheerless planets, and he didn't like his cousin Rolo, who had been sent with him to oversee the signing of the contract. So he closed his eyes and pretended to doze while his headset streamed images from the Empress's Martian pilgrimage straight to the visual centers of his brain.

If things had gone according to plan, he and Threnody would have been celebrating their wedding about then. It was only meant to be a business marriage, but Kobi had loved his Thren, he really had. He couldn't believe his luck when their families' matchmakers first introduced them. He had done his clumsy best to impress her, and made a fool of himself, and probably failed, but after the Spindlebridge disaster she had needed him, and he had really thought she was starting to like him. And then she'd suddenly been whisked away and elected Empress, and it was thanks but no thanks, Kobi Chen-Tulsi.

And the worst part was that nobody seemed to understand that his heart was broken. His mother was more worried about the damage to the Chen-Tulsi brand. The family image consultants told her Kobi shouldn't even be allowed out in public, in case he gave more ammunition to the Sundarbani gossip feeds, which were all having a ball with this, of course. That was why he'd been packed off with Rolo on this trade mission to the Prell Consortium on their frozen, half-finished worlds at the edge of the Network. That was how he came to be slumped on the uncomfortable seats of the *Heavy Weather*, scrolling through stories about Threnody on his headset, while Rolo ate almond pastries in the seat beside him and wiped his sticky fingers on the armrest.

*

No one remembered for sure whether it was the Guardians who had created the corporations, or the corporations that had created the Guardians. One thing was certain: the Guardians had created the K-gates, and when humanity started to travel through them it was the corporations that had built the stations and the trains and rolling stock, and laid some of the rails that linked the gates together. Doing business in those wild times on worlds that might be half a galaxy apart, when laws were always changing, the corporations found they needed more than trust to build their business deals on, so they had started to seal their alliances with marriage, and the corporate families were born.

During the centuries that followed, some of the families had thrived, while others withered away. The most important these days were the Noons (of course), the Albayeks, the Nguyens, and the Khans. There were thousands of smaller houses too—families like the Chen-Tulsis, with power in a single station or system, and dreams of growing greater. And then there were the Prells, lurking in their cold worlds out on the western branch lines, nursing their old grudges, stubbornly convinced that they deserved more power, more say in things. "We built this Network," the Prells would grumble, sooner or later, whenever the talk turned to politics. "We were the pioneers, we went where no one else wanted to go, and once we'd built stations there and set about terraforming the worlds we found, some other family would breeze in and take over. Those Noons. Those Albayeks. Noses in the air, acting all ethical, cutting us out, cheating us. Like they'd be anything without us Prells . . ."

The Prells had never made their peace with the other great families or intermarried as the others had. They traded, but they stayed aloof. Fifty years ago they had backed the separatist rebels on the Spiral Line and started a nasty little war that almost won them the Empire, until Railforce smashed their armored trains at the Battle of Galaghast.

Many people had wondered why the Guardians didn't just give the troublesome Prell-controlled worlds to other, more civilized families and be done with it. Perhaps it was just that nobody but the Prells wanted the bother and hard work of ruling the Trans-Chiba branch lines.

*

"Kobi! Wake up, cousin! Straighten yourself up a bit, for the Guardians' sake. We're here!"

Kobi turned off his headset and pretended to wake. Rolo was heaving himself to his feet, scattering crumbs and pastry wrappers. He was older than Kobi by five or six years, but Kobi always thought he looked like an overinflated child, with his plump face and his love of sweets.

"Do stir yourself, cousin Kobi," he blustered. "We mustn't dawdle. We can't afford to offend the Prells, and the Prells are very easily offended. I know these people, remember. I've been working on this deal for years, making friends, making contacts, while you paraded around with that stuck-up Noon girl."

"Threnody isn't stuck-up. She's just shy . . ."

"All right, cousin. Don't bite my head off! Maybe we'll find you a nice Prell girl, eh? They have hearts of ice, but I'm sure you could melt them . . ."

Kobi scowled and reached for his coat and hat.

Broken Moon was a little larger than most of the Prell stations they had passed through, and the lowering portraits of Elon Prell above the platforms were a little more imposing. A squad of the Prells' Corporate Marines was waiting to meet them on the platform. A car drove them away through a delta of rail yards and engine sheds and up winding roads into the mountains.

There, among the crags, crouched Karkatagarh, the family home of the Prells. People called it "Crab Castle" according to Rolo, and it *did* look a bit like a crab: a long, low bio-building, the main section tucked in under a shell-shaped roof, two crescent guest wings forming its pincers. Across the sky above it were strewn the fragments of the broken moon that gave this world its name. It must have been nearly as big as its mother planet once, but some long-ago impact had shattered it into a permanent, ragged crescent, surrounded by rings of rubble.

Its bone-cold light lay on the snow and on the curved crab-shell roof of Karkatagarh.

A cable car took Kobi and Rolo up to the house. They stepped out into a circular entrance hall walled with black stone and decorated with the heads of gigantic hairy animals—some kind of gene-teched Old Earth prehistorics. "All shot in the family game reserve on the far side of the mountain," said the young woman who was waiting there. "I'm told you like to hunt?"

Kobi wondered if she'd heard the stories about him. He *had* liked to hunt, but he'd done some stupid things in the Noon preserve on Jangala and ended up nearly getting himself killed by one of their game beasts. The sight of all those tusked and glaring heads brought the memory of it back: the terror and the shame. When the young woman said, "I'll take you out tomorrow, if you like," he thought he was going to be sick.

"We'd love to!" said Rolo.

"I'm Laria Prell," she said, bowing. She was not much older than Kobi. White-blond hair and pale gray eyes, and the unflattering purple dress uniform of the Prell CoMa, which did nothing for her sturdy figure. Kobi had not met many white people before. It was hard not to stare at her pasty, blotchy face, her long pink nose. But she seemed to be his partner for the evening, so he smiled as gallantly as he could and followed her through into a dining room, where there were more people to meet: Prells, Prells, Colonel somebody of Railforce, the Stationmaster of somewhere, then more Prells, and finally the old man himself, Elon Prell, as ugly and unwelcoming as his house, his face creased into deep lines by years of scheming.

The servants were human, not Motorik, and they seemed to come in matching pairs. The man who showed Kobi and Laria to their seats had a doppelganger who came a moment later to pour their drinks. More pairs of identical servants brought in the food: thin soup, then mammoth steaks, served rare and oozing blood. Behind Elon's chair stood two thugs with identical grim faces and shaved heads.

"My uncle only employs twins here," said Laria softly. "Those two behind him are Shiv and Enki Mako, his favorite bodyguards. Whenever twins are born on the Prell worlds, their parents know they can find work with our family. It is to honor the Twins themselves: the great Twins, in the Datasea. The Twins have always been very good to our family."

That figured, thought Kobi. Everyone said the Twins were the strangest, most difficult of the Guardians. The Prells were just their kind of people. At least there was only one of Laria . . .

After dinner they went into a small conference room, where Rolo turned on a holoprojector and gave a presentation about how much money the Prells and the Chen-Tulsis could make if they worked together, extracting minerals from the various Prell-owned systems. "Don't imagine that, because we are based on Sundarban, we don't know what hard work is. The Chen-Tulsi family has built its fortunes in the hardest places there are: asteroid mines, remote moons. My grandmother, our glorious founder, spent most of her life in space, building anti-matter farms in the magnetosphere of the star Vajrapani . . ." Holographic planets whirled past Kobi's face. A miniature asteroid belt appeared above the projector like a halo of airborne granola, with threads of orange to show the paths Chen-Tulsi mining ships could take between the larger asteroids.

Rolo was good at this. He looked less childlike, rattling off figures and statistics in answer to the questions the Prell family executives fired at him. And there was nothing for Kobi to do but sit there sleepily, half watching, slyly calling up images of Threnody on his headset, wondering if he would ever be happy again.

"A few weeks ago you were ready to ally yourselves to the Noons," grumbled Elon Prell. He pointed a thick finger at Kobi. "*He* was scheduled to marry the girl they just shoehorned in as Empress. Is that why you're here? Prells are your second choice, are we?"

"I don't deny that we were disappointed when the marriage to Threnody Noon fell through," said Rolo smoothly, before Kobi could think of a reply. "But we've decided to look on it as an opportunity. The girl is Empress, but will she *stay* Empress? Everyone knows she is only Lyssa Delius's puppet, and no one likes the reforms that Delius is planning. Who knows what might happen? We feel that it might be best to link ourselves to a more *adaptable* family."

What that meant exactly, Kobi wasn't sure, but the Prells seemed pleased. There were murmurs of agreement from around the table. A couple of people even raised their glasses, drinking to Rolo's health with their sour local wine. Kobi smiled and nodded, trying to look intelligent.

"Well said," growled Elon Prell, and twin servants stepped forward to fill his glass, and Kobi's too. "Contracts will be arranged tomorrow, and a formal announcement next week, but I think we're agreed. An alliance between our two families: the Chen-Tulsis to have exclusive development rights to our off-world possessions, while we gain access to your rail-freight yards and other facilities on Sundarban. The arrangement to be sealed by marriage between Lady Laria Prell and Kobi Chen-Tulsi."

Which was the first Kobi had heard about it, and, judging by the look of horror on her plain face, the first that Laria Prell had heard too.

*

"I thought you realized!" Rolo kept saying, later. "I thought your mother would have told you that she had found a new match for you!"

"If she had told me, I would never have come to this horrible place!"

"Ah. Well, I expect that's why she *didn't* tell you, then."

They were in Rolo's room, which was next door to Kobi's, on one of the upper floors of Crab Castle. Rolo was sitting on the bed, one shoe off, as if he had been starting to get undressed when Kobi burst in.

"But I don't *want* to marry the Prell girl!"

"Do stop calling her the 'Prell girl.' Call her Laria. That's what you will have to call her when you're married."

"I . . ."

"I know, I know. You don't want to marry her. But that's the price you pay for being the heir to an up-and-coming family like ours. You are like a counter in a game, dear cousin; your mother must make the best play she can with you."

"And this is it? Marrying me to that shovel-faced ice princess so we can work our butts off for the Prells?"

"For one thing, Kobi, it pains me to hear you talk about your future wife in that way; she is probably a very lovely girl. Looks aren't everything, you know. And for another thing, an alliance with the Prell Consortium is the very best hope for our family at the moment. You don't know everything, cousin of mine. Believe you me, these Prells are going places."

"What's that supposed to mean?"

Rolo yawned and shook his head. "I've said too much. Now *do* go to bed, Kobi, dear fellow. It's very late, we've had a long day, and these frosty savages seem intent on taking us hunting in the morning."

Kobi went and stood at the window. He had a vague idea about climbing out of it and finding his way off this chilly rock, but Mother would be furious, and it was snowing hard outside.

Down in the courtyard Elon Prell himself, in a massive fur coat, was saying goodbye to one of his guests. His twin bodyguards stood behind Elon in the shadows. As the visitor's flyer took off, the glare from its running lights flashed on their shaven heads, pale and shiny as a pair of matching skulls.

7

By dawn the shattered moon had moved to another part of the sky, but Kobi could still see it hanging there, its gigantic ruin filling the frosty clear air above the distant rail yards. The sun was small and low and gave no warmth. *Why on earth did the Prells insist on making their home here?* Kobi wondered. Was it plain stubbornness? Or maybe they just liked being uncomfortable. The bed in his big, underheated room had been as hard as a slab of slate.

Hunting was uncomfortable too. No snow boats or hound-drones for the Prells. They hunted with real hounds, and they did it on the backs of actual horses. It was years since Kobi had ridden one, but he wasn't going to let his new future in-laws see how scared he was, so he scrambled up somehow into the big beast's saddle and tried to look as if he knew what he was doing. The horses were artificial, with a twist of zebra in their DNA. Their coats matched the chameleon ponchos that the riders wore, the black and white stripes camouflaging them against the snow-slashed screes of Broken Moon.

Long before they'd crossed the ridge into the hunting reserve, Kobi's thighs were aching and his face was numb from the icy wind. Still, he seemed to be handling the horse all right, cantering along with the rest of the party. And the game they were after was not as big or as fierce as he'd feared: just a troop of lanky, white-furred monkeys that lived on the tops of the mountains.

They turned up a steep-sided valley, following the clamor of the dogs and the distant, echoing howls of the monkeys. Kobi found himself riding beside Laria Prell, who said stiffly, "I wasn't expecting that announcement last night."

"Me neither," said Kobi. "I'm sorry."

"That's all right. I don't want to marry you, either."

That startled him a bit. *Why not?* he thought.

"I don't want to marry anybody," she said. "Maybe one day, but not yet. I've been with the family marine corps for a couple of years. I'm enjoying it. I want to command a wartrain one day."

"I suppose you could be married and still be a soldier," said Kobi. He thought her white face made sense out here in the cold. Her cheeks and the tip of her nose had turned red, which sort of suited her, and on horseback she had a kind of big-boned grace. He supposed it didn't matter who he was engaged to, now that he had lost Threnody. Why not Laria Prell?

But she had already ridden on ahead. He lost sight of her in the blur of identical striped horses and striped ponchos and hoof-scattered powder snow. Then guns started going off far up the valley and the field broke up, pursuing individual monkeys as the troop scattered across the slopes. Ten minutes later he caught a glimpse of Laria again, standing up in her saddle, taking aim with her carbine at a big male that was whooping and jabbering at her from a claw of rock. He turned his horse uphill toward her, but it plunged through a crust of new snow into a hollow and he was thrown over its head.

He landed hard. By the time he had floundered out of the snowdrift his horse was gone, heading for home with its stirrups flying. Kobi dropped back almost gratefully into the snow, waiting for the Prells' drones to spot him and their servants to bring a bike or flyer and fetch him home. But slowly, as the sounds of the hunt faded over the ridge above him, he started to realize that wasn't going to happen. These stupid Prells with their love of hardship probably didn't have any drones on watch, or any rescue flyers waiting to ferry fallen riders home. He tried his headset, but a damping field blocked all connection to the local data raft; there was just an emergency site where serious injuries could be reported.

Kobi checked himself over. He wasn't injured. He was about to log in and ask for a flyer to come and fetch him anyway when he suddenly wondered if the Prells were testing him. Maybe this ordeal was designed to see if he had what it took to be a proper Prell. He didn't want to confirm their prejudices about soft Sundarbanis. And he didn't want to have to go home and face his mother with the tale of another failure, another disastrous hunting trip.

So he was going to have to walk back to Crab Castle.

Great.

*

It was a long walk, and a lonely one, and Kobi was not used to long walks or loneliness. For the first hour or so he played the music that was stored in his headset, but he didn't much like music really, and he grew bored with it. When he turned it off the mountains were silent except for the squeak and crunch of his boots on the snow. He had changed the chameleon settings on his poncho so that it was bright orange, in the hope that someone would spot him trudging across the snowfields. But if the hunt was still out, they had moved far away from him. He thought he caught the baying of the hounds at one point, but it might have been only the wind moaning through the crags.

The low sun sank lower still. Blue shadows crept across the snowfields, and the ruined moon toppled across the sky. It was like living under a permanently collapsing tower, thought Kobi, glaring up at it. No wonder the Prells were all half crazy.

When the last of the daylight faded, he finally admitted to himself that he was lost. He was considering pinging the emergency site again when a familiar sound came echoing over the ridge ahead of him: the squeal of train brakes and the dull clash of couplings. He stumbled up the ridge and looked down onto a rail yard, patched with light from tall gantries. There were stacked freight containers and a dozen tracks vanishing into an opening in the mountainside. It was a strange place for a freight terminal, but Broken Moon was a strange world. Maybe there were mines in there. There would be people, at least, or machines that would be able to connect him to Crab Castle. He bounded down the slope toward the tracks in a cloud of powder snow.

But at the foot of the slope, between him and the tracks, there was a fence. Chain link, many feet high, topped off with razor wire. He'd never seen security like it. What were the Prells afraid of, out here in the mountains? Maybe the monkeys were a problem?

Angrily, he started to trudge along beside the fence, following the rails toward the place where they went into the mountain. He could see lights in there, and movement: big lifters piling things onto flatcars. He turned on his headset, but there was still nothing. Thought about shouting, but the underground loading bays were still too far away, and too loud for anyone inside to hear him.

Then the nearest set of rails began to thrum, the way rails did when a train was coming. He looked over his shoulder and saw it approaching up the line with its lights out, moving slowly. He turned to face it, and was about to wave his arms and shout when something made him think better of it.

Why would it not have its lights on?

He stood in the shadows and watched as it rumbled past. It was a wartrain, small but heavily armed, and towing a long line of armored carriages and flatcars. On every flatcar squatted a tank, or a gun, or an assault hovercraft. Kobi had never seen so much military equipment outside an action threedie. And there was more inside the mountain; he turned his headset on and zoomed in on the loading bays, and in each one there was a Prell wartrain.

So this was what Rolo had meant when he said the Prells were going places. They were getting ready to go to war.

Light blazed down on him from the sky. He looked up at the descending belly of a flyer. He must have triggered some trackside security system. The Prells were happy enough to take him off their mountain now.

Back in Crab Castle, after he'd eaten and been checked over by the Prells' medics, Kobi talked to Rolo—lowly and urgently in his room, knowing the heavy carvings on the walls might hide spy cams and microphones that would feed every word straight into the Prells' security net.

"They have wartrains, Rolo! Dozens of them. They're getting ready for something . . ."

Rolo was sulky, angry at him for getting lost, annoyed at being dragged away from the drinks and food downstairs. "Well of *course* they're getting ready for something, dear cousin. Why do you think we want this alliance? Everything's changed: the Noons have been weakened, and it's time for someone else to seize power. That someone will be the Prell Consortium. They've been waiting a generation for this. Your future father-in-law knows he'll never get a better chance."

"Don't call him that!"

"Why not? You seemed to be getting along all right with Lady Laria at the hunt today, before you fell off."

"This isn't about Laria. It's about Threnody. What's going to happen to her, if the Prells take over?"

"She'll be killed, I expect. Or sent into exile. Why do you care? That stuck-up Noon cow . . ."

"She isn't stuck-up."

"She dumped you fast enough when a better chance came along."

"They made her the Empress! She didn't want it! They made her break the engagement! They had to! Our family isn't big enough to marry into the imperial household!"

"But we *will* be!" said Rolo. "Don't you see? By the time your marriage to Laria Prell goes through, her uncle Elon will be sitting on the Flatcar Throne. That's what this is all about, Kobi. Getting our feet under the table at the dawn of a new dynasty. We're going to be one of the great families of this new era."

Kobi sat down on the bed. He picked miserably at the embroidered covers. "I don't see how they can expect to get away with it," he said. "All those wartrains and troop movements. The Guardians will notice."

Rolo smiled. It was the rather self-satisfied smile of someone who knows a secret. He sat down beside Kobi on the bed and said, "Cousin dearest, you must know that some of the Guardians have always had a soft spot for our chilly friends out here in Trans-Chiba. The Twins are protecting them, making sure they can prepare in secret for their move against the Noons. Which, when it comes, will be swift and ruthless. The other Guardians will grumble, but Guardians value stability above everything else. Once the smoke clears, Elon Prell will be

Emperor, and as long as he doesn't try to rule too brutally, the Guardians will accept him. It doesn't make too much difference to them who sits on the Flatcar Throne, so long as someone does."

Kobi thought of Threnody. How pretty she had looked in those portraits from Mars. Did she know what the Prells were cooking up? Surely her Railforce guards would be ready for it? But if even the Guardians didn't know . . .

"You see?" said Rolo, springing up, as if he was too excited to sit still for long. "You see? Poor old cousin Rolo, banished to the Winter Stars to talk to savages, but I've been getting to know these people. I've been building bridges, making deals. As soon as the old Emperor died I went straight to your mother and said, 'This is our chance, forget those old Noons, the Prells are the people to back.' You see?"

"Yes," said Kobi meekly.

"And you're going to thank me for finding you such a bride?"

"Thank you, Rolo."

"Don't mention it! Now, I don't know about you, but I could do with another drink tonight, so I am going to go back downstairs. Coming? Just keep what I've told you to yourself."

Kobi grinned. "All right. You continue down; I'll see you in twenty minutes."

He waited until his cousin had had time to walk along the corridor to the elevators, then started to change. He pulled on his traveling clothes. Over the top he put the camouflage hunting poncho. When he left, he went out through the window onto the balcony and down an outside staircase, heading for the cable car.

He told himself there was nothing to be afraid of. He was a guest in the Prells' home, and an important guest at that. If he wanted to take an evening stroll alone (despite the cold, despite how tired he was), then no one could object. All the same, as the cable car let him off at the small station below Crab Castle, he pulled up his hood and chameleoned his poncho to the same dull gray as those of the workers who were waiting there for a connection to the station city.

He stood in the shadows and wondered what his plan was. He hadn't had much experience with making plans. He had never needed to. When you were the son of a corporate family you did what you wanted, and left others to clean up the mess.

Well, now he wanted to warn Threnody, and give her a chance to get away from Grand Central before whatever it was that the Prells were planning happened. He didn't have to actually go there himself. There was a Railforce post on Broken Moon;

he'd tell the commander what he knew, then get a train back to Crab Castle before morning, and explain at breakfast that he had been too tired to rejoin the party.

It felt good to have that sorted out in his mind.

The train arrived and he shuffled into it, trying not to look too shocked at the shabbiness of the standard-class carriages. He had never traveled in standard class before. There were no compartments, just rows and rows of seats. Keeping his hood up, he sat in a corner one with his face turned to the window, looking out at snowfields and dark buildings while he used his headset to search the local data raft for the Railforce office. He wasn't going to risk messaging them, but he needed to know where to go and who to talk to so that he could deliver his warning in person.

There it was. A bland black block in the business district, not far from the station platforms. The local Railforce commander was a Colonel Bairam—a good Sundarbani name. Kobi called up a bio of him, and his plan fell apart.

He recognized the colonel's photo instantly. He was the same old, white-haired soldier who had been at the Prells' dinner.

"Broken Moon Station City," the train said, slowing. The other passengers all started pulling on coats and picking up bags, but Kobi stayed staring out of the window, watching the trackside clutter go by. Of course the Prells would have made sure that the local Railforce officers were in their pocket. Of course Colonel Bairam was a welcome guest at Crab Castle, a friend of the family. His junior officers too, most likely. Kobi groaned. How could he have been so stupid?

"You all right, friend?" asked a man, leaning down to touch his shoulder. Kobi stood up hastily, nodding, but the man followed him down the carriage and into the vestibule, where the other passengers were lining up to leave. "You're not from around here, are you?"

"I'm just visiting," said Kobi. "Doing some work for my family."

"Sundarbani, are you?" asked the man, recognizing Kobi's accent. A couple of others turned to look at him. "Bet you find it cold out here!"

The doors had opened. Everyone was shuffling out. In the hard white light under the station canopy, Kobi saw another train waiting on the neighboring platform, and heard the station's automated announcement booming, "All passengers for the zero forty-five to Golden Junction, stopping at Frostfall, PityMe, Lifthrasir, Chiba, and Golden Junction . . ."

"My train," he said, breaking free of his new friend, shoving a woman out of the way. "Excuse me . . ."

He sprinted across the platform and jumped aboard the express just as the doors sighed shut. One of the train's subroutines opened a window into his headset and asked for his travel credit. He pinged it the number of his family's account without thinking, and sat down. There was a slight delay—the doors closed, then opened again—and Kobi spent the time wishing he had been smart enough to buy some basic credit before he boarded. He was not cut out for this sort of adventure; he did not think fast enough. But it was all right; the train was finally pulling out of the station, leaving the city behind.

He pushed his way through the sticky sliding doors that led from the vestibule into the main part of the train car. He sat down in an empty seat, and looked out of the window for a last glimpse of Broken Moon's broken moon as the loco began to sing, accelerating hard into a tunnel and down the long straight to the K-gate.

A door slid open at the far end of the car and Elon Prell's twin bodyguards came through, making their way forward from the back of the train. They were moving slowly, looking into each bay of seats, glancing quickly at the face of every passenger. When they passed under the lamps set in the car ceiling, the light bounced from their shaved scalps.

I'll bluff it out, Kobi told himself. *I'll tell them I'm going down to Golden Junction to meet a girl. They'll understand that . . . I'm a Chen-Tulsi—they won't do anything to me . . .*

The twins were closer now. They moved in unison, but their heads turned in different directions, one checking the passengers on the left of the car, the other those on the right.

I'll pretend I'm asleep, thought Kobi. *I'll put my head down and close my eyes, and they won't even notice me.*

But he knew they would.

He felt the rhythm of the wheels change suddenly, and knew the train was hurtling into a gate. As the un-light of K-space shone through the windows he started to move, pulling himself out of the seat in the weird slow-motion timeless instant when his carriage was passing through the gate. By the time the train was across the threshold and racketing out of a tunnel on some minor moon, he was on his feet, moving toward the dining car at the front end.

He knew it would be a mistake to look back, but he looked back anyway. One of the Mako brothers saw him. Kobi pushed his way out of the car, through the swaying concertina coupling, into the next. Passengers in the seats he passed glanced up at him, and he was sure they could tell that he was scared. Through another door, another vestibule, another roaring coupling. Past stacked-up suitcases in a baggage car. The Motorik attendant there looked at him expectantly, but he shoved it out of his way and went on into the next car, and the next, and then turned sideways into a bathroom, hoping the Makos would go past.

After a moment he heard their voices outside. Something that sounded harder than a fist knocked on the door. "Sir?"

"Just a minute . . ." Kobi backed against the window. Lights were flashing past outside, but the glass was frosted so that he couldn't see out. Up through the drain from the sink in the corner came the thin, throbbing hiss of the wheels on the tracks, like music seeping from a cheap headset. The knocking on the door started again. It was loud and confident sounding— the knocking of men who were used to the doors they knocked on being opened.

Kobi messaged Rolo, who answered almost instantly. His image appeared, streamed by the headset into Kobi's visual cortex, so that Rolo's face seemed to hang in the air between him and the bathroom wall. He looked frazzled and angry. "Kobi? Where are you? What do you think you're—?"

"They're after me!" Kobi whimpered. "I'm on a train, and there are these two—"

"Of course they're after you!" shouted Rolo. "They think you're a spy! What the hell . . . Where are you?"

"Sir?" said one of the men outside the door.

"On a train . . . I don't know," said Kobi. "There are these two thugs, the Mako brothers . . ."

"Elon Prell's personal enforcers," said Rolo. "What did you expect? Did you think you could just sneak out, knowing what you know? Did you think they wouldn't be watching you?" He shook his head. "There's nothing I can do for you, you poor fool. When I think of all the work I put into this alliance—"

Kobi cut the connection. Stood there trembling, staring at his own stunned face in the mirror above the tiny sink.

There's nothing I can do. They were going to kill him. It didn't feel real. It couldn't end here. *Not in a bathroom . . .*

"Please come out, sir," said the voice outside the door.

Kobi talked to his headset, getting into the train's systems. The loco was called *Decision Trees*, an old AG-90 from the Foss trainworks on Kalina B. He did not know if he could trust it, but it had not locked any doors in his face on his way down the train, or unlocked this one yet, so he sent it a desperate message. "Train, tell Threnody Noon the Prells are going to attack Grand Central, tell her I—"

A sudden weightless feeling took hold of him. Beyond the frosted glass the light had changed to the unknown color of K-space. The train poured itself through another gateway, and in the timeless instant when it was between two worlds, there was a loud bang and the bathroom door burst open. One of the men stayed outside, keeping watch. The other came halfway in, pointing a chunky silver gun at Kobi.

"I am Kobi Chen-Tulsi!" shouted Kobi, brandishing his family's name like a weapon. It had always worked for him before, when he had been in minor trouble with the police on Sundarban, or wanted a table for his friends in a crowded restaurant. He shouted it half to the train, in the hope that it was listening, and half to the gunman. "I'm important!"

But the train did not answer, and the gunman shot him anyway.

PART FOUR
RAILWAR

10

Sometimes Chandni worried that if she went on living with rich people she would end up acting like a rich person, and caring about the things rich people cared about: poetry and curtains and stuff. Sometimes she thought that might not be such a bad idea, because the people at the palace seemed a lot happier and healthier than the low heroes she had mixed with in the past. But each time she started to enjoy her new life, something would happen to jolt her out of it.

The midsummer ball was like that. Chandni had been looking forward to it. The Empress's own dressmakers had made her a new gown for the occasion. Her hair had grown back just enough that she no longer had to wear a wig or headscarf. As she made her way downstairs to the Azure Room with all the other ladies, she kept catching glimpses of her reflection in mirrors and polished wall panels and thinking that she had come a long way since the freezers. But when she entered the massive room, her heart hardened again. No one had bothered telling her that the ball was ice-themed.

It was a rich people idea of a joke, she guessed: marking the longest day of Grand Central's long summer in a room full of icebergs. The floor had been covered with black sand, and the icebergs were so big that she imagined the room must have been demolished to let them in, then rebuilt around them. Some had been hollowed out and musicians were playing inside them, strange bing-bongy music on those modern instruments whose names Chandni could never remember. Some had spiral staircases carved up their flanks, and partygoers were gathering on their summits, reaching up to touch the painted ceiling. On a long central dais stood icy sculptures of birds and animals, and a centerpiece in the form of the smiling sun symbol of the Noons, which was hollow, and appeared to be full of red and gold butterflies. On ice-carved tables stood blocks of ice in which delicious-looking snacks had been embedded. They were designed to melt during the first few dances, so that people could reward themselves with some refreshment when they came off the dance floor.

For a moment Chandni stood in the doorway as if she had been flash-frozen again. She was wondering if it was all some cruel, elaborate joke about her past. But it wasn't. The only people who knew about her time on ice were Kala Tanaka and the Empress herself. Kala Tanaka was dancing with Threnody's uncle Nilesh, who had arrived from Khoorsandi that afternoon. There was a silly smile on her plain old face, and she looked as if she had forgotten that Chandni Hansa even existed. Threnody was dancing too, more formally, with Lyssa Delius. She wore a silvery dress cut low behind, and intricate white frost patterns had been stenciled on the brown of her shoulders and her back. She must have sat for hours while someone sprayed those on her, Chandni thought, and it had never once crossed her mind that for a girl from the freezer prisons, all this ice might bring back chilly memories.

"Do you like the music?" asked a young officer in Railforce uniform, nerving himself to ask Chandni for a dance.

"It's music?"

"Yes! That's Lufthansa Terminal—you must have heard of them? And I hear Cranberry Morpheme will be playing later . . ."

"I prefer real bands," she shouted, over the music. "Like The Radical Daylight . . ." But The Radical Daylight had split up because of artistic differences while Chandni had been doing her first stint in the freezers, and she could tell from the uncertain look in the young man's eyes that nobody under fifty had even heard of them.

She turned and left. The palace corridors were empty except for patrolling security drones, but Chandni pinged them her clearance code and they did not bother her. She helped herself to a priceless little Old Earth artifact from a niche beside the entrance to the Waterfall Room. Outside the windows, fireworks were rising above the city, silver and white, drawing enormous snowflakes on the sky.

*

Threnody was not enjoying the party either. It had seemed like a good idea to decorate the ballroom in the style of her mother's iceberg portraits, but they just made her homesick for the black sand beaches of Malapet, and her mother had preferred to stay at home and paint—she did not like parties. Of course, an Empress could not storm off to her room, so Threnody stayed, and danced, and smiled, and said all the usual pointless things to all the usual pointless people. But she was glad when the partygoers started making for their cars and flyers and the guest rooms on the lower floors, leaving the palace staff to start melting the icebergs with hot air blowers and sweeping up tons of wet sand.

She sent her ladies-in-waiting to bed, wondered vaguely what had become of Chandni Hansa, and took the elevator to her own quarters on the top floor. A message pinged into her headset on the way. She waited until all her servants and her security team had left before she threw herself down on one of her enormous sofas and checked to see who it was from. Blissful alone time, much better than parties. She was a little drunk. Her room spun around her, not unpleasantly. The message was from the *Crystal Horizon*, the train that had taken her to Mars. It must have been given her private channel while she was a passenger. It was a nice old train, but she wondered why it would ping messages at her in the middle of the night.

Empress Threnody—please contact me.

Threnody slipped her shoes off and flexed her toes, which had been trodden on by many important people during the dancing. (Not enough people for Lyssa Delius's liking; a lot of the corporate families had stayed away, unhappy about the new laws that the Rail Marshal had pushed through the senate while the media was busy covering the Mars trip.)

Threnody pinged a reply to the *Crystal Horizon*. The waiting signal flashed for a moment in the corner of her eye, then a still image of the old train appeared and its voice said, "Empress Threnody! I am sorry to interrupt you. I have returned to normal service, as you know, and I am just leaving Grand Central. I am the three twenty express to Coalsack Junction . . ."

"Three twenty?" Threnody yawned. "Is it really that late? I mean, that early?"

"I can't talk for long, Empress Threnody; I'll be going through the gate in a minute. But I heard something very odd in

Chiba yesterday. A loco called *Decision Trees* told me that one of its passengers got shot. Two Prell security people came aboard, told the *Trees* this young fellow was a terrorist. Well, after what happened to the *Wildfire* and the *Time of Gifts* we're all a bit on edge about that sort of thing, so the *Trees* let them carry on. It thought they were going to arrest him. But they shot him! Dead!"

"Go on."

"Well, just before it happened, the young man talked to it. He said his name was Kobi Chen-Tulsi. He said, 'Tell Threnody Noon that the Prells are going to attack Grand Central.'"

Threnody, who had only half been concentrating, sat up and opened her eyes. She stood and crossed her suite, the windows folding back automatically as she went out onto the wide balcony. The lights of the city sprawled across the deep blue night; road surfaces glowing gently with the sunlight they had stored during the day, and the moving chains of amber lights that were the windows of trains.

"Kobi? Kobi Chen-Tulsi? He . . . *what?*"

"He said, 'Tell Threnody Noon that the Prells are going to attack Grand Central.' And then they shot him. The *Decision Trees* pinged me a recording. It's somewhat graphic . . ."

"Show me," said Threnody.

*

Chandni was really leaving this time. Her ball gown lay over the back of a chair like a sloughed-off skin, and she had changed into black pants and a black tunic. Not that she was planning to sneak out of the palace. She would just borrow one of the cars from the staff garage and tell it to drop her at the nearest K-bahn platform. But the black clothes looked good on her, and they would attract no attention on whichever world she decided to alight.

She was not taking much with her. The Old Earth artifact she had picked up at random in the corridor was a little golden figurine that fitted snugly in her tunic pocket—she would sell it at Ambersai or K'mbussi. She had packed a bag with spare clothes: rolled underwear and balled-up socks. It was only a small bag, but it was more than she had owned for a long time. Now she was waiting for 3:30 a.m., when she figured the last party guests would finally have cleared off.

When the knocking started, she jumped right out of her chair. It took her a second or two to figure out that nobody was knocking at her door—they were pounding on the door of Kala Tanaka's suite, just down the corridor. Pounding and shouting. "Kala! Kala!" Pounding and shouting and sobbing.

There was no way Chandni could pretend to have slept through it all. She went to her door and opened it. The Empress Threnody herself stood in the corridor, barefoot but still in her ball gown, fist raised to punish Kala's door some more. She turned to Chandni a face streaked with mascara and twisted in some kind of misery. Her drones tried to get between her and Chandni and she swatted them irritably aside. "Where's Kala?" she sobbed.

Chandni thought fast, looking for some excuse that would save her from getting entangled in whatever rich person craziness was going down. There wasn't one, not that she could see. She said, "I think she's probably spending the night with your uncle Nilesh in his guest suite. They seemed pretty happy to see each other at the party. You've tried her headset?"

"Kobi's dead!" said Threnody. "A train sent me footage! They murdered him! He said the Prells are planning an attack . . ."

"Maybe this is something you should be telling security? You know, all those security people and drones and things you keep?"

"But I don't know if it's true! It might be a hoax or something; I don't want to start a whole alert, not about the Prells—it'll cause an incident, and if it isn't true . . . but it can't be true . . . he can't really be dead, can he?"

"Show me," said Chandni. She opened her door wider and let Threnody into her room. The bag lay on the floor where she had left it. She kicked it into the corner, hoping Threnody wouldn't notice.

As she did so, the video file pinged from Threnody's headset into her own. It showed grainy snatches of footage from ceiling cameras in a train vestibule. A young man came running through, two more men close behind. The pursuers had shaved pale heads. Then the view switched to a narrow bathroom. The young man was staring up at the camera. "Train, tell Threnody Noon the Prells are going to attack Grand Central, tell her I—" Then a bang—a *gunshot*—the kid shouting, panicky, "I am Kobi Chen-Tulsi! I'm important!" Another shot, kicking him backward against the window. A smear on the starred glass as he fell sideways, out of sight.

Chandni cursed. "Where's the train who sent you this?"

"Gone offworld. It has to be a hoax, doesn't it? Kala can always spot these things—she'll know . . ."

Chandni let her babble on. She opened a K-bahn timetable in her headset. Arrival data for all the platforms on Grand Central popped up. Next to one was a red flag: the 3:44 from Chiba was delayed. That wasn't in itself unusual. A long-ago biotech screw-up on Chiba meant that most of the planet was covered by one enormous plant, the Weltkraut. Trains were sometimes delayed there by a leaf on the line. But this particular morning it seemed somehow sinister, because Chiba was the hub that linked the Prell worlds to the rest of the Network.

"Call your security people," she told Threnody. "Call Delius. I don't think it's a hoax."

Threnody stared at her a moment, then blinked a couple of times and started tearily explaining things all over again to her headset. Chandni went out onto the balcony. Cool night air, three moons stacked up over the mountains like stratocruisers waiting for a runway. On the many viaducts of the station city, trains were moving. Too many trains for this hour of the morning.

"Empress," she said, and as she turned something terrifyingly fast and loud came shrieking through the sky above her and slammed into Threnody's suite on the floor above. Fire and debris came down around her as she dived into the room, but the room was tilting, as if it were trying to throw her back out onto the balcony—which had gone, smashed off the side of the palace by another balcony falling from above. Threnody was shouting something. Chandni swore steadily. Then she heard that shriek again, racing through the air, coming at enormous speed, and something grabbed her and plucked her off her feet and *threw* her. She screamed and barely noticed the floor hit her, and her scream was lost in a stunning flare of light, a storm of brutal noise.

11

One moment Threnody was talking on her headset link to a man on the palace security team, the next it was dark and she was lying awkwardly in a corner. It was *really* dark—she couldn't see anything except a fading red smear, the after-image of some colossal flash. She couldn't hear much at first either, but then her ears popped and there were far-off firecracker noises and a rustling cellophane sound much closer that she worked out was fire.

So why was it dark? Why weren't there flames? There must be flames—she could feel the heat of them on one side of her face, she could smell the burning—but she couldn't see them, because she was blind.

"Chandni?" she shouted. "Chandni Hansa?"

No reply. Threnody pushed herself up onto all fours, wanting to run and not knowing which way. *An explosion,* she thought. She started crawling like a baby, away from the heat and crackle of the fire. The carpet under her hands felt crisp, like fried seaweed. A siren was blaring somewhere. She thought she could hear the little wingbeats of her hummingbird drones still circling her, but she couldn't contact them, and when she reached up to where her headset had been she found that it was gone.

"Chandni?" she shouted. "Help me!"

A lot of loud bangs were happening, far off, but not far enough. Every time she heard one, memories of the Spindlebridge hit her like shrapnel. For a moment, she wondered if she was still on the Spindlebridge. Because such things couldn't happen twice, could they? This must be all one great, ongoing catastrophe, and the strange interval in which she had become Empress and moved to the imperial palace had been just a hallucination brought on by the noise and the fire and the fear.

Someone grabbed hold of her. She screamed, and couldn't stop screaming, even when she recognized Chandni's voice saying, "It's all right, it's all right . . ."

"Where were you? I called for you . . ."

"I was knocked out for a moment. It's all right now."

"It's not all right—I can't *see!*"

She struggled to break free, and Chandni hit her a single hard, stinging blow with the flat of her hand. That stilled Threnody long enough for Chandni to press something to her face. She felt terminals slip into place, audio behind her ear, visual against her temple. Chandni held her head steady with one hand while she fumbled with the headset.

Suddenly Threnody could see again. Not through her eyes, which were still throwing up after-images and felt like they'd been grilled, but through the headset's camera, which fed its images straight into her brain. She saw Chandni as a dim green ghost against swirls of deeper green smoke and bright blank patches that she guessed were flame.

"We have to get out of here, because it's on fire," Chandni was saying, grabbing a bag from the corner, shaking bits of ceiling off it before she swung it onto her shoulder. Threnody looked down and saw Chandni take her hand. It was like watching a screen—something happening to someone else.

"What happened?"

"Missiles or something," said Chandni, pulling her to her feet. "Prells, I'm guessing."

"They must be crazy! Railforce will crush them. This will mean the end of their family . . ."

They moved together through the shattered room. Some of Threnody's drones had survived the blast and went ahead in a V formation as Chandni pushed the door open and stepped out into the corridor. Where Kala Tanaka's suite had been there was just a dizzy view past twisted girders to the city, where several big fires were burning. Lyssa Delius's HQ on the top floors of the Railforce tower was blazing like a torch. Jagged, fast-moving flying things flicked through the smoke, the roar of engines rumbling after them only when they were out of sight.

"But security said there was no danger of an attack," said Threnody. "They told me everything was under control . . ."

"They were wrong, then," Chandni said, dragging her past the hole and out into a wider corridor that seemed undamaged. "There were delays on the O Link and the Spiral Line. The Prells must have been stopping traffic to get their wartrains through."

They went along the corridor. It was surprisingly quiet. Where were the rescue drones? Where were the guards? A flock of little origami birds, folded from gold and silver leaf, hung from the ceiling, fluttering wildly in the odd winds that were gusting through the palace. Voices echoed up a stairwell ahead, bellowing orders in Railforce battle code.

"Oh, thank the Guardians!" said Threnody, hurrying to meet the squad of blue-armored troopers as they came up the stairs.

Chandni hung back. She had been thinking. If *she* had been able to check the K-bahn timetable and tell that something bad was about to go down, why hadn't the security people seen it coming? Why had they told Threnody not to worry?

She hit the Empress from behind with a flying tackle that brought both of them crashing down on the hard floor. Threnody's indignant yelp was drowned by the hard crack of a gun as the leading trooper raised his pistol and shot at her, the bullet slicing through empty air where her head had just been. At the same moment her hummingbird drones reacted to the threat, folding their wings against their bodies and transforming themselves into little missiles. They flew at the Railforce squad on tails of fire. There were small sonic booms, flares of light, wet bangs, and the heavy sound of bodies falling. When Chandni and Threnody raised their heads, they saw that parts of the corridor were on fire and that the Bluebodies were dead.

"But they're on our side . . ." Threnody said, in a tiny wondering voice that seemed to come from somewhere else entirely, like dialogue from a kid's show overlaid on a bloodthirsty war story.

Chandni stood up and went warily through the smoke to where the bodies lay. She took a gun from one of the dead men and pulled a medipak full of battlefield surgical supplies from another's belt. As she came back to where Threnody cowered there was more shouting from downstairs, then a sudden quick burst of gunfire like demented hammering. Chandni helped Threnody up and started dragging her on along the corridor.

"I don't think the Prells would make a move like this unless they were sure they could win," she said. "They probably have half of Railforce on their side. They must have friends in the K-bahn Timetable Authority too, to clear the way for their wartrains."

"But . . . then we can't trust anyone!"

"I never trusted anyone to start with." Chandni thumbed open the doors of an elevator and pushed Threnody inside.

"You're not supposed to use elevators when there's a fire . . . ," Threnody said.

"There is a fire," agreed the elevator. "Please use the stairs."

"Shut up," said Chandni, to both of them.

The elevator dropped for a time, then stopped. "Next time you are in a burning building," it said tartly, "please consider taking the stairs instead."

They stepped out on an administrative level. There was nobody around, just the tireless wailing of alarms. They hurried along wide service corridors where gilded chairs were stacked, through a door marked THIS DOOR NOT IN USE. They entered a maze of scruffy, silent offices that Empresses weren't ever meant to see.

"What about the Guardians?" asked Threnody. "They'll stop it, won't they? How could they let the Prells do this?"

Chandni didn't answer, but she didn't need to. Threnody could figure it out for herself. The Guardians must have known what the Prells were planning, because the Guardians knew everything. If they let this happen, they must approve of it. It wasn't just the Prells and their friends in Railforce who were out to get her. The gods themselves had turned against her.

"What will we do?" she asked.

Chandni looked her up and down. "Get out of that stupid party dress, for a start," she said.

Threnody obediently started to take off the ragged, stained ball gown. Chandni opened her bag and dumped out a small heap of clothes—good clothes, but ordinary: black and gray. "How did you have time to pack?" asked Threnody. But she continued before Chandni could think of an answer, saying, "I'm so glad you're with me. Without you . . . thank you."

Chandni watched her dress, wondering if she should tell her that she had been planning to leave anyway. Wondering if she should tell her that she hadn't been stunned by the explosions earlier. She'd stood there watching for what felt like ages while Threnody crawled blindly around in the burning room shouting for her, and she hadn't said a thing. She'd been on her way to the door when something made her turn back and help. She still didn't know why she had done it.

In the bottom of a locker she found an ancient pair of shoes, near enough Threnody's size. In a drawer she found some scissors, which she used to crop Threnody's hair down to a black stubble even shorter than her own. Threnody, who was used to having other people decide what she should look like and then make it happen, said nothing; she just shut her eyes and stood there while the heavy blue tresses fell on the floor around her feet.

Chandni worked in silence too. She was wondering how to break it to Threnody that this was where they parted. If she left on her own, she could vanish into the war-torn city, and maybe take advantage of whatever local chaos the Prell assault had bred. She certainly wasn't going to risk getting caught with a fugitive Empress.

But when she put the scissors down and Threnody blinked at her, trusting and somehow childlike, the same strange feeling that had made her help the Empress the first time took hold of her again. She resented it, but she could not ignore it.

She kicked open the doors to an access stairway. Noises drifted down from floors above. Ceramic stairs descended into shadow.

"Come on," she said, stretching out her hand for Threnody to take.

And they went down the stairs together, into the dark.

12

The Prell wartrains reached Grand Central in three waves. The first were assault trains, packing heavy weapons and towing lines of flatcars that launched swarms of drones and missiles as they emerged from the K-gates. Behind them came troop trains: carriage after carriage filled with infantry in the unfashionable purple battle armor of the Prell CoMa.

Laria Prell arrived with the third wave, riding in the command car of her uncle's train, the *New Maps of Hell*, as it came tearing through the K-gates from Frostfall, past stations full of stranded travelers and indignant passenger trains cowering on sidings. News of the attack was already out—the Prells had posted a press release in the data rafts of all the central worlds—but no word had come back yet from Grand Central of how the battle was going. So Laria was tense as they roared into the last gate. If things had gone badly, the *New Maps of Hell* might be under attack as soon as it emerged on the far side.

Everything had happened so fast. Kobi Chen-Tulsi had triggered it, running away from Crab Castle the other night. Laria was secretly glad that he had gone—she had felt sorry for him, and she hadn't wanted to marry him—but the family security people feared he might have sent some message to the Noons. Suddenly the plans that had been in slow, careful preparation for so many months were all being put into action.

In the timeless blink of K-light between Kisinchand and Grand Central, Laria wondered what had become of Kobi. There was a rumor that the Mako brothers had gone after him when he fled, and another rumor that they had killed him, but Laria did not want to believe that one; the House of Prell were warriors, not murderers.

The glow of the K-gate faded. No turning back now. Not that turning back had ever really been an option. They were in a tunnel, the slightly heavier gravity of Grand Central pulling Laria deeper into her seat. Sudden sunlight stabbed the narrow windows. She couldn't see anything outside, but her headset fed her a drone's-eye view of the city. It looked pretty normal from out here on the Chaim Nevek Viaduct. Until you realized that those ten or twelve black towers, all leaning at the same slight angle away from the prevailing wind, were towers of smoke. Combat hovercraft flying the Prell battle flag were pouring off a train on a neighboring line. Northward, part of the imperial palace had been engulfed by an upside-down cascade of golden flames.

She looked at her uncle Elon, who was scowling in concentration as he listened to battle reports. After a moment his craggy face turned red and he slammed his fist down on the livewood armrest of his seat and shouted, "Yes! They were taken by surprise! Organized resistance has collapsed. Our ground troops are mopping up a few last pockets of Delius's people . . ."

"Already?" asked Laria, while the other officers in the carriage began cheering. "We've beaten Railforce, sir?"

He was busy with his headset feed again and didn't hear her question. But his bodyguards did. Shiv and Enki Mako were sitting nearby, out of uniform as usual and sprawled in their seats in that lazy way that Uncle Elon would never have tolerated from anybody else. They smiled at Laria, and Shiv said, "Railforce don't give in that easily!"

"But we weren't fighting Railforce," said his brother. "Not all of them. The marshals of the third and twelfth divisions are as unhappy as we are with the new Noon Empress. Their troops are fighting alongside ours."

The train was drawing into a station. People were shouting, "Victory!" But it didn't feel like victory to Laria. She had been expecting a real battle, like the big murals of Galaghast on the wall of the schoolroom when she was little: blazing wartrains, burning drones. Of course, Galaghast had been a glorious defeat for the family, and she wanted to win, but winning because the enemy's army turned out to have been on your side all along didn't feel like victory. It felt more like politics. Or just plain *cheating*.

More reports were coming in. As Laria stepped off the command car behind her uncle, Prell CoMa generals came hurrying up to salute and tell him that this or that objective had been secured. A few Railforce units loyal to the Noons were still making trouble near the senate gardens. An old Noon wartrain called the *Hairy Panic* was fighting a running battle with Prell locos on the viaducts of the Jauhexine Quarter, but they expected news of its surrender shortly.

"What about Threnody Noon?" he asked.

The commanders grew uncertain. One said, "We are still identifying bodies from the missile strike on her suite."

Another admitted, "Her private rooms were extensively damaged, but unfortunately it seems she may not have been in them at the time. It is possible that she is still at large."

Laria felt oddly relieved. Kobi Chen-Tulsi had cared about the Noon Empress; he had become a much nicer, more interesting person when he talked about her. Wherever he was, Kobi would be happy that she had escaped.

Elon Prell, however, was not. He gave a sharp sniff that people who knew him recognized as a sign of danger. "Find her," he said.

It was the first order he gave as Emperor of the Network.

*

The dinosaurs were nervous. Spooked by the smell of smoke on the breeze, and by the occasional sounds of gunfire still drifting from the city, the great sauropods stretched their necks high into the air and let out hooting cries.

Threnody had explained that the creatures weren't dangerous. This wide crescent of parkland north of the palace was not stocked with any carnivores, just big, decorative creatures like those brachiosaurs, gene-teched replicas of beasts that had once roamed Old Earth. But Chandni was wary of them anyway. They were massive. If they stampeded and she was in their way, well, it would be just her luck to escape the freezers and the Prell assault only to get herself trodden on by a dinosaur.

Still, Chandni was glad to have the park. Prell scout drones were wheeling above the city. Here in the park, the dense foliage and the presence of so many animals might help to hide her and Threnody.

They walked north all day, keeping to the trees as much as they could, lying in deep, shady places whenever drones came overhead. The smells of soil and growing things reminded Threnody of her family's game reserves on Jangala, where she had gone with Kobi and Zen Starling on a disastrous hunting trip. Every time she thought of Kobi, she thought of Kobi dying, and it made her feel that all this walking was a waste of time, because if Kobi could die then she could die too. Sooner or later one of those drones would spot her, and the Prell soldiers would come and shoot her just as they had shot Kobi. But she didn't want to be left behind, so each time Chandni Hansa started moving north again she got to her feet and followed doggedly, feet blistering inside her stolen shoes.

At least Threnody's eyesight was returning. Chandni had treated her eyes with something from the medipak she'd looted, a spray that felt cold against her eyeballs. She could see now without the headset's help: dim, smeared sight, but enough to make her hope that, if she came through this day alive, she would not be blind. The sunlight stung, but that was another reason to stay under cover of the trees. She followed Chandni and thought about the way her drones had killed the medipak's owner. Violence like that was something everyone liked to say the human race had long grown out of—the stuff of historical threedies, wars on Old Earth. But it was still there, just beneath life's settled surface. The Guardians only had to take their eyes off the game for a moment . . .

Chandni took the headset back and used it to access the Grand Central data rafts. A lot of sites were down, replaced by infomercials telling everyone to stay in their homes and cooperate with the Prell CoMa, who had joined with Railforce to liberate the city. On the newsfeeds Elon Prell delivered a speech about how the Prell family had acted in the interests of the whole Empire, overthrowing the usurper Delius and her Noon puppet.

Drone footage showed Lyssa Delius lying dead on the floor of a shot-up office in the Railforce tower. She looked smaller and older and more fragile than she had alive. Prell soldiers posed beside her body like hunters showing off their prey.

Chandni checked a few maps, then took the headset off and threw it into a wallow where some triceratops were enjoying a mud bath. She did not know much about modern headsets, and she was afraid the Prells might be able to track her through it if she used it for too long. The maps were safe in her head, though; she'd always had a good memory for maps.

*

Toward evening, as the twin suns sank redly through the drifts of smoke that still hung over the heart of the city, two young women emerged from the northern end of the Imperial Sauropod Park and looked down into the industrial district of Gallibagh. They wore the shabby clothes of workers or servants. They both had raggedly close-cropped hair, ordinary faces crusted with ordinary dirt.

At the foot of the slope a branch line from the Gallibagh rail yards led to a bunkerlike ceramic building with the Railforce logo glowing on its roof.

"What's that?" asked Threnody, sitting down in the shadow of some bushes and pulling off her shoes to rub her feet.

"Railforce retirement home," said Chandni. "It's where they store some of the old locos they don't have a use for anymore. I can't imagine the Prells have much use for them either. Hopefully they won't be watching this place too closely."

Threnody followed her quickly downhill through the dying light. High overhead, in the smoky haze that hung above the city, a Prell surveillance drone noticed the movement and zoomed its cameras in. It fed the grainy footage to intelligence systems in the Datasea, which started running it through facial recognition filters.

*

The lines that led in through the big hangar doors of the retirement home were screened by high wire fences. The building itself was an unwelcoming block of gray ceramic dug into a hill.

"How do we get in?" asked Threnody.

Chandni reached inside her tunic and pulled out the gun she had brought from the palace.

"You're not going to kill anyone, are you?" asked Threnody.

"Hope not. It depends how things work out."

"But you have, haven't you? Before, I mean?"

Chandni shrugged her shrug, which had so many meanings. "You heard of Ayaguz? I don't suppose you ever did an imperial visit to Ayaguz. They wouldn't wave flags at you there. It's a deep-ocean waterworld: a bunch of undersea mining habitats, rough as they come. A different gang controls each pressure dome, all looking to expand their territories the whole time. I wound up there after my first time in the freezers—ran with the Deep Six Crew for eight or nine months. So this isn't my first time in a turf war, Empress."

Threnody was about to explain that railwar between two great corporate families was nothing at all like a squabble between two gangs of hoodlums in a mining town, but while Chandni was talking they had been creeping along the side of the building, past low scrub and big trash bins, and they had come to a ceramic door, stenciled with warning decals. Chandni hammered on it with the handgrip of her gun, then stuck the barrel into the face of the man who opened the door.

She wrenched his headset off with her free hand and tossed it into the bushes behind her.

The man was old, with a flop of white hair, a wrinkled brown face, and wet brown eyes that crossed when he looked at the gun and came uncrossed again when he looked past it at Chandni.

"You on your own here?" she asked.

He nodded nervously, half raising his hands. "I am the caretaker. This is just a storage facility . . ."

"You know who this is?"

"No. Another bad young woman like yourself? Your sister, maybe?"

"Come on, you must have seen her. She has her face on money and buildings and things."

The caretaker looked again at Threnody. "It can't be . . . they are saying on the newsfeeds that she is dead—I don't want trouble . . ."

"Nobody *wants* trouble," said Chandni. "Trouble just finds us." She shoved him backward, gesturing with her head for Threnody to follow her inside. The door shut behind them. They stood in a corridor, lit by ceiling panels. The hum of big power units, underground smells. A holoscreen in a cluttered little office showing news footage of Elon Prell. It felt strange to be indoors again. The caretaker kept staring at Threnody as though she were a ghost. He seemed more interested in her than in the gun, which Chandni was now poking into his ribs.

"Take us to the trains," she said.

13

It was always a problem, what to do with old trains. You couldn't just scrap them when they became outmoded. Trains were at least as self-aware as people. So you kept them running for as long as possible, upgrading and reconfiguring, rehousing old brains in shiny new bodies. And if there was really no way they could be kept on the rails—if they were hopelessly antiquated or eccentric, or if they were designed for war and there were no wars going on—then you stored them. There were facilities all over the Network where old trains dreamed away their retirement in slow-state sleep, or surfed sections of the Datasea designed to please them: virtual tracks and railway playgrounds, strange chatrooms where the ancient locos could discuss their adventures and grumble about the fancy newfangled models that had replaced them.

The caretaker led Chandni and Threnody down a bit more corridor and peered into a lock beside a door. The lock scanned his retina and the door slid open. For a few seconds there was darkness on the other side, then lights sensed they were needed and came flickering on all across a high roof. They were inside the hill, Threnody realized. The building outside was just a kind of porch. The real facility was this cavernous hangar, its floor covered with rails. On every set of rails at least one train was sleeping. There were de-fanged wartrains with gaping holes in their armor where weapons had been removed, and locos whose whole hulls had been stripped off, baring doughnut-shaped reaction chambers and the boxy housings of their brains. Others looked whole, though most were connected to webs of cabling and ducts that trailed down from the shadows overhead.

"What are you looking for?" asked Threnody, as Chandni forced the poor caretaker ahead of her across the rails, staring at each of the silent trains in turn.

"Something that'll get us off Grand Central fast, without attracting too much attention."

Threnody patted the prow of a towering black thing, all sleek armor plate and lidded weapon hatches. "What about this one?"

The caretaker shook his head. "Oh no, Lady Noon, you don't want that one. That is an unstable train."

The loco seemed to sense Threnody's touch. It sort of *purred* deep down inside itself, and two red lights glowed like fiery eyes up among the complications of its armor.

"It looks fast," she said.

"It is," said Chandni, "but we're not in *that* much of a hurry, and it's not exactly inconspicuous." She went on across the hangar, forcing the old man ahead of her. "What else do you have hidden in here? Come on, the sooner we find something, the sooner we'll be on our way."

Threnody looked up at the black loco. She could feel it watching her. The name on its flank was *Ghost Wolf.*

Chandni had stopped in front of a shabby little Foss 500. It was the sort of train that usually hauled freight—the sort of train nobody looked twice at. "I have some old ammunition cars over on track nine," the caretaker was saying eagerly. "Give me ten minutes; I'll soon have it hitched up and fueled."

The Foss was waking up. "I am pleased to be back in service," it said. "I am the *Courageous Snipe*. Where shall we be going?"

"Anywhere," said Chandni. "The timetables will be all over the place. If anyone complains, you can tell them you're carrying urgent supplies for the Prell CoMa."

"Gate two hundred and sixty-five," said Threnody. "It's not far from here."

Chandni looked back at her. "Where does it go?"

"It leads to Toubit," said Threnody. "At Toubit we could get onto the old Dog Star Line." The Dog Star zigzagged through the Network's heart, linking dead stations and dead worlds. "We could use it like Raven did, and maybe get to Sundarban before the Prells do."

"The Dog Star Line?" Chandni shook her head. "It'll be blocked off. No, we'll head for Gosinchand or one of those worlds, get on the Spiderlight Line or the Eastern Doubt. Nobody will think to look for us out there."

"We should go to Sundarban," insisted Threnody. "It's my family's homeworld. They'll be organizing a fight-back against this Prell takeover. When they hear how you rescued me, you'll be rewarded."

"I'm not doing this for a *reward*," said Chandni.

The huge doors at the front of the train store opened with surprising speed, rattling up into the roof like window blinds. The setting sun streamed in so brightly that it dazzled Threnody for a moment. People came running into the facility, their helmet-amplified voices shouting things about surrendering and getting down on the floor. She recognized the purple combat armor of Prell Corporate Marines.

She started to raise her hands, feeling almost relieved that she did not have to run anymore.

What happened next—what started it—she was never sure. Maybe the Prell CoMa were just eager for a chance to shoot someone. At any rate, Chandni shouted something, the old man went running forward, also shouting, there was a stutter of gunfire, bullets pecked at his clothes, and he stumbled and fell. Chandni was running across the tracks, firing her pistol. The Prell troopers scattered into cover. Behind the hard thump of guns and their echoes there was a pretty chinkling sound as spent cartridges hit the rails. A shadow heaved itself across the sunset. Something big was entering the train store. A brutal-looking armored loco with Prell banners fluttering on its nose. As Chandni reached her, Threnody saw its guns swing around to point at her. Then a black wall slid across her view.

The *Ghost Wolf* had rolled forward, putting itself between the Prells and their prey.

"Get aboard," it said, in a big, hard voice. A narrow doorway opened in its armored hide.

Something burst on the far side of it, sending a sheet of flame up into the gantries overhead. Chandni thrust Threnody toward the black train. She scrambled up the steps, through the doorway, with the whole loco shaking as more shots from the Prell train slammed into it.

Someone in the Prell squad must have had their wits about them, because the facility doors were starting to close again. The *Ghost Wolf* gave a contemptuous-sounding snort and shouldered its way out, shearing through the ceramic like a blade through wet cardboard. In its cramped little cabin Threnody clung to seat backs and door pillars, flung from side to side as it went rattling over points outside the facility.

"Where are we going?" asked the train. "The Prells have already sent messages to their forces in the city. I'm picking up two more of their wartrains leaving the central platforms."

"Gate two-six-five," shouted Chandni.

"But you said—" Threnody began.

"Two-six-five is the only gate we can hope to reach before those wartrains cut us off."

Physics tugged them sideways as the *Ghost Wolf* went too fast around a curve of the track. "There are drones patrolling at gate two-six-five," it said, with what sounded like dark amusement.

"Can you handle them, train?" asked Chandni.

"Got nothing to handle them *with*," said the train, sulkily. "I'm decommissioned. The only reason I've got fuel is 'cause I stole it from other stored trains. All my weapons have been removed."

"Can those drones pierce your armor?"

"I doubt it. Let's find out, shall we?"

A fiery surf broke over it as a missile hit. The cabin rang like a huge bell, then rang again, the screens glitching for a moment the second time.

"Nah," said the *Ghost Wolf.* "They're rubbish."

*

Gate two-six-five was under a wooded hill in a quiet northern suburb of the station city. The Prells had not sent a wartrain to guard it, since it led nowhere but Toubit. A small squad of drones was on sentry duty there instead. The ugly, stubby-winged machines circled like sullen bees above the tunnel mouth where the line vanished into the hillside. A few children from the district came to watch them for a while, but they were not very interesting drones, so they soon began to drift away. The war had seemed exciting when it started, but now everyone was saying it was already over. There would be school again tomorrow.

So there were only three children left when the black loco came tearing up the line. They heard it coming and ran to the trackside fences, twining grubby fingers through the chain-linked wire. The train was moving faster than any train they'd ever seen. It was moving so fast that when they described it to their friends the next day they would not be believed. The Prell drones fired *actual missiles* at it, but the black wartrain did not want to stop, and the missiles didn't seem to do much harm; they just started a few fires on the surface of its black armor, which only made it look *even cooler*.

As the train came past the place where the children were standing, a drone swung itself in to try a close shot, and the train, as if it knew it had an audience, flipped open the hatch cover on one of its weapon bays. The bay was empty, but the edge of the hatch cover was as good as a blade at that speed: it sliced the drone in half. One half went tumbling away in the train's slipstream while the other spun upward, making that whiffling, chirruping sound doomed drones always made in games. The children looked up, round-eyed, as it spun helplessly into another drone, and both slid sideways across the sky and hit the cliffs above the tunnel mouth with a very satisfying explosion. A few rather big rocks came tumbling down, rebounding from the black train's armor. As it went into the tunnel mouth, the cliff face above it seemed to shrug and sag. Trees up there began to glide downhill, upright and dignified at first, then tilting and tumbling as the ground beneath them broke up and collapsed in rubble across the tracks.

Bits of debris from the wrecked drones pattered through the leaves of the trackside trees. The children scampered to collect the fragments. They clutched the hot shards in their hands and watched in awe as the dust settled. More trains were coming—Prell wartrains—that slowed, and stopped, and sent out fresh drones to buzz furiously above the blocked line.

14

The colorless pulse of the K-gate faded. The *Ghost Wolf* was on another planet.

"You've dropped your speed, train," Chandni said. "Something wrong?"

"We're underwater," said the train.

Threnody looked out through one of the narrow windows. She saw a shifting soup, blue-green, filled with bits of weed or stirred-up sand or something. She remembered Toubit from her lessons now; the K-gate there lay at the bottom of one of the deepest trenches in the planet's ocean.

"Why would the Guardians have made a K-gate at the bottom of the sea?" Chandni wondered.

"Maybe it wasn't sea back when the gate was opened," said Threnody.

"Some bozo wants to talk to you, ladies," said the train, and opened a bright screen in the air in the middle of the cabin.

"Unknown train?" A man's face filled the screen, middle-aged and faintly pompous, a few thin hairs bravely clinging on above a bald dome of forehead. It peered into the *Ghost Wolf*'s cabin like a nosy neighbor spying through a window. "Administrator Ozcelyk of the Toubiti Transit Authority. Please identify yourself."

"Chandni Hansa," said Chandni. "Railforce," she added, unconvincingly. "There's been an attack on Grand Central by the Prell CoMa. They were repulsed after heavy fighting. We're here to secure your station city, in case the enemy tries to strike here."

Administrator Ozcelyk frowned. "But a freight train from Grand Central came in a few hours ago. It told us that the *Prells* have secured the city. It said Elon Prell is now Emperor . . ."

"It was wrong," said Chandni. "The situation is changing very fast. The Prells have been defeated."

The Administrator blinked helplessly. "I presume your train can provide proof of this? Media updates from the Grand Central data rafts . . ."

"Not me," said the *Ghost Wolf*. "I'm a wartrain, mate. I've got better things to do with my brain than store a load of boring updates for your news sites."

Ozcelyk killed the sound for a moment and talked to someone off-screen. The sea outside was shallowing. Shafts of sunlight shone down through it, lighting up a plain of silvery sand, kelp plantations, and some seafloor settlements under snow-globe domes. Threnody could feel the track rising under the *Ghost Wolf*'s wheels as it approached the island where Toubit Station City stood.

"You will stop," said Ozcelyk, turning the sound on again. "There is a siding half a mile ahead of you. You will stop there until we can find out what the truth is. Submarines of the Toubiti Defense Force are closing in on your position; if you do not comply, they will open fire on you."

"*Ooh, I'm frightened*," sneered the *Ghost Wolf*. It muted the screen, and Ozcelyk went on talking in silence, opening and closing his mouth like a rather stern fish. The siding shot past.

Threnody said, "Train, can you take us onto the old Dog Star Line?"

"I see it," said the *Ghost Wolf*. "It's not in the updated maps I'm pulling from the local raft, but it's still in my tactical database. The spur branches off from this line just before the main station . . ."

The light outside grew brighter and brighter and then suddenly they were in open air, water streaming down the window glass, palm trees and bio-buildings flickering past under an afternoon sky. On the screen, Ozcelyk yelled and waved like someone trapped in a soundproof booth.

"Is it safe—this Dog Star Line?" Chandni asked. "Won't they have taken up the rails?"

"Nobody takes up rails," said Threnody. "It's too difficult. It costs too much."

"But won't the K-gate be blocked?"

"That won't be a problem for me, darling," bragged the *Ghost Wolf*.

The sky outside was full of flying things: media drones and maybe gunships too. Light flickered from some of them, but whether it was camera flashes or weapons, Threnody couldn't tell. If they were shooting at the *Ghost Wolf*, its armor absorbed the energy of their beams and bullets so efficiently that she didn't even hear them hit.

"What is this train, Chandni?" she asked. "You spoke as if there's something wrong with it?"

Chandni looked at her. "It's a good train," she said.

"So why were you going to take that little Foss 500 instead?"

"Because this one is a Zodiak," said Chandni, reluctantly. "You heard of those? The fighting C12s? Thickest armor, biggest engines, best weapons in the business. I didn't think there were any left. Thought they'd all been broken up long ago. I guess Railforce kept a few mothballed for a rainy day, though it's hard to imagine a day *that* rainy . . ."

"But if they're so good, why break them up?" asked Threnody. She liked this train: the way it had rescued them, the way it scoffed at the Prells. She thought it was a bit like Chandni herself; they were both common and a little scary, both had been in storage for a long time, and now they were both awake and helping her.

Chandni kept her eyes on the window and spoke very softly, as if she didn't want the train to overhear. "Zodiak trainworks tried to build the ultimate fighting locos, but there was some glitch in their minds. Most of the C12s turned out to be psychopaths. Killing machines who weren't that bothered about who they killed."

"WaHOOO!" said the *Ghost Wolf* just then, sounding more like a kid than a killer. The cabin rocked from side to side. "Points," it explained. "We've crossed onto the old Dog Star Line. The switching gear had been locked against us but I managed to get into its brain and get it working. I'm trained for cyberwar, I am."

"Very nice," said Chandni. "Can you switch those points back? Stop any Prell trains from following us?"

"Already done," said the train smugly. "Switched the points, killed the switching gear. Nobody's going to come through there without some *serious* help from tech support, know what I mean? Guardians alive, they've got another tank on the line ahead—do they *never* give up? If I still had my missile batteries I'd light up their whole crappy city for them . . ."

There was a bang and more swaying. Bits of something airborne and mostly burning flashed past the windows. *Do tanks have human crews?* Threnody wondered. *Probably not. Hopefully not . . .*

"Tunnel ahead leading to the K-gate," said the train. "It's walled up. There's a forty-five percent risk of heavy damage if I go through."

"Let's chance it," said Chandni. She killed the holoscreen, where Ozcelyk had given up shouting and buried his face in his hands. She looked back at Threnody and grinned. "Hold on tight . . ."

They hunkered down, grabbing handholds. The *Ghost Wolf* started to sing. It hit the barrier with such force that, even though she was bracing for the impact, Threnody was flung through the air. She tumbled, landed hard, thought, *This is it, we're derailed, we're dead . . .* The song of the train swirled up and filled her thoughts, and the light of another K-gate flared outside the windows.

*

But they were not dead, not yet. The *Ghost Wolf* ran on, plunging through K-gate after K-gate, world after world. Mostly the Dog Star Line ran underground. When it broke the surface it was usually on stripped-out industrial planets: litter on empty platforms, cold smokestacks on the skylines, faded ads on the station walls for snacks and threedies that Chandni remembered from before she was first frozen. Sometimes the wartrain had to shunt aside a heap of debris or speed up and ram its way through another barrier.

There was a place called Fugazi where it rained gasoline and the line ran on an embankment between lakes of napalm;

the *Ghost Wolf* went through at a crawl, careful not to shed a single spark from its wheels. *"I'll* be all right if the atmosphere ignites," it said cheerfully, "but I can't promise you two won't get roasted."

Threnody watched the brown rain trickling down the windows, but she was too tired to be scared, or maybe she was just beyond fear after all the terrors of the past day. She found a hard bunk in a little cabin just behind the main one and lay down on it to sleep, drifting in and out of strange dreams till Chandni came and looked in on her.

"You all right?"

"All right ish," said Threnody.

"This is where they put the prisoners," said Chandni, looking at the narrow cabin with its tiny window. "When the Bluebodies picked me up on Ayaguz I got taken up the line in a train a bit like this. The captain's cabin is up the other end."

Threnody couldn't be bothered to move. Her stomach rumbled, and she realized that one of the unpleasant sensations she was feeling was hunger. She could not remember ever being hungry before. She had never gone for so long without food. She said, "If the Prells catch us, I'll have to get used to being a prisoner."

"You should be so lucky," said Chandni, sitting down on the floor and resting her chin on her knees. "If they wanted you alive they wouldn't have started their war by chucking missiles at your bedroom window. But don't worry, we'll get you safe to Sundarban or wherever." There was a kind of glee about her, an energy that Threnody had not seen before. Her eyes did not look too old for her anymore. "I've never gotten away with a whole train before," she said.

15

It was strange having no headsets. They were both used to dropping into the local data raft in idle moments or scrolling through photos and vids. Of course, there was no Datasea on many of the worlds they were crossing now, but each time they reached a living one, the *Ghost Wolf* would grumblingly open holoscreens so they could see the local newsfeeds. They heard about the death of the Empress Threnody in an accidental missile strike. They saw the footage of Prell wartrains arriving in all the major stations on the O Link, then in the outlying hubs of Golden Junction and Tusk. On Grand Central, the fighting was already over. On most other worlds it had not begun: the Prells had moved too swiftly. One good piece of news was that Uncle Nilesh had escaped from Grand Central—Threnody felt sure that the redoubtable Kala Tanaka had helped him—and he was back on Khoorsandi, appealing for other corporate families to help the Noons. But none were, and the remaining Noon-controlled worlds could not fight the Prell CoMa and their

Railforce allies alone. It had been a neat, quick, almost bloodless little war, and now it was over.

"But things will be different once we get to Sundarban," said Threnody. "The family will gather there. They won't give up the throne so easily. When they see that I'm still alive they will rouse people up against the Prells."

"If anybody cares," said Chandni. "I never cared who the Emperor was. Most people will just be glad the fighting hasn't spread and the trains are running again."

"You'll see," said Threnody.

But what they saw when they reached Sundarban was the worst news of all. The *Ghost Wolf* didn't have to be cajoled into opening a holoscreen; it picked up the report as soon as it came through the K-gate, and slowed to a stop well outside Sundarban Station City. "You need to see this, little Empress," it said.

It sounded sorry for her.

Threnody stood in the cabin and stared at the images. They showed her sister Priya standing next to that smug toad Elon Prell while camera flashes lit up her beautiful, haughty face. She wondered why Priya was in the news, and tried to remember some occasion when Elon Prell and Priya would have met. And then, slowly, she started to realize that this was new. The date stamp in the corner of the screen showed that it had been broadcast only yesterday on Grand Central.

". . . Prell forces also discovered the secret location where Threnody Noon had been keeping her half-sister Priya under house arrest," the newscaster was saying. "Priya Noon is the rightful heir to the late Emperor Mahalaxmi XXIII. Now, with the help of the Prell family, she will sit at last on the throne Threnody tried to steal from her . . ."

"I didn't!" said Threnody, as if there was some use arguing

with a story that was being put out across every media platform in the Empire.

". . . but she will not rule alone. Elon Prell has announced that he will be marrying the Lady Priya, and founding a new imperial dynasty, the Prell-Noons."

Threnody gasped as if the newsreader had just reached through the holoscreen and slapped her. Chandni said, "So Elon Prell gets to claim he's just done his duty and restored the real Empress, and he still gets to be Emperor himself." She snorted, almost admiringly. She knew a clever thief when she saw one, but she'd never seen anybody steal an entire empire before.

"What now, Empress?" she asked.

"I don't know," said Threnody. "I don't know." All the way from Grand Central she had been telling herself that it would be all right when she reached Sundarban. She would be welcomed, and when everyone saw what the Prells had done, her cropped hair and ragged clothes, they would rally to her and drive Elon Prell all the way back to Broken Moon. Now she knew that would not happen. Her family did not need to fight anymore. Elon Prell had given them a way to save face. They could let him have the throne, and there would still be a Noon Empress. The next Emperor would still have Noon blood. The old Noon homeworlds and a few little places like Khoorsandi and Katsebo would stay in the family. The House of Noon would lose a lot of money when Elon rearranged the Empire's trade rules to favor his own family, but not as much as they would have lost fighting a long, difficult war.

What a fool she had been, to head for Sundarban. She suddenly knew that what she wanted most was to go home to her mother on Malapet. Malapet was a small, quiet world; the Prells would not need it, and perhaps they would let

Threnody live there in peace. She would walk on the black sand beach again, and sit in her mother's studio in the smell of paints, and stroll out to the café on the point on summer evenings to eat skewers of grilled tofu and trilobites baked in their shells . . .

But before she could ask the *Ghost Wolf* to turn back and find a way across the Network to Malapet, she felt the train start moving again. Red lights flashed on the cabin walls as it instinctively tried to arm weapons systems it no longer had. It said, "Uh-oh."

"What?" asked Chandni.

"Something just came through the K-gate behind us. A Prell wartrain, I'm guessing. They must have sent it through from Grand Central. Missile range in another thirty seconds."

It cursed. Threnody had never heard a train swear before. She felt slightly shocked by it, even while she was figuring out what to do. Surrender? She felt defeated enough, tired enough, hungry enough. Maybe the Prells would feed her if she surrendered. But maybe they wouldn't. Maybe Chandni was right and they'd just want her dead. And what about Chandni herself? They would kill her too, or put her back in the freezers . . .

For the first time, she understood that she was responsible for Chandni as well as herself.

"Run," she said.

The *Ghost Wolf* was ready. It took off so fast that Threnody would have been thrown off her feet again if Chandni had not caught her.

"Where will we go?"

"Only one place we can go," said the train. "Keep on down this Dog Star Line . . ."

A K-gate took it, and then the pale milk-white glow of moonlight on snow was pouring through the windows.

On through high, snowy mountains, then curving around the shore of a bay where the waves had frozen white and solid, like meringue ruffled up with a fork.

On the next world the rails had been almost swallowed by the forests crowding in on either side. Among the trees was a crumbling station complex where the *Ghost Wolf* stopped. It had picked up the beacon belonging to a refueling facility that still had some fuel cells in stock. The train had no maintenance spiders, though, so it had to send Threnody and Chandni out into the cold, resinous air to fetch them. The cells were the size of coffins, and their handles were designed for spiders' clamps, not human hands. Somehow they struggled two of them onto the train. Threnody had never thought much about how trains were powered before; everything happened automatically—they just *went*. Now she had a quick lesson in their mysterious undersides, loading the fuel cells into a silo where an automatic conveyor would carry them into the fusion chamber.

"That Prell train just came through behind us again," said the *Ghost Wolf,* as they scrambled back into its cabin. "It's not fast, but it's persistent."

They went on. Beyond the next gate lay a vegetable nightmare of overgrown bio-buildings where the fermented air pressed moistly against the window glass. "Interesting," said the *Ghost Wolf* as it shot through what had once been a station, "there's been fighting here; train on train by the look of it, and not that long ago. Something strange in the Datasea here too. Something *really* strange . . ."

Threnody looked out of the window, but they were moving too fast to see much. Then, abruptly, the *Ghost Wolf* braked.

"Flippin' hell," it said.

When they asked it what the problem was, it didn't seem able to explain. It opened a holoscreen instead and showed them the view from its nose camera. The line led up a long slope toward the tunnel mouth that must lead to the next K-gate. In front of the tunnel stood a huge mobile gun, two mechanical legs on each side of the line, and its muzzle aimed straight at the *Ghost Wolf.*

Then the screen went out, and a figure in golden armor appeared like a flame in the middle of the cabin. It was a hologram, but so perfect that it seemed someone really was standing there; there were even reflections of Chandni's and Threnody's startled faces in its burnished breastplate. The only thing that made it unreal was the fact that it seemed lit by sunlight instead of the dim glow of the *Ghost Wolf*'s lamps.

"This is a closed world," it said sternly. Its face was invisible behind its visor, but its rich, kindly voice filled the cabin. "The gate ahead is barred. Reverse, and return to your permitted lines."

It was a Guardian, or the holographic interface of one. Chandni, who had always talked so cynically about the Guardians and never seen one, dropped to her knees in front of it, went down on her face on the hard floor, trembling. Threnody stayed on her feet. She was awed, but she had talked with an interface before, and she felt almost glad to meet this one. Perhaps it could explain why the Guardians had let everything turn so bad.

"We cannot go back," she said. "We are being chased by another train. It is a Prell wartrain, and if it catches us, it will kill us."

"Hmmm," said the hologram. "You are the former Empress, Threnody Noon. You have done something to your hair. It does not suit you."

It wavered and changed shape. It was still golden, still flame-bright, but now it had the head, arms, and torso of a young man, and the legs and body of a horse. Threnody knew it now. That centaur was the avatar that it displayed above its data shrines.

"You are the Mordaunt 90 Network!" she whispered.

The centaur's beautiful face looked sadly down at her. "I am. I have known your family a long time, Threnody Noon. I watched over your many-times-great grandfathers in the pioneer camps when the Network was young . . ."

"Then why . . ."

"Other Guardians have their favorites too. My sisters the Twins felt that the time had come to allow the Prell family a turn in the sun. I tried to prevent it, but many of the other Guardians agreed with them, and in the end a small war between humans is far less terrible than a fight between two Guardians would be."

Threnody found that she was weeping. The tears trickled saltily into the corners of her mouth and dripped off her chin. She said, "But it was terrible for *us*. They killed Kobi, and Lyssa Delius, and the old man at the train store. And they will kill me if they catch me . . ."

The *Ghost Wolf* spoke, quite softly, with none of its usual swagger. "The Prell train has just come through behind us. Missile range in fifty seconds."

Another tear ran down the side of Threnody's nose. In the time it took to make the journey, Mordaunt 90 considered the situation. It noticed that the oncoming train was the Prell CoMa's light rail cruiser *Ambush Predator*, armed with the new PlanWrecker 5000 train-to-train missile system, capable of punching through even the *Ghost Wolf*'s armor. It called up details of the *Predator*'s ten-person crew. It considered how angry the other Guardians would be if it destroyed a Prell train, and weighed that against how angry they would be if it took a different course of action. It made a wistful journey in its memory back down Threnody's enormous family tree, remembering all the Noons it had known, all the way back to Surita Noon, a barefoot stowaway stepping off the *Varanasi* onto the sands of Mars.

The tear reached the end of Threnody's nose, thought about hiding in her nostril, then fell with the faintest sound onto her tunic.

"Go through the next gate," said Mordaunt 90. "You will be safe there."

The centaur vanished, like a flame blown out. On the tracks ahead the mobile gun stirred like a waking dinosaur, swung its massive turret away from the *Ghost Wolf*, and stepped with surprising daintiness off the line. The *Ghost Wolf* moved forward, gathering speed, a few of the Guardian's drones flying alongside as it ran toward the K-gate.

"What is the next world, train?" asked Threnody. "Where is the Guardian sending us?"

"End of the line," said the *Ghost Wolf*. "A world called Tristesse. A station called Desdemor."

When it had passed, the monstrous gun squatted over the rails again. Through its sights, Mordaunt 90 watched the Prell wartrain approach, slowing as it came in visual range. It projected its armored sentry hologram into the crew compartment and said, "This is a closed world. The gate ahead is barred to you. Reverse, and return to your permitted lines, or you will be destroyed . . ."

16

In the afternoons, when the rings of the gas giant Hammurabi stood like emerald arches above the Sea of Sadness, Yanvar Malik would sit on the balcony of his suite at the Terminal Hotel and play chess with the golden man. He always lost, because the brain of the golden man was linked to the vast mind of Mordaunt 90, which now took up almost all Desdemor's data raft. But Malik did not mind losing. He felt flattered that Mordaunt 90 respected him enough not to take pity on him and let him win.

Malik had arrived on the water-moon Tristesse with a mission led by an interface of the Guardian Anais Six. They had been trying to stop Raven from opening a new K-gate, but they had failed. Malik sometimes thought he could see the colorless glow of the new gate reflecting from the clouds on the southern horizon. Raven had died out there, on the island where his new gate stood. The interface of Anais Six had died too, and Malik had let Raven's young companion, Zen Starling, and the Motorik Nova take their old red train and vanish through the gate.

Then he had walked back along the viaduct to the city of Desdemor.

When he reached it, he found that Mordaunt 90 had already taken control of the place; it was filling up the water-moon's empty data raft and sending surveillance drones to examine the new gate. Carlota, the Motorik who had kept Malik company on his walk back to Desdemor, had her memory wiped of everything relating to Raven's schemes and went calmly back to her job as manager of the hotel. The other survivors of his team, who had been left to guard the station and had no knowledge of Raven's gate, were sent home. But Malik was ordered to stay.

The Guardian spoke to him from the Datasea, through the speakers in the hotel lobby. It questioned him about what he had seen when the new gate opened, and he told it everything. The only thing he kept from it was the fact that he had killed the interface of Anais Six himself, to stop it from harming Zen and Nova—but perhaps Mordaunt 90 guessed that part.

Malik assumed that the Guardian would kill him when it had finished with its questions. He had learned a lot about matters that the Guardians had long kept secret; it could hardly risk sending him back to share what he knew with other people. He did not much care. He had spent a long time hunting Raven, and now that Raven was dead, he felt that he was ready to die too.

But he did not die. He moved into Raven's old suite, high in the hotel. He wore the clothes he found in Raven's wardrobes: crisp summer shirts, suits of white linen. He swam in the hotel pools, walked on the beaches. And one day the golden man arrived to keep him company.

Sometimes, in the months that had followed, Malik had wondered if he was dead, and this was some sort of afterlife, because everything was very pleasant and nothing ever changed.

But this particular afternoon, something did. Just as the light was fading, and Mordaunt 90 was getting ready to checkmate him, he suddenly paused and looked up.

"What?" asked Malik.

The eyes of the interface were like small golden suns. They looked through Malik, concentrating on new information that was spilling into the data raft. "A train just came in on the old Dog Star Line," he said. "Not one of mine. It seems that the version of me that was guarding the gate on Pnin has decided to let us have some visitors."

The Terminal Hotel was built directly above Desdemor's K-bahn station, but it was a very tall hotel—its architect had won an award for taking full advantage of Desdemor's low gravity—and by the time Malik and the Mordaunt 90 interface had made their way down to platform level, the *Ghost Wolf* had already pulled in.

The interface waited in the hotel lobby while Malik walked out along the platform to meet the newcomers. Two young women, not much more than girls. One tall, the other short and runty. The runty one was holding a gun in her hand, but it was not pointed at Malik, just hanging there by her side as if she were too tired to lift it. They both looked exhausted. Malik thought there was something familiar about the tall one. He could not place her at first, and then he remembered that night on Sundarban, just before he came here. The proud, angry girl whom Lyssa Delius had said she would turn into an empress.

The short one squared up to him like a fighter and said, "Hey, is there anything to eat on this planet?"

*

There was. The Terminal Hotel had five restaurants, and their freezers had still been half full when visitors stopped coming to the water-moon Tristesse. Carlota and her Motorik staff were able to provide just about any meal you could think of. But Threnody and Chandni were almost past thinking, so Malik ordered for them: big bowls of red and saffron rice, flatbreads, spicy little curry dishes that made their eyes stream, fish from the Sea of Sadness cooked in coconut milk, sweet fried seaweed and rice dumplings. He sat with them in the empty restaurant while they ate, checking the news updates that the *Ghost Wolf* had just uploaded to the data raft.

That was how he learned that his old friend Lyssa Delius had been killed.

"Where's the interface gone?" asked Chandni Hansa, looking around the big, dark restaurant while she helped herself to another heap of honey-fried banana chips.

"It's listening, I expect," said Malik. "It's not just a cloned body. It's everywhere. The drones that shadowed your train when you arrived were Mordaunt 90; it's in the Datasea, the raft, the hotel's systems . . . It's listening."

"I don't know why he's a golden man," said Threnody. "Mordaunt 90 is supposed to be a centaur, isn't it? The Shiguri Monad is the one who appears as a golden man."

"He's cute, though. Maybe he's designed to appeal to you," said Chandni.

Threnody blushed, saying, "He looks like the boys I had posters of on my bedroom wall when I was twelve. I used to like ponies better in those days. It should have stuck with the centaur."

"I think he's designed to appeal to me," said Malik.

"Oh," said Chandni and Threnody, and were quiet for a bit, because although they'd heard stories about human beings who had love affairs with the Guardians, they had never expected to sit down at table with one, and if they had, they certainly wouldn't have imagined that he would look like battered old Yanvar Malik.

"Why is it here?" asked Threnody after a while. "What's been happening? Is Raven still here? Zen Starling? That Moto girl?"

Malik shook his head. "They're gone. I don't want to talk about it, though. If I tell you too much, Mordaunt 90 might never let you leave."

Threnody shrugged, a gesture she had picked up from Chandni. "I can't leave anyway," she said self-pityingly. "Where would I go? What would I do? I'm nothing now. I've gone from a Noon to a no one in the space of a few days . . ."

(Chandni rolled her eyes and started to play a tiny invisible violin.)

"Except I was always a no one, really," Threnody went on. "I was just Lyssa Delius's puppet, and now she's dead and there's nobody to pull my strings—"

Malik banged the flat of his hand on the table. "You think she chose you at random?" he said. "Of course she didn't. She saw something in you. I did too, that night on Sundarban, after you'd walked out of that crashed shuttle. Most people would be helpless with shock after something like that, but not you. You wanted a fight. That's why Lyssa made you Empress. Because she knew you were strong."

Threnody looked up at him half hopefully. She wished Lyssa Delius had told her that in person. She didn't *feel* strong.

"You too," he said, turning his fierce eyes on Chandni Hansa. "I know who you are. Last time I saw you, it was through the window of a freezer. You worked for Raven, and Raven was the smartest person I've ever come up against. He picked his little helpers carefully. You're both extraordinary. That's how you made it here. And that's why you're going to be all right."

There wasn't much to say after that. Even Malik seemed a bit shocked by his outburst. After a while he said, "You should get some sleep. Carlota has made up rooms for you. Rest. Maybe tomorrow Mordaunt 90 will let us know its plans for you both."

*

They went to their rooms. Threnody was asleep on her feet in the elevator, but Chandni never slept easily. It was as if her body knew that she'd had enough sleep in the freezers to last her a lifetime. She dozed for an hour in the big hotel bed (not as soft as the one she'd had at the palace, but not bad). Then she woke and lay trying to process what had happened in the past few days, but it was all just a blur of noise and fear.

Long after midnight she got up and went out onto the balcony. Weird birds were hooting somewhere. Yanvar Malik walked alone in the hotel gardens. Chandni watched him climb a little ornamental hill that looked out through a wide space between other buildings to the sea. The sky was dark, but a faint greenish phosphorescence showed in the waves, making a silhouette of him. He lifted a glass he had been carrying, drained it, and raised it high, saluting the night or the ocean or something—saluting, she suddenly realized, Lyssa Delius. She thought about how kind he had been, even though he must have wished that the *Ghost Wolf* had brought his old friend here, not two lost girls. She liked the old soldier, and she almost trusted him. He was the first person she'd met who seemed as out of place as she was.

Far off, where the sea met the sky, a light the color of nothing at all reflected very faintly on the clouds.

17

On the line from Coalsack Junction to Luna Verde there is a station called Baidrama where nobody ever gets on and nobody ever gets off. Most trains race through it without stopping, but sometimes the Timetable Authority makes one wait a few minutes there to ease congestion farther up the line. It is a night-bound planet, far from its sun, lifeless and airless. The huge blocks that the lamps of passing trains light up as they race across its surface are not houses or offices but data storage centers.

From a spur that runs away into darkness between some of those blocks, a strange locomotive makes its way onto the mainline. It is long and featureless, striped in black and yellow like a wingless wasp, and it hauls no cars. It heads through one of Baidrama's K-gates to Nokomis, then Glorieta. It is night on both those worlds, and people living in the trackside towns hear the train go by and stir in their sleep, wondering if it really was a train. It makes almost all the noises they associate with trains:

the engine roar, the whoosh of air over carriage roofs, the rattle of couplings, the thin sewing machine sounds of wheels on track. But the noise that really makes a train a train is missing. This loco does not sing.

And on the next world, Przedwiosnie, it vanishes onto the Dog Star Line, and no one hears it at all after that. Not until it rolls through the K-gate into Desdemor, where the interface of Mordaunt 90, out for a stroll on the empty seafronts, feels another Guardian uploading itself into Tristesse's Datasea.

*

The hotel had printed a new headset for Threnody, but she had taken it off when she went to bed. Chandni had to come into her room and shake her to wake her up. The green light of the gas giant Hammurabi poured through the big windows like mint sunshine. Chandni said, "It's nearly midday. You've been asleep fourteen straight hours. A new train's arrived."

Threnody rolled over and tried to rub the sleep out of her eyes. "What train?"

"I don't know. It hasn't come into the station; it's waiting back up the line, near the K-gate. Malik and his boyfriend seem to think it's important."

Threnody went to use the bathroom and splash cold water on her face, then down to the ground floor wearing the loose summer clothes that the staff had left in her room for her while her own were being cleaned. Breakfast or lunch or something was being served on the veranda, but Malik and the Mordaunt 90 interface looked so serious that Threnody abandoned any thought of eating and said, "What's happened?"

"Another visitor, Empress," said Malik. "A new train just came in carrying a Guardian."

Threnody looked around, expecting to see some weird fairy-tale figure lounging at one of the veranda tables. There was only the golden man, who said, "Not an interface, Threnody. Our guests have arrived in information form; they are waiting in the Datasea to talk with me. I think you should join me."

Threnody thought differently. She'd dipped in the Datasea to meet a Guardian before, and it had been a frightening experience. But she could not think of any way to say no to the Mordaunt 90 interface, who was smiling kindly and holding out a golden hand to her. He was beautiful, she thought, as she went toward him. His skin didn't look as if had been painted gold; it actually was golden, as if the color lay just beneath the surface, or he had honey-colored light instead of blood.

She reached out, his fingers closed around hers, and suddenly she wasn't on the veranda anymore.

The last time she dived in the Datasea it had looked like an actual sea, and then there had been a room where Anais Six was waiting for her. This time, she found herself in a garden. It had high, dark hedges and black trees. Snow was falling steadily from a sky that was almost white. There was a fountain, but it was frozen and festooned with thick icicles. The air wasn't cold, though. It wasn't even air. Everything here was an illusion made of code. Even Threnody herself. She looked down and saw the virtual body that Mordaunt 90 had given her. It seemed to be based on one of her coronation photos, and was dressed in a long gown of red silk with an embroidered K-train spiraling around the skirts and up onto the bodice. She had hair again too! But when she reached up to touch it she felt the tufty stubble of the emergency haircut Chandni had given her, and sensed for a moment the veranda tables around her, and Malik and Chandni looking on.

"You are in no danger, Threnody Noon," said Mordaunt 90, its golden interface looking the same in this virtual world as it did in the real one. She smiled at it nervously. It was certainly a more reassuring sort of Guardian than Anais Six had been. It was not looking at her, though, and when she turned to follow its golden gaze, she saw something approaching down one of the long paths that stretched away between the hedges. She wasn't sure what at first—a cloud of butterflies? Birds? Drones? Then she saw that they were fish: two shoals of small black and white fish, swimming through the virtual air the way real fish swim through water.

The fish came closer, circling the fountain.

"This?" said Mordaunt 90 suddenly, answering a question that Threnody had not heard. "This is a meeting place I have made, where our human guest can feel at home. Talk so Threnody can hear. You are the ones who drove her here, you and your cruel Prells. You owe her that."

The fish darted toward each other, scales shimmering in snow-light. They poured past each other, and somehow each shoal solidified and became a girl. One was black with long white hair, the other white with long black hair. They were both naked. The black and white hair tangled, blown on breezes Threnody could not feel, until the two girls were knotted together by its ends.

"As you have probably guessed," said Mordaunt 90, "these are the Twins. None of us is quite sure if they count as one Guardian or two. Some of us constructed Twin 1 soon after the first K-gate was opened. It was designed for security purposes—a warrior who would defend us in case we found anything beyond the K-gates that posed a threat. Perhaps we made it a little too paranoid, because it instantly made a backup copy of itself, and it has existed as a dual personality ever since . . ."

"Are there any more of our secrets you wish to share with your new pet?" asked the Twins, stalking toward Threnody, parting to pass on either side of her so that she had to duck to let the scarf of their knotted hair pass over her head. They turned behind her, looking her up and down. "Why *did* you bring her here?"

"It was a whim," said Mordaunt 90. "The version of me on Pnin felt sorry for her. Poor child, hounded halfway across the Network by those beastly Prells. I can't think what you see in that family."

"The Prells are a useful tool," hissed one of the Twins, the white one.

"More use than your soft Noons!" sneered the other.

Mordaunt 90 sighed. "We have been through all this. We agreed—at least the others agreed—that you should be allowed to install your Prells as the ruling family, and you promised a bloodless takeover. But a hundred people died, Twins!"

"A hundred!" scoffed the black Twin. "What are a hundred humans, for we who have seen a hundred billion live and die! Humans are all the same, anyway. A hundred will not be missed."

Mordaunt 90 leaned in closer to Threnody and said, "The Twins have never been what you'd call a people person."

"And Mordaunt 90 is a sentimentalist," the Twins chorused. "Why are you keeping that man Malik alive?"

"Because I'm fond of him," said the golden man. "He is a tough old soldier, but he has a kind heart."

"A bit like us then," said the white Twin, with a fake smile.

"Except with a kind heart," growled her sister.

"When we agreed that you were to take charge of this

moon," they said together, "we thought that you would undo the damage that ninny Anais Six had caused. We did not realize that you meant to turn the place into a holiday resort for yourself and your human playthings. So we have come to relieve you of your responsibilities. The new gate will be blocked."

"You can't block K-gates!"

"There is a way; there has always been a way," the Twins said. "It is only that our brothers and sisters would not let us use it. But the means exist. We have brought one with us."

The golden man had a face that was made for smiling or looking handsome in repose. It tried to twist into a look of horror now, but it didn't quite work. "You've brought a Railbomb?"

"The gate will be blocked," said the white Twin.

"Then the viaduct that leads to the gate will be destroyed," said the black Twin.

"The humans will be eliminated."

"The water-moon Tristesse will be sealed off entirely."

"You can't," said Mordaunt 90. "I won't permit it."

The Twins smiled their most simpering smiles. "But you are alone here!"

"And there are two of us . . ."

"And there is only one of you . . ."

18

Mordaunt 90 started to say something, and suddenly it was gone, vanished out of existence, not even leaving a footprint on the virtual snow. The Twins high-fived each other and turned toward Threnody with triumphant grins, and then she was expelled from the garden too, blinking and gasping on the hotel veranda with Chandni holding her by the arms and saying, "What is it? What did you see?"

Something hit the pavement behind her like a dropped bucket. Bits and pieces of it went skittering away across the flagstones. It was one of Mordaunt 90's golden drones. Another, which had been circling the hotel, shot off course and punched a hole through the glass wall of a neighboring building. The noise of the falling glass was very clear and sharp in the silent city. The interface of Mordaunt 90 put a hand to his face. "I can't—" he said, and stumbled sideways, Malik stepping forward to catch him as he fell. "It is the Twins. Something is spreading through the Datasea. I can't—"

He thrashed wildly in Malik's arms and weird sounds came from him. "They're attacking him," said Threnody, and she remembered something his hologram-centaur version had said the day before—that a war between humans was far less terrible than a fight between two Guardians. "They're *deleting* him . . ."

"Why?" demanded Malik. "What happened in the Datasea?"

"The Twins were there. They were angry. They said they were taking charge, and that we would be eliminated."

Malik was already moving, easing the half-conscious interface upright. Chandni ran to help him. Threnody followed them back into the hotel, where the Motorik staff all stood around like mannequins, looking up, as if something they had just heard had turned them all to statues. Threnody opened a headset channel to the *Ghost Wolf* and said, "We have to leave!"

"Make it quick," came the train's voice. "Something's happening in the Datasea. Some kind of virus. Weird stuff. Guardian stuff. It's busy with Mordaunt 90 at the moment, but it looks like it's winning. Then I'm guessing it'll turn its attention to me."

"Get your firewalls up," said Threnody.

"They won't hold out long against something that can take down a Guardian," said the train. "But yeah. Come quick, little Empress."

It went silent, hidden behind its firewalls.

They struggled on through the hotel's elaborate ground floor, through the bars and lounges, the interface stumbling along with one arm around Malik's shoulders and one around Chandni's, their progress hampered by the fact that Chandni was so much shorter.

"Are you armed?" asked Malik, as they reached the lobby.

Chandni shook her head. There was no room in her nice new summer clothes to hide a gun; she had left it in the safe in her bedroom. Just thinking about it made her feel sad that she could not go back to that nice, soft bed. Also stupid, for having let herself believe that she and Threnody were out of danger.

"Me neither," said Malik. He looked back at Threnody. "There's a gun cabinet. Door on the left there . . ."

Threnody ran to it. The door was unlocked. It wasn't really a cabinet, more a small room. On the parts of wall that weren't covered with racks of guns were framed pictures of hunting parties in old-timey clothes, posed grinning with those same guns and the monstrous manta-ray things they must have killed with them. The guns were rifles, very retro-looking, with carved wooden stocks. She slung one by its strap over her shoulder, took another, then started looking for ammunition.

In the lobby, Malik and Chandni reached the door and paused, sitting the interface down on a livewood chair. The golden man looked up at them in confusion. "I can't stop it," he whispered. "It gets past every barrier. The blackness . . ."

Malik knelt beside him. "You'll be all right."

"It's eating my mind, Yanvar Malik."

"It's eating the mind of the Mordaunt 90 in the Datasea." Malik stroked the golden face. "You have your own mind, in here."

"That's too small! It can't hold all of me! I'll be only a human!"

Malik held him close, and Chandni looked away, embarrassed. Behind the reception desk, one of the frozen Motorik had started to shake. The movement spread to another, then another. There were a dozen Motos in the lobby and within a few seconds all of them were making the same fluttering, quivering movements, like leaves in a gale.

"Malik . . ." said Chandni.

A Motorik in a bellboy's uniform leaped at her from behind, wrapping his mechanical fingers tightly around her throat. Chandni yelped in shock, but she'd been jumped like this before and her instincts knew what to do, jerking her body forward and flipping her attacker over her head. He hit the ground hard and lay there, doing his twitching and quivering routine again. The other Motos had turned to stare at Chandni and Malik. As they started to advance, Chandni looked around for a weapon and picked up a chair. Tristesse's gentle gravity made it light and easy to throw, but it also meant that it didn't knock down the Moto receptionist it hit, just bounced off her face and made her stagger back a few steps. She came on again with blue gel trickling from her broken nose, clutching a pair of scissors like a dagger.

"The Twins are controlling them," said Malik.

"You think?" Chandni flung a small slate-topped table at a manicurist and started backing toward the doors. If the Twins had their wits about them they would have taken control of those too, she thought. But perhaps Mordaunt 90 was still in the fight and able to protect the doors' small brain somehow, because they slid open obediently enough when she got close. "Threnody!" she shouted.

The glass in a nearby window starred suddenly, the crack of a gunshot coming straight afterward. Carlota, the hotel's manager, was coming down the stairs from the mezzanine level, as dignified as ever in her long blue dress, holding some antique sort of rifle in her hands. A spent cartridge casing tumbled lazily end over end in the air above her head and hit the ground at the same time as she reached the bottom step. "Mr. Malik, Miss Chandni," she said, "I am so terribly sorry. Some sort of interference . . ." She raised the gun again, aiming this time at the Mordaunt 90 interface, slumped in the livewood chair.

Was it the low gravity that made everything seem so slow? Chandni saw it all in intense detail: the spurt of flame at the rifle's mouth, the way Malik's eyes widened as he stepped between the golden man and the oncoming bullet. She heard the crunch as it went through his chest. The spurt of blood made pretty red shapes on the air. And as he crumpled, Carlota was already lifting the gun again and swinging it to point at Chandni this time, but then Carlota's head snapped sideways and a long spray of blue gel flew out of it and she was falling too, her gun shooting pointlessly into the ceiling.

Threnody was running across the lobby, a rifle in her hands and another on her back. She stopped midway to shoot down the other Motorik, the big slugs kicking them backward, gel splattering the carpets and the long livewood curve of the reception desk. She shot them with a cold fury, as if they were Prells, and when they were all down she kept shooting until the old gun clicked emptily.

It was the first sign Chandni had seen that Malik had been telling the truth when he'd talked about Threnody being tough. She ran and took the empty gun, and Threnody tremblingly passed her a cartridge of bullets to reload it with, but no more Motorik came at them. Maybe the Twins had given up on that idea, or maybe Mordaunt 90 had blocked it somehow.

The interface had come out of his chair. He knelt over Malik, blood on his golden hands. "Why did you do that?" he was asking him. "There are so many of me, and only one of you! There are versions of Mordaunt 90 in the Datasea on every world . . ."

Malik couldn't answer. There was blood in his mouth. There was a red flower on the breast of his white jacket. Chandni said, "He doesn't care about those others. Only you."

Malik heard their voices, but he wasn't really listening. He felt very tired. Strangely, there was not much pain. He had been shot before and it had always hurt a lot. This time there was just a warm, spreading numbness, as if he were falling asleep, but he knew he mustn't fall asleep, because Mordaunt 90 and the two girls needed him. He could worry about himself once they were all on the train. But when he tried to get up, the girl Chandni Hansa held him gently down and said he shouldn't move. The interface knelt beside her, looking down at him, as beautiful as sunlight. *Like unexpected sunlight at the end of a long, hard day,* thought Malik. The interface looked so afraid that Malik wanted to tell him it was going to be all right, but the numbness had reached his mouth by then and made it difficult to speak. *I'll just rest here for a few seconds,* he thought, *and gather my strength.* And he closed his eyes and slipped away.

The interface didn't understand. He kept shaking Malik, trying to wake him, until Chandni said, "We have to get going. He'd want us to go. Otherwise it was for nothing."

Threnody helped her pull the interface to his feet again and lead him away from Malik's body. He seemed to move more easily now, as if he was losing his connection with whatever chaos was going on in the Datasea. They left the hotel and crossed the station concourse, guns held ready in case more Motos came, but none appeared. One of Mordaunt 90's drones had crashed through the station canopy and lay wrecked near the end of the platform where the *Ghost Wolf* waited. They crunched over the broken glass and made their way to the old loco, afraid it would be dead or turned against them. But its engines were already running, and it opened its door for them. When they were aboard it said, "I'm glad you made it. What about the other bloke?"

Chandni shook her head. The interface wept. Threnody said, "Just pull us out."

"That's going to be tricky," said the *Ghost Wolf*, reversing away from the platform, out into the green gas-giant light of a Desdemor afternoon. It opened a holoscreen and showed them a view of the tracks leading back toward the K-gate. There on the rails sat a silver loco. "That thing's been sitting out on the down-line since it arrived. It won't talk; it just sits there. If it were an ordinary train I'd say the hell with it and go past it, but I don't know what this stripy thing is, nor what weapons it's carrying."

"If it had weapons you'd think it would have used them by now," said Chandni, scowling at it.

Threnody said, "Maybe it doesn't have any weapons. Maybe it *is* a weapon."

She was looking at the interface, who had been sitting miserably on one of the *Ghost Wolf*'s hard little seats, staring at the floor. When Threnody spoke he raised his head and looked at the screen without much interest. "Yes," he said. "It's a Railbomb."

The *Ghost Wolf* went very slowly back onto the mainline. "And *what*," it said, "is a Railbomb?"

"A loco carrying a massive antimatter warhead," said the interface flatly. "It doesn't have the same sort of mind you do, train. All it wants is to explode."

"Nice to have an ambition in life, I suppose," said the train.

"It is supposed to target a K-gate and detonate itself the instant it passes through. The idea is that, even if the gate itself is not damaged, the tunnel it's in and the rails will be put out of use. It is something the Twins devised."

"Why would they want to do that? Who'd want to block a gate?"

"Why is it here?" asked Chandni.

"There's another gate on this world," said Threnody. "A new gate that's been opened somehow. The Twins want to block it, but Mordaunt 90 wants to keep it open. So the Twins are shutting down Mordaunt 90, and when they're finished they'll send the bomb to do its stuff."

"The gate's south of here," said the *Ghost Wolf.* "I picked it up last night, but I thought my sensors must be acting up."

"Where does it go?" asked Threnody.

The interface shook his head. "We do not know."

"But the Guardians know everything!"

"Not this. The gate must not be used."

"The gate's going to have to be used," said the *Ghost Wolf,* "because in a few more minutes the Twins are going to get tired of ripping Mordaunt 90 to little bits in the Datasea and come after me."

It was moving south through the silent city, out onto a viaduct that stretched away toward the horizon. Big shapes swooped past the windows, making Threnody fear a drone attack, but it was just some of those ray things, flapping like ungainly bats out of their lairs in the arches of the viaduct.

"We mustn't," said the interface.

"It's that or die," said Chandni. "It's worth a chance, isn't it?"

"What's on the other side," said the interface miserably, "might be worse than dying . . ."

"Here comes trouble," said the *Ghost Wolf.*

Behind them, the Railbomb had begun to move. The rear-view cameras showed it nosing its way out onto the viaduct. The *Ghost Wolf* cursed. "I thought it was creepy the way it didn't talk or sing, but it's singing now, and I wish it had stayed quiet. Listen . . ."

The voice of the Railbomb came over the speakers and filled the cabin. It wasn't singing words—trains never did—but its meaning was clear. It was singing of death, and speed, and the splendid light it would make, and the crater it would leave behind. It was singing of its pity for lesser trains, who would never know such glory.

"It's coming fast," said Chandni.

"It's got powerful engines," said the *Ghost Wolf.* "But it's heavy. I bet I can stay ahead of it . . ." It put on speed, shouldering aside great waves that were bursting over the viaduct out there in mid-ocean. It opened another holoscreen to show its passengers the view ahead. Something was coming into view there, far away still, vague behind the veils of sea spray.

"There is an island," said the interface. "I think that was where Raven built his Worm. Where the gate was opened."

"Did Raven and Zen Starling go through that gate?" asked Threnody. "Is that what happened to them?"

"Malik told me that Raven died," the interface said. "But Zen Starling, yes. He has already gone through."

"But you must have some idea where it leads?"

The interface looked up at her with wide, scared, tearful eyes. Mordaunt 90, the great mind for which he had just been a sort of terminal, was gone from Tristesse now; the Twins' virus had left nothing but a few strands of corrupted code looping mindlessly in the Datasea. All the knowledge the interface had once been able to call on was erased. "I am just a fragment," he said. "There is not room in my head for a millionth part of what I was. I am mortal, and I am going to die . . ."

Threnody took his hand in hers, trying to comfort him. The *Ghost Wolf* said, "Nobody's dying, not if I can help it," and did something with its engines that drove it to a screaming new level of speed. It was singing its own song now, excited in spite of itself by the wind and spray that slammed against its nose. The island drew closer. Chandni and Threnody saw for the first time the gate, a bony archway standing naked under the green sky. Gaunt, skeletal machines littered the island, and two mobile guns stood like sentinels on either side of the gate, not aimed at the *Ghost Wolf* but at the gate itself. *They had been stationed there to destroy something coming through from the other side,* Threnody thought, *but their minds had been linked to Mordaunt 90.* They stood motionless as the *Ghost Wolf* tore past, trailing litter and salt spray in its slipstream, and plunged through the billowing curtain of light that filled the archway.

"*Death!*" sang the Railbomb, speeding down the viaduct behind it. "*Death!*" it wailed as it crossed the island its weird voice rebounding from the armor of the silent guns. "*Death!*" it shrieked, and vanished through the gate after the *Ghost Wolf.*

And Desdemor was quiet again, except for the wash of the waves, and the wingbeats of the rays as they circled above the empty island.

But in the tunnel on the far side of the gate there was sudden thunder as the *Ghost Wolf* emerged from K-space and hurled itself at the tiny circle of daylight far ahead. It was still running at unfeasible speeds as it burst out into the low, raking light of the alien sun. Something broke, down underneath it, the noise lost in trainsong and engine roar. Clouds of sparks spewed out between its speeding wheels, then red flame, black smoke. Smoke filled the cabin too, lit by the red flicker of emergency warning lights that made everything look like cheap animation. Threnody and the interface choked.

Chandni choked too, but found an extinguisher while she was doing it and sprayed foam at the places the smoke was coming from. "Stop!" she shouted at the train.

"Not till I've put more distance between me and the Railbomb," said the *Ghost Wolf*, but it was already slowing, rolling to a stop on scorched wheels.

"*Death!*" sang the Railbomb, piercing the K-gate behind it, and did the thing it had been longing to do for the whole of its short life.

The explosion filled the tunnel with a violent light, hot as a newborn sun. Rock flashed into vapor. The mountains shrugged. A vast red fist of flame punched its way out into the startled sky, wearing splintered crags like brass knuckles. For six hundred miles around the tunnel mouth, the ground jumped like a drum skin. Then the thunder came, outpacing the rolling dust clouds to go rumbling away around the curve of the world.

The *Ghost Wolf*'s cabin electrics had failed. Dust blinded the windows. Threnody and Chandni and the interface sat in darkness, listening to the rattles and thuds as bits of mountain that had been on exciting pleasure trips into the high atmosphere remembered they were geology rather than weather, and came tumbling down again, rebounding off the *Ghost Wolf*'s armor.

"What's out there?" asked Threnody. "Did anyone get a look? Did you see which world it is?"

Nobody had.

"I think I picked up some kind of signals," said the *Ghost Wolf*, "but I couldn't make heads or tails of them, and the dust is blocking reception now."

"What part of the Network are we on?" Threnody asked the interface. "If there are Prells around . . ."

"We are not on the Network," said the interface. "We are elsewhere."

The bombardment was slowing. The things hitting the hull now sounded more like gravel than boulders. A few shy sunbeams peeped in through the windows.

Chandni said, "You realize we've forgotten to bring anything to eat, again."

PART FIVE
STRANGE STATIONS

19

"Are you going to swim?"

"I don't think we both need to. You swim, and I'll watch."

They were walking down a steep path to the shore. Behind them, the last sunlight lit the crags. Ahead, the worldwide ocean spread out, glittering and inky blue. The path led to a horseshoe-shaped tide pool and a jetty of Railmaker glass. Zen went to the end of the jetty and started taking off his clothes, dropping them on the glass at his feet. The sea didn't scare him. He had learned to swim on the beaches of Santheraki, the year he had lived there with his mother and Myka when he was eleven. Nova smiled, thinking of that, imagining what he must have been like back then. He had told her all about it, everything about his past, while they'd been riding the Web of Worlds. Quite often he forgot something that he had told her, and told her again, but Nova didn't mind; she wanted to know everything. It felt wonderful to know so much about someone, to have them trust you with all their memories and dreams. Especially Zen, who had never really trusted anyone before.

He pulled off his headset and put it on top of his carelessly heaped clothes, glancing back at Nova with a quick, half-nervous grin. He looked beautiful, standing naked there at the jetty's end, his lean brown body dark against the twilight sea. "Be careful," she started to say, but he was already diving, plunging into the slow upward heave of an oncoming wave.

They had been together for nine months. Nine whole months since that beautiful first night on Yaarm. They had almost forgotten who they had been before they came through Raven's gate. Whole days went by when they did not think about Raven or the Noon train job, or ask themselves if things might have gone differently.

It had been difficult at times. Neither of them had been in love before, and all that they knew about it came from stories. Stories usually *ended* with people falling in love. What happened next? They had nothing in common except for the adventures that had brought them together. Nova liked things neat and tidy, which Zen didn't care about at all. She liked to know things, while Zen seemed happy to stay ignorant. She was filled with curiosity about how the Web of Worlds had come to be, and kept trying to find out more about its history, but Zen was only interested in the present, and seemed quite glad that they had come too late to meet the mysterious Railmakers.

If they had still been in the Network Empire, Nova thought, they would have split up after a week or two. Their differences would have made them fight, and there would have been the pressure of what other people thought too; humans and Motorik were not supposed to like each other, let alone fall in love.

But there were no other humans here to judge them, and they had needed each other too much to fight. She had learned to ignore all the things about Zen that she didn't like. When you loved someone, she was discovering, you loved all of them, the good parts and the bad. Sometimes, when she was with Zen, she had the feeling that nobody had ever loved anyone as much as she loved him. That made her feel special and unique and more human than she had ever felt before, because she was pretty sure that all humans felt that way when they were in love.

He surfaced several feet offshore, sleek as a seal with his wet hair plastered flat. He called out to Nova and waved. "They're here!" The sun had set, but she could see him clearly, lit by a soft pastel-colored light that streamed up through the waves from somewhere beneath him. She ran to the end of the jetty in time to see a huge animal passing below him, turning over as it soared through the water. Pulses of blue and amber light flickered along its flanks and the long trailing banners of its fins. "They're *big*," Zen shouted, diving again. And, although she knew the Night Swimmers were friendly, Nova felt grateful for the floor of clear Railmaker glass that separated him from the deeps.

*

They had come a long way since Yaarm. Down all the shiny lines to Priina-Réae: the countless gates, the untold alien stations. They'd stopped at Yashtey in the Tides of Gmylm, and Semiimiliiip, and Groosht. They had seen the *morvah* nurseries on Iehíín where some of the Web's strange living locomotives were hatched and young ones trundled around on training rails, trying out their new wheels. They had traveled the New Porcelain Line all the way to the Rainbow Half-Worlds, then struck out along the spur called Makers' Ladder until it had brought them here, to Night's Edge, a waterworld where only one mountain range rose high enough to break the surface of the ocean. The Railmakers had left a K-gate at one end of the long, rocky landmass, three more at the other, and one of their stations in the middle. A colony of Deeka lived there, acting as middlemen for trade between visiting trains and the Night's Edge natives, the immense, whalelike Night Swimmers.

There were two of the Swimmers beneath Zen now, and he suddenly saw that there were others beneath *them*: tiny moving lights that must be more of the creatures coming up from some immense depth. The lights seemed to ripple as the glass floor of the tide pool trembled to their subsonic calls. Zen spread out his arms and legs and drifted. The Night Swimmers were curious about humans, just like everyone he had met on the Web of Worlds. But unlike the others, the Swimmers felt they couldn't really start to understand a new race until they had seen them *swim*.

So he hung there for a moment, naked in the darkening sea, letting the things below get a good look at him with whatever they used for eyes. All around him now the light of the watchers in the deep shone upward through the waves.

He wondered how he was doing. How did the Ambassador for Humans compare to all the other races who had found their way to Night's Edge and displayed themselves in this ancient pool? *Better than the Hath,* he thought; those friendly tents would have just skated across the wave-tops like living flotsam. The Herastec would have swum like horses with their three legs flailing and their horned heads held high out of the water. The Deeka would have done better; they were half at home in water. And the Ones Who Remember the Sea were basically just octopuses, which was cheating . . .

He swam toward the entrance of the pool, where the two arms of rock that encircled it ended and the waves rolled in from the open sea. But he was getting cold, so he decided that the Night Swimmers had seen enough and turned back toward the glass jetty.

"Did you see them? The Night Swimmers? They're the size of trains!"

"I think they might have *been* trains once," said Nova, crouched beside his heap of clothes, frowning down through the water. "A Deeka I talked to back at V'rey said they evolved from *morvah* that were stranded here after the Blackout. It seems possible."

That was so Nova, thought Zen, as he scrambled out of the water. Always coming up with theories, always asking questions . . .

"You should go in," he said. "There are tons of them, circling way down deep; you can't see from up here. Go in and swim."

"Better not," said Nova. She wished she could, but if she stripped off and dived in, then the Night Swimmers, and anyone looking down from the walkways and terraces on the cliffs above, might notice that her body had none of the same details as Zen's. She had never managed to personalize it in the same way she had her face, so it was still a standard-issue Motorik body with no nipples, no navel, none of those cute patterns of moles. Aliens would probably just attribute that to differences between the human sexes, but she did not want to risk them guessing the truth. People on the Web of Worlds were wary of machines.

Luckily, that meant that they didn't have any very complex ones of their own, and nobody seemed able to figure out that Nova was not a female human, or that the *Damask Rose* was anything more than a strange, inferior sort of *morvah* that needed a mechanical housing to protect it. The *Damask Rose* was not happy about that, but she played along, making sure her maintenance spiders only crept out to do their work on lonely stretches of line where they would not be seen, or making Zen and Nova do it themselves. She was learning the wordless, hooting songs of the *morvah*, and sometimes joined in with them. In her siding on Night's Edge she was singing soft duets with a *morvah* of the Herastec as Zen and Nova walked back up the sloping paths to the station. Behind them, the rainbow glow in the tide pool faded as the Night Swimmers sank back into the depths.

They had made new friends on their journeys: fellow travelers whom they met from time to time at different stations. As they crossed the footbridge above Night's Edge's main platforms, a Herastec trading pair called out a whinnying greeting. They were Koth/Atalaí, who had been on Yaarm when the *Damask Rose* first arrived.

Nova had long since upgraded Zen's headset to translate the Web's trade language and several other alien tongues, so he was able to understand what the Herastec were saying; their words appeared like glowing subtitles superimposed across his view of them as they came cantering up the ramp onto the bridge, towing their wares in spherical baggage carts.

"Ambassadors for Humans! Nova/Zen! It is good to meet again upon the rails! Have you opened the gateway to your own Network yet? Remember, we are eager to trade with your people!"

"Not yet," said Nova, as she always did. "Soon, I hope."

"You are on your way home now perhaps?" asked one of the Herastec. (Which one was Koth and which was Atalaí, Zen could not tell, and perhaps it did not matter. Herastec pair-bonds were so strong that, once they had mated, the two became almost one. Anyway, they all looked pretty much the same in their black glass masks.)

"There is a fast line from this world back to Yaarm," said the other. "You can go home and tell all humans that the people of the Web are waiting eagerly to meet and trade."

"The recordings you traded with us have been very profitable," said the first. "*Casablanca* is a big success with the Chmoii. They keep asking if there is a sequel . . ."

Koth/Atalaí were traders in entertainment. They bought dramas and stories and songs and strange, alien art forms and sold them all over the Web, recorded on little crystalline wafers that had to be read by a special viewing device. Nova had a whole collection of old movies stored in one of the attics of her mind, and she had traded some of these with Koth/Atalaí, curious to see what aliens would make of human love stories and sci-fi. She was glad that the Chmoii liked *Casablanca*; it had always been one of her very favorites. "I don't think there ever was a *Casablanca 2*," she said, "but they might enjoy *Forbidden Planet* . . ."

Together they went on up the winding pathways of the city. Zen offered to help pull the Herastec's luggage, but it was surprisingly heavy. The Herastec seemed untroubled by the weight; they leaned patiently into their harnesses and the trolleys trundled along behind them. They had come to Night's Edge to record the songs of the Night Swimmers—sequences of weird subsonic rumbling noises that went on for weeks, and were popular with the sort of people who liked listening to the sort of music that their friends weren't even sure *was* music. Koth/Atalaí had arranged for a Deeka submersible to take them down into one of the deep ocean trenches for a recording session the following night.

"And you, Nova/Zen?" they asked. "You are bound for Yaarm and your own dear homeworlds, yes?"

"We don't know where we're going," Nova replied, hoping to avoid a return to the awkward subject of when she and Zen would be going home. "There is so much of the Web that we still have not seen. The line to Yaarm is not the only line that passes through Night's Edge . . ."

"Ah, but you don't want to take the others," said one of the Herastec. "One goes only to a string of scruffy places, the homeworlds of the Kraitt. You would not like the Kraitt. They are as likely to be raiders as traders. They are . . ." (Zen's headset struggled to find a translation for the scornful snorting sound, and settled upon "hooligans.")

"And what about the other lines?" asked Nova.

"One goes through some empty worlds to Iaheí-Iahaa, but you could get there more speedily via Yaarm," said Koth/Atalaí. "As for the other, no one takes it. It leads to another Kraitt place, then some Neem Nestworlds, and then . . ."

"We don't want to go there," said Zen. The Neem were a mysterious race who kept to themselves, but he had glimpsed some from a distance on Yashtey and they had looked like something from his nightmares: crab-spider-insect things the size of small ponies, scuttling about on nasty, segmented legs. He didn't want to travel any line that passed through their stations.

"And after the Nestworlds?" asked Nova. "Where does the line go then?"

Koth/Atalaí tossed their heads uneasily. "Nowhere, Nova/Zen. It may have gone somewhere once, in the days of the Railmakers, but now it is impassable, for it leads into the Black Light Zone, and no *morvah* will venture there. Night's Edge is as close to the Zone as we like to go. Look, you can see it from here . . ."

The Herastec stopped and pointed to the sky. The moon was sinking, and the stars shone in their bright constellations over the endless sea. But at one point, low on the horizon, there were no stars. It looked as if a cloud hung there, blocking them out, but Nova knew the night was cloudless. She was looking at a wide region of space where there simply were no stars.

There was something, though. She could sense it, like a sound at the very edge of hearing. Not quite a signal, not a voice exactly, but *something*, singing to her out of that darkness.

And then it was gone, and Zen was saying, "The Black Light Zone? That has something to do with the Railmakers, doesn't it?"

"It's where the Railmakers' homeworlds must have been," said Nova. "It's the region at the very heart of the Web. It must all have started there. There must be great hubs there from which lines once reached out to stations like this. But when the Railmakers died—when the Blackout came, whatever that was—well, the legend is that the suns that lit the Railmakers' homeworlds just went out."

"How could that happen?" Zen asked.

The Herastec were tossing their heads nervously. They did not talk of the Blackout. "It happened so very long ago, Zen/ Nova, and it was so very bad, that nobody now remembers."

"But the *morvah* remember. They will not pass through any gate that leads into the Black Light Zone. As the old song about the Railmakers says, 'Lost are their lodges, lost every line, and no train runs where the black suns shine.'"

"But let us not talk about the Blackout. Let us find friends, and eat and drink."

They moved on, the wheels of the baggage carts squeaking slightly on the pavement. Nova looked back at that black hole in the sky, but it was slipping below the horizon. Whatever it was that had whispered to her from it was silent now.

21

The Blackout had left a long shadow of fear across the Web of Worlds. Zen and Nova had noticed it before. People might joke about it sometimes; they might say, "Blackout take it!" when they dropped a drink, or when a wheel fell off a baggage cart, but the fear was real. The civilizations of the Web had grown up in the ruins left by an event too terrible to understand, a disaster that had swallowed up the Railmakers themselves. That was why they were so uneasy about any machine more complicated than a simple computer—the Railmakers were said to have had incredible machines, and no one wanted to be too much like the Railmakers, in case another Blackout came and swallowed them up too.

For the same reason, the buildings that stood at the heart of every station—the ancient Railmaker buildings, covered in that glowing weed—always stood empty. Children dared each other to creep a little way into the silent halls, and adults built lesser buildings against the outer walls, but no one wanted to live in a place the Railmakers had built. Just in case.

Night's Edge was no exception. The old glass towers stood abandoned between the platforms, and around their feet more modest structures had sprung up. There were Deeka lodges like fat little clay ovens, and Chmoii tents, and the rambling scruffy shelters of the Hath. There were Herastec longhouses, which always had one open side, because the Herastec had evolved on a world that was all prairie and hated to be enclosed for too long. There was an open space between the buildings where colored lights had been strung, perhaps to obscure the pale ghost-light from the creepers on the ruins, and there were food stalls and a Deeka bar selling whiffs of intoxicating gas, and small pools where the Hath stood like grounded kites with their feet in baths of tasty nutrients.

"Look—there are Kraitt here!" said one of Koth/Atalaí, as they made their way between groups of squatting Deeka and Herastec pairs standing quietly at tables piled with subtly flavored grasses. None of the beings Zen and Nova had yet met upon the Web used chairs, but the Kraitt looked as if they might; Zen felt a thrill of recognition when he first caught sight of them, moving through the crowds on the far side of the square. They looked almost human at first; they were the first living things he had seen in nine months who had two arms and two legs and one head and kept them all in more or less the right places. But as they drew closer—watching him with their yellow eyes just as intently as he was watching them—he saw that they were as alien in their own way as any of the rest.

There must have been a planet somewhere where dinosaurs had evolved, and no asteroid had dropped in to wipe them out, so they had gone on evolving and turned into the Kraitt: muscular, man-sized lizards with flat faces and wide mouths, and a lot of crests and spines and fins that might be part of their clothes or part of themselves, it was hard to tell. One was taller than the rest, and Zen thought at first that it had wings, but it turned out to be just a leather cape, with a wide red collar that framed the creature's clever, reptile face.

"There is a female with them," said Koth (or Atalaí). "That is good."

"The males are less intelligent," said Atalaí (or Koth). "They make trouble without a female to lead them."

"They sound a lot like humans," said Nova.

The Kraitt matriarch came closer, with two of her males behind her. Her amber eyes were cold and curious, and her voice was a collection of snarls and hisses that must somehow have formed words in the Web's trade tongue, because a translation appeared in Zen's view.

"You are the Ambassadors for Humans. We have heard news of you. Very interesting things."

Nova gave her usual speech, about how she and Zen were exploring on behalf of the Network Empire, which would soon be ready to open trade with the worlds of the Web.

"Yes," agreed the Kraitt, baring her gleaming teeth in what looked to Zen very much like a sarcastic smile. "Soon you will go home through your gate on Yaarm, and return with trains full of more people like you."

"It is not unusual for a new race to send envoys onto the Web long before it opens its gate for trade," said Koth/Atalaí, and then fell silent. Zen glanced at the Herastec and saw that they were both standing very stiffly with their heads held high, alarmed by the closeness of this toothy predator.

The Kraitt ignored them. "When your traders come," she said, "tell them not to bother with these prey species. They should trade with the Kraitt. We are not bound by the old fears and the old customs, as they are. We are a young race, like you, and the young races are the future of the Web. We are very interested in your *technology* . . ."

She lingered over that word, and her eyes slid from Zen to Nova. For a moment Zen was afraid that she had guessed what Nova was, but perhaps it was just a coincidence; perhaps there was nothing sinister in the way her black tongue flickered between her teeth while she looked Nova up and down.

"I am the Tzeld Gekh Karneiss," she said. "You should come to my home station on the Shards of Kharne. If you are not too eager to go home . . ."

And again there was that hint of sarcasm about the way she said "home," as if she knew full well that Zen and Nova never could go there. But she couldn't know, Zen told himself; she couldn't possibly have guessed that much about them. It must just be that she was more humanoid than the people he was used to; he was reading human meanings into expressions and body language that probably meant something quite different to the Kraitt.

"We'll think about it," said Nova sweetly. "We still haven't decided where we're going next."

The Tzeld Gekh Karneiss suddenly tipped her head back to bare the soft, leathery folds of her throat. Perhaps it was the equivalent of bowing, if you were a Kraitt. Then she turned and went away, with her males behind her.

"Well, she seemed nice," said Nova.

The Herastec shivered inside their robes.

They moved on through the busy square, through the scents from the alien food stalls. Koth/Atalaí were greeted by another Herastec pair and went off to drink three-leaf broth with them and swap gossip about their complicated clans. Nova, who could eat things for their taste without having to worry about digesting them, bought a slab of spiced bread from a Chmoii kitchen, but Zen had tried some of that on Yashtey and still remembered its side effects. They sat down together with their backs against the wall of a Deeka lodge while Nova ate the bread and drew things in the dust.

"So this is the Web of Worlds," she said. "It's like a big snowflake. It started here, on the homeworld of the Railmakers. They made a bunch of lines that led from there to hub-worlds, and from those more lines go out to other hubs, where lots of lines branch off, forming the different networks—the Herastec Network, the Human Network. Only I can't draw all those here, because it's a three-dimensional shape, fractal and amazingly complex . . . And the middle part is just guesswork, because that whole section, the inner hubs and the center, is all lost, hidden in the Black Light Zone . . ." She wiped out the center of her diagram and stared at what was left. "We have no idea what's in there."

"Why do we care?" asked Zen. "It's just history."

"History is interesting," said Nova. "Don't you want to know how all this started? Who the Railmakers were?"

Zen shrugged. "Not really."

He could be disappointing sometimes. Nova wondered if she should tell him about the whisper coming from the Black Light Zone. She couldn't even find the right word for it, let alone make him understand. She sought for some way to catch his interest.

"What if there was a way home?" she asked.

"Home?"

Zen had trained himself to stop thinking about home. At first, he had not been able to think of anything else, but it had been too painful; he had stopped himself, and slowly the nagging ache of it had faded, driven from his thoughts by Nova and the strange new places they had traveled to.

"We can't go home," he said uneasily, wondering how she could have forgotten. "We're criminals, remember?"

Nova shrugged. "Half the corporate families started out as criminals of some sort. Once people realize what we've found here and the trade that could be done with the Web of Worlds, they'd soon forgive us."

"But they wouldn't ever realize, would they? We'd never get a chance to tell them because the Guardians will be watching Raven's gate and as soon as we go back through it they'll stomp on us. They've been lying to everyone for centuries, claiming they made the gates. They're hardly going to let us tell the truth."

"That is a worry," said Nova. "You're right—we couldn't go back through Raven's gate. But what if we could find another? What if we could find a gate that led to a busier world, where people would notice us as soon as we arrived? The Guardians couldn't blow us off the tracks if we were on Grand Central or somewhere. It would be all over the news sites."

"But how could we get to Grand Central?"

"Maybe not Grand Central itself. But the Web of Worlds must have been linked to our Network at some stage, long ago," said Nova. "Remember the walls Raven told me about, the walls they found on Marapur when they were building the new station city? Those must have been Railmaker structures. I bet there were lines that used to link our network with the Railmakers' hubs, deep in the Black Light Zone. The Guardians have hidden the gates on human worlds, but what if we could find the other end, and go through anyway?"

"You mean go into the Black Light Zone?"

"Why not?"

"But you heard what the Herastec said. Trains won't go there."

"*Morvah* won't go there. They have some instinctive phobia. But the *Damask Rose* isn't a *morvah*."

Zen shifted uncomfortably. It seemed to him that the *morvah* might have good reasons to shun the Black Light Zone. He had heard enough about it to share their fear. Something terrible had happened there. So far, the Web of Worlds had turned out to be a much less frightening place than he had expected; he had met no monsters, no poison-planets or hideous diseases. But it seemed to him that all those things might be waiting for him among the sunless homeworlds of the Railmakers. The Herastec and the Deeka might not be as technologically smart as humans, but they weren't stupid, and you didn't find *them* trying to get into the Zone.

He didn't want to admit to Nova that the idea scared him, though. He still had too much of his old street-kid pride for that. So he said, "It wouldn't work. Even if we found a way home, the Guardians killed the story about the walls on Marapur, and they'd kill us too. They aren't ever going to let news about the Web of Worlds leak out. So there's no point risking the Black Light Zone."

"All right," said Nova.

But it wasn't all right. They'd often had disagreements while they had been traveling, even little arguments sometimes, but this felt different; it was the first time the two of them had wanted two different things, and it made them both feel sad.

The *Damask Rose* broke in, her voice coming simultaneously into Zen's headset and Nova's mind. "Zen? Nova? I am being *pestered*."

"Pestered?" asked Zen.

"By *hooligans*," said the train, and she showed them the feed from her hull cameras. Some Kraitt were creeping around on the siding where she was parked for the night. They gawked up at her painted hull and reached out with clawed hands to try her carriage doors. From time to time one looked right at a camera and his eyes shone yellow.

"What are they up to?" Zen wondered.

"There's no sign of the Tzeld Gekh Karneiss," said Nova.

"We should get back there and see what's happening . . ."

"But carefully. They might be dangerous."

They stood up and made their way back through the marketplace. As they passed Koth/Atalaí and their friends, Nova called out to say that they were returning to their train because they thought the Kraitt might be making trouble. Then they were hurrying past the weed-clad buttresses of the Railmaker ruins, heading downhill to the sidings. Below them the dark sea boomed, patched here and there with flickering light where a Night Swimmer drifted near the surface. The path twisted steeply between jags of rock and wind-hissing vegetation. In the shadows just off it Zen saw a pair of eyes catch the starlight and shine like twin lamps.

"Nova," he said, "there's—"

Something hit him hard from behind. He fell and rolled and scrambled up, stunned, indignant, wondering who to hit. Kraitt were emerging from the shadows all around. Nova was struggling with two of them. They seemed surprised by her strength. Zen heard the splintering dry-branch crack of snapped bone as she broke one's arm, but his scream brought more running. They carried a net, which made slinking metal noises when they threw it over her. Zen ran at them, but one turned and saw him, and something like a club swept around at knee height and tripped him, slamming his face into the dirt again. *A tail,* he thought, as he rolled out of the way of scuffling feet. He had not noticed till then that the Kraitt had tails.

Nova was trussed in the net, which one of the Kraitt carried over his shoulder. Zen caught a glimpse of her face as she was swung past him, the Kraitt all around her, hurrying down the path. He heard her voice in his headset: "Zen, no, don't try to fight them; there are too many, they're too fierce . . ."

"Help!" he shouted, giving chase. The Kraitt moved fast, their knees bending the wrong way as they ran. They crossed a bridge, heading toward one of the outer sidings where a *morvah* waited under the glow of the rail-yard lamps.

Morvah tended to resemble their owners. Herastec *morvah* were gentle, with long, backswept horns, while those bred on the Deeka worlds had fins and gills. This Kraitt *morvah* looked like a prehistoric reptile, armor plated and bristling with spines. Its front end was sheathed in rusty metal, from which more spines and tusks jutted. Its three carriages were armored in the same haphazard way, with scruffy little forts on their roofs where more Kraitt stood. The train was already moving, and the Kraitt who had captured Nova started running to keep up with it. The ones on the roof cheered them on. Others leaned from doors and windows, reaching out helping claws. Nova thrashed in the net like a landed fish, making one last desperate bid to break free, but the mesh was too strong.

Zen ran hard and flung himself at the rearmost of the raiders. He and the Kraitt went down, and when they came up again the Kraitt had a silvery crescent blade clenched in its claws. He slashed at Zen with the blade and his own steel-tipped tail, his mouth wide and toothy, breath stinking of heat and blood. But other people had heard the commotion on the platform by then;

Zen could hear the hooting alarm calls of frightened Herastec behind him. As the Kraitt feinted again, one of the big squidlike creatures who called themselves the Ones Who Remember the Sea arrived in a whirl of whipping ghost-white tentacles and grabbed the Kraitt by his arms, legs, and tail. Zen stepped past him and went sprinting after the departing train.

"Nova!"

She saw him behind her for a moment—a jolting, upside-down glimpse through the mesh of the metal net. Then she was in midair, tumbling. The Kraitt who had been carrying her had flung her sideways through an open door into the train. Her vision glitched as she landed hard on a rusty deck with Kraitt trampling over her as they piled in behind. The train was gathering speed, leaving the station behind, shooting between high crags and into a tunnel. Dim red light, the stamping of clawed feet, the hot stink of the big lizards.

She sent one last message to Zen. "It's all right, Zen. I'll find a way to escape. I'll be back soon. Don't—"

Don't come after me, she had been about to say. But just then the light of a K-gate flared outside the gun-slit windows, time stretched and snapped, and when things righted themselves she was alone with the Kraitt, speeding through an unknown world.

Zen kept running long after he knew he could not catch the Kraitt train. He shouted through his headset to the *Damask Rose*, "They've taken Nova! Stop them! Head them off!" But the Kraitt had thrown the whole station into chaos; *morvah* were maneuvering in every direction and there was no way the *Rose* could do as he asked.

"It's all right, Zen," said Nova's voice in his headset suddenly. "I'll find a way to escape. I'll be back soon. Don't—" And then a silence that stretched on until he knew that it was permanent.

He turned back. The One Who Remembers the Sea who had helped him was nursing a slashed tentacle and waving the red leather tunic that the Kraitt warrior had left behind when he tore himself free. Others were gathering around to hear what had happened; the paths and sidings were full of bobbing lights. Zen caught the Kraitt tunic as the angry squid threw it aside. It was heavy, perhaps made out of the skin of a Kraitt its owner had defeated. He kept hold of it as if it were a clue and stumbled through the gathering crowd until he met Koth/Atalaí. He started shouting at them, "They took Nova! Where does that line go? Where does that K-gate go to?"

The Herastec shied away, staring at him. They didn't understand how he was still alive. Their own bond was so strong that if they were ever separated they would both die. They knew that it was different for other species, but it still felt wrong to them, as if Zen were a ghost. And perhaps he was, in a way, because, without Nova, he could not talk to them; his headset translated what they said to him, but his mouth could not make the sounds their language needed. Anyway, they were not listening. They had some news of their own to tell him.

"Another bad/surprising thing has happened," he read, watching the headset translation scroll across his sightline while Koth/Atalaí tossed their heads uneasily and took turns to whinny at him.

"A train came in from Yaarm shortly before the Kraitt attacked you . . ."

"The Herastec who were on this new train brought us news. They say your gate on Yaarm is gone. There has been a great disaster there. The mountains sat down upon your gate and buried it . . ."

"What?" Zen couldn't take it in, this new bad news.

More Herastec were shambling up, some of the ones who had come from Yaarm perhaps, eager to add more details to the story. "Before the mountains sat down another human *morvah* came through the gate. It carried three humans, but none of them was like this human's pair-mate . . ."

Their voices came at Zen like blows. They left him punch-drunk.

"The new humans on Yaarm know of this human Zen. They say he is not an ambassador at all, he is only a thief and a murderer, no better than Kraitt!"

"They say his pair-mate Nova is not a human at all; they say she is some type of (untranslatable) machine!"

Zen heard Koth/Atalaí's dung hit the floor and smelled its sweetish scent. Making dung was the ultimate expression of surprise if you were a Herastec. "Is this true, Zen/Nova?" they asked. "This cannot be true! We talked to her, she moved, she was not a thing, she was a living being . . ."

"The Kraitt do not take living beings," a Deeka pointed out. "But they do steal things."

"The humans are more clever with machines than Zen/Nova has been telling us," said someone else. "We are lucky their gate has been sat on by the mountains and no more of them can come; they might have brought a second Blackout down upon us all!"

"It's not true," said Zen, but he wasn't sure which part he was denying, and they didn't understand him anyway. He wanted to curl up in a ball and shut his eyes and block it all out. Herastec and Deeka crowded in, all talking at once so that his headset could not translate properly. Hath flapped their speaking membranes at him like faded bunting. He looked around and saw painted angels sliding by. A babble of alien shouts broke out behind him as he turned and ran, and his headset flashed confused translations at him: "Stop him let him go (untranslatable) bad strange/bad (untranslatable) where is he going?"

Zen didn't know where he was going; only across the tracks to where the *Damask Rose* was waiting. Only in through the door she opened, into the cluttered little house on wheels that he had shared with Nova for so long. Only to a seat, where he slumped, shaking, while the *Rose* carried him out of the station.

"We must go after Nova," he said after a while. He made himself stand up and go back through the train to the rear car, to the locked cabinet where Raven had stored his guns. "There's a line that leads to the Kraitt worlds," he said. "Can you tell which one it is? The Kraitt boss said she came from a place called Shards of something . . ."

"The Shards of Kharne," said the *Damask Rose*. "But think, Zen; you are alone, and my weapons are empty. How are we going to tackle a planet full of these Kraitt? How can we rescue Nova on our own?"

Zen didn't know. He was still shaking with the shock of losing her. He didn't have a plan. He thought love and anger would be enough.

The *Damask Rose* sent a maintenance spider scuttling ahead to alter a set of points, then started to gain speed, singing to herself one of the stirring songs she always sang when she was heading for a K-gate. "We are not going after the Kraitt," she said.

"But what about Nova? Don't you care about her? They don't even know what she is; they might damage her somehow . . ."

"I think they know exactly what she is," the train said. "I think the Tzeld Gekh Karneiss or whatever she calls herself got word somehow of the news from Yaarm a while before your Herastec friends did. I think they took Nova because they heard she was a machine."

"Yaarm," groaned Zen, remembering. "How can there be humans on Yaarm anyway? Who are they?"

"That's what I think we need to find out," said the *Damask Rose*, "before we go and do anything hasty. So that is where we're going."

On the Kraitt train, lizard warriors rolled Nova out of the net they had caught her in and heaved her to her feet. One put a claw-shaped knife to her throat and shoved her ahead of him along the dim, dirty, rusty carriage and through a door into the carriage behind it. It was brighter and cleaner in there. Three Kraitt skulls were displayed in an alcove high on one wall, and there was a saddlelike chair where the Kraitt female from Night's Edge station sat waiting. She was the Tzeld Gekh Karneiss, Nova remembered. Her translation software guessed that "Gekh" was a title, like "Queen" or "General," and "Karneiss" probably meant "from Kharne." As for "Tzeld," it seemed to mean "vicious," which she supposed must be a compliment in Kraitt.

The warrior forced her to her knees and backed away to the end of the carriage.

"So," said the Tzeld Gekh Karneiss. "Is it true? Are you a machine?"

Nova looked up into the clever yellow eyes. She decided that there was no point in lying to the owner of eyes like that. "How did you know?" she asked.

The Gekh folded her jeweled claws in front of her. A little sine wave of self-satisfaction ran the length of her tail. "The lesser races have been talking about you ever since you arrived on our Web. Some of them had noticed that you were different from your male. Different smell; different ways of moving. Many thought that you were augmented with machinery in some way. So quick at translating our languages! But now more humans have come to Yaarm, and it seems they have told the lesser races there that you are not a human at all."

"More humans?" asked Nova.

"Yes. Two females and a male, they say, and they will be the last ever to venture onto the Web of Worlds, because your gate has gone. That is good—we do not want new races on the Web. But we do want new machines. The lesser races are scared of machines, but I think that such superstitions hold us back. I believe that it is our duty to explore the opportunities that such machines might bring. My own people have already made many advances, but I see that humans are far ahead of us. That is why I sent my males to fetch you."

"There was no need," said Nova. "If it's help of that sort that you need, I can help you. We can reach an agreement."

"You mean trade?" snorted the Gekh. "We are the Kraitt. We are the Hunters of the Dawn. All other races are our prey. What they think is theirs is really ours, we just have not bothered to take it from them yet. You have always been mine, machine. Now I have taken you. I will learn from you how the Kraitt can build machines that think."

How strange, Nova was thinking. *Imagine sharing the galaxy* with all sorts of interesting people like the Herastec and the Night Swimmers and still believing that you're better than them. She listened to the silly rant with just a small part of her mind, while another small part wondered who the new humans on Yaarm could be.

The rest got busy studying the Kraitt train. She could dimly sense the electrical impulses sparking through the big, weird mind of the *morvah* up at the front, but it was not controlling the systems in its carriages the way a K-bahn loco did. The lights and ventilators and door controls were all running on little electronic circuits, controlled by a computer as clumsy as something from Old Earth. By the time the Gekh said, "You have always been mine . . ." Nova had already hacked through its flimsy firewalls. Better still, she had detected a faint signal from a Deeka train. It might be too far away for her to catch, but it proved that other trains did cross whatever world this was; she'd just have to find one, and start making her way back to Zen.

"That's all very interesting," she said politely when the Gekh paused. "But I'm afraid I must be going now." She tweaked the subsystems that controlled the door. It hissed open, and wind came blustering into the car. "It's been *lovely* talking to you . . ."

She moved quickly toward the door but, to her surprise, the Tzeld Gekh Karneiss was quicker. The floppy leather ruff around her neck went rigid with a loud snapping noise, not part of her robes at all, but part of her. She crossed the carriage with the speed of a sprung trap, slamming Nova against the far wall. She bellowed something that Nova could not translate. The Kraitt male sprang forward to pin Nova's arms, and more started swarming into the car. For a moment Nova felt warm green sunlight on her face; then the door she had forced open shut again.

"You think we are *stupid*, machine?" said the Gekh. "We are the Kraitt. No prey escapes us." She ran her black tongue carefully over all those shark-white teeth as if her instincts were prompting her to rip out Nova's throat. "You will come with me to the Shards of Kharne and I shall study you. I shall examine your body"—a long black talon tapped Nova's breastbone—"and I shall examine your mind"—the tip of the talon touched Nova's temple—"but, of course, I do not need to examine them both in the same place."

She made a sharp clicking sound and one of her males jumped forward. He was smaller than the warriors, a technician of some sort. He carried tools, in particular a sharp thing like a motorized pizza cutter that made a high whining sound when he switched it on. The air around it filled with a fine mist from the water it sprayed to cool the whirling blade.

Nova could not feel pain. She could feel fear, though. She could feel panic. She arched her back and kicked, she tried to twist herself away, but the scrum of Kraitt was too strong for her. Some of the blue gel she used as blood squirted over them as the blade went to work on her neck. Sparks sprayed when it bit into her ferro-ceramic spine. She was almost too distressed to engage her emergency shutdown and damage limitation routines, but she did, and watched her body go limp and still as the males dragged it away.

The Tzeld Gekh Karneiss picked her severed head up by the hair and carried it across the car. She placed it in the alcove beside the three Kraitt skulls. "No more escapes, machine," she said.

Okay . . . thought Nova's head. *What now?*

24

Raven's Worm still stood on the siding it had made for itself, just beyond the place where the spur that led to the new gate joined the mainline. The Worm was not much more than a hill now, with grass and small trees growing on it. On either side the lagoons spread their mirrors for the stars of Yaarm. Nearby, on the bright new rails, an old black loco stood.

Zen had known that he would find the newcomers there. On the worlds he had crossed since he left Night's Edge, the local media had been full of images of the black train. The *Damask Rose* had picked up crude TV pictures taken by Herastec photographers leaning perilously out of circling flying machines, and by Chmoii camera teams that had ventured close enough to capture the writing on the loco's flank that said GHOST WOLF. He knew that it was damaged, which was why it had stopped here— although it probably would not have been welcome in Yaarm station, because the Herastec's aerial footage had also shown what had happened to the mountains where the new K-gate had been. The members of the Yaarm traders' council were distinctly less friendly to Zen than they had been on his first visit. Humans were dangerous, it seemed, and what was the point of being friendly to them when the only gate to their homeworlds was buried forever?

The *Damask Rose* rolled slowly toward the black loco, her seven shadows spread around her in the glorious Yaarmish night. A Deeka documentary team who were camped on the shore beside the line peeked from their bubble tents at the sound of her engines and started fetching out cameras. The *Rose* ignored them and kept her own cameras focused on the other train.

"It's a Zodiak all right," she said. (The TV images had been so crude that she had not been sure till then.) "Just like Raven's *Thought Fox*," she added. "And maybe just as dangerous . . ."

"It doesn't *look* very dangerous," said Zen.

And it didn't. Its weapons hatches were open, but no guns or missiles targeted the *Rose* as she approached. And was that someone's laundry, strung on lines between the hatch covers?

"I am the *Ghost Wolf*," it said, in answer to the *Rose*'s hail. "It's nice to meet a real train here at last. Have you seen these local jobs—these biotech things? Like slugs on roller skates."

"I am the *Damask Rose*," said the *Damask Rose*.

"Oh yes, I've heard all about *you*," the wartrain said. "Are Zen Starling and the Motorik Nova on board? My passengers want a word with them."

The TV pictures had shown three passengers, but Zen could only see two. The two young women climbed down out of its cabin as the *Rose* drew to a halt about two hundred feet away. Both carried guns, which even Zen could tell weren't military guns but old-fashioned hunting rifles. He had already chosen a weapon of his own from Raven's gun cabinet: a stylish Bandarpeti pistol.

He took it with him when he climbed out of the train and held it where the strangers could see it as he walked along the track to meet them. A wind came across the lagoons, ruffling the starlit water into little cat's-paws and reminding Zen of his first night on the Web of Worlds.

"Stop there!" shouted one of the strangers.

Zen stopped. They were both quite familiar to him from the alien media broadcasts, but he had not seen them in color before—the Herastec broadcast only in black and white, the Chmoii for some reason in soft shades of blue. Peering at the lo-res images on the *Rose*'s holoscreens, Zen had wondered if these two were sisters, because they both had the same spiky, bad-girl hair and scruffy summer clothes. But now that he was looking at them in real life he saw that they were quite different.

One looked like trouble, with a hard little face like a clenched fist. The other was Threnody Noon. That stopped him as if he'd walked into a wall. He'd always felt bad about the lies he'd told Threnody and the things he'd done. He'd consoled himself with the thought that they would never meet again.

"Is that him?" asked the short one.

"That's him, Chandni," said Threnody.

She had spent so long hating him. She had spent so many sleepless nights remembering how he had lied to her and the chaos that he had caused. She had spent so much time imagining the punishments that she would demand if Railforce or Noon security ever found him. And now she had found him herself, and she had a gun in her hands, and all she could think was how glad she was to meet another human being, and one who had found out how to survive in this strange place. It was all she could do to stop herself from laughing and crying and begging him for help.

Chandni spat on the rails and went closer, staring at Zen.

"So it's real, then? This place?" she asked. "Because I've been having this argument with the Empress. I said it could all be some kind of virtual world in the Datasea that someone's running to trick us. Full of monsters and stuff."

"It's real," said Zen. "We've been here eight, nine months. We've traveled all over . . ."

"Telling everyone that you're the ambassador for all humanity," said Threnody. "That's a step up. You were just pretending to be Tallis Noon when I met you."

"He *does* look a bit like Tallis, to be fair," said Chandni. "He doesn't look like an ambassador for all humanity, though. He's too young."

"The people here don't know that," said Zen. "They don't know anything about humans, except what me and Nova told them. At least, they didn't, till you arrived and ruined everything. Now they don't trust me, and they know that Nova's a Motorik . . ." He hesitated. He had so many questions of his own, not the least of which was how the Empress of the Network came to be stuck here like a castaway. But he sensed that the answer to that one would be long and complicated, so he said, "What happened to the gate?"

"The Guardians destroyed it," said Threnody. "The Twins sent something called a Railbomb through behind us. Now we're stuck here. The *Ghost Wolf* is damaged . . ."

"Don't tell him that!" said the *Ghost Wolf*.

"So we couldn't go any farther. We'd been here a few hours when this *thing*—"

"This *train*," said Chandni.

"This sort of train came with *creatures* in it. I suppose they wanted to see what had happened. They didn't seem pleased.

The *Wolf* was able to translate some of the noises they made. It explained who we are, and they told us about you, and then we explained who you are. Who you *really* are. And they didn't seem pleased about that, either, and they cleared off and left us here."

"Who's with you?" asked Zen. "I saw three people on the broadcasts."

"Just the interface," said Threnody. She looked behind her. "Oh," she said. "He's wandered off again."

*

Beyond the place where the Worm was turning into a landscape feature, the ground sloped downward again to meet more mirror-water. Along the shoreline there, the interface of Mordaunt 90 had been piling up round, flat stones in little towers. He was still very sad about the death of his friend Yanvar Malik. The Guardians knew that humans died, of course—a human lifetime was like the brief flaring of a match to them—but it was only now that he had become mortal himself that the interface truly understood what that meant. He was in mourning for Malik, and in shock that he too was now trapped in a fragile human shell. Piling up stones gave him something else to occupy his thoughts. It was surprisingly difficult to stack more than four or five. You had to choose your stones with care. The biggest went at the base, and the smallest at the top. The towers often fell down, but the interface was very patient, and some had already grown as tall as him.

It was all very fascinating for the small colony of Hath who lived just offshore with their stalklike legs planted in the rich silt. They liked pebbles more than anything, and good ones were passed from hand to hand for hundreds of miles between neighboring Hath in the great colonies that stretched along the shores of Yaarm's lagoons. They had never seen anyone pile them up so elegantly before. In the few days since the interface began his work, hundreds of Hath had come wading down the coast to watch. They stood in the shallows in a wide, fluttering crowd, buzzing their appreciation each time a new pebble was added to the latest tower.

When he saw Zen, Threnody, and Chandni coming toward him, the interface said, "Oh, a visitor!" and put down the pebble he had been holding.

Zen looked at his golden skin, his golden eyes. "Is that . . . ?"

"It was," said Chandni. "He can hardly remember anything now."

"That is not fair, Chandni Hansa," said the interface mildly. "I am only a fragment of my old self and no longer connected to the great data centers of Mordaunt 90. But I can remember all sorts of things."

"Nothing useful, though," said Threnody. "Like why the Guardians never told us there were places like this, and how we get home again."

"It is true that I don't know the answers to those questions," said the interface, looking embarrassed. Then he cheered up, as a small Hath came carefully between the pebble towers and placed something in his hands—not a pebble, for once, but a little silvery fish thing. "Oh, thank you!" he said.

"They've been quite kind to us, these tents," said Threnody. "We cook the fish on an open fire. They seem edible enough."

"They give me the runs," said Chandni Hansa.

"I have food," said Zen, without quite meaning to. "Aboard the *Damask Rose*. You'd better come and eat and tell me what's happened. And I'll tell you . . . I'll tell you how to get home."

Threnody's tired face lit with hope. "Then there's a way? Another gate?"

"Don't trust him," said Chandni. "Remember what he did to your family."

"He was working for Raven then," said Threnody. "Now we need him. Sometimes, to survive, you have to make alliances with people you don't like."

That shut Chandni up. Her mouth went tight and narrow and she kept on glowering at Zen, but she didn't say any more.

"So is there a way?" Threnody asked. "A way back to the Network Empire?"

"Nova thinks there is," said Zen. He'd been thinking it over on the way from Night's Edge. He hadn't liked Nova's scheme when she'd suggested it, but he needed to offer these newcomers something, because he needed them to help him get her back. The promise of a way home was all he had. But now that he had said it, he found that he suddenly wanted very much for it to be more than a promise. He had missed other human beings; he had not even realized how much. The scent of their sweat, the texture of their skin, the way they stood. He wanted Nova to be right. He wanted there to be a way home.

"Nova has a plan," he said.

"Where is she?" demanded Threnody. "Let's hear this plan."

"She's not here," said Zen. "She's on a place called the Shards of Kharne. If you want her to show you the way home, we'll have to go and get her."

The Shards of Kharne turned out to be the remnants of a shattered planet that had once orbited a small, golden sun. The Shards orbited it still, but now they orbited one another too: moon-sized chunks of what had once been a world, locked in a complicated gravitational ballet. The fact that they had never flown apart or collided with one another, and that they were all encased in one envelope of atmosphere, made Nova wonder if the Railmakers had been at work here long ago. As the Tzeld Gekh Karneiss's servants carried her from the train, she saw a rugged worldlet tumble slowly across the sky above the station, spurting black smoke from a score of small volcanoes. Could those vents be acting like thrusters to prevent the various world-splinters from colliding?

She would have liked to stop and watch, but she had no choice now in what she looked at. She was just a head, being carried in the claws of a Kraitt, following three other Kraitt who bore the polished skulls from the Gekh's private car. Nova assumed the skulls were ancestors, or battle trophies, for they were treated with elaborate care.

The Kraitt servants went through the shabby, half-derelict station, which was built inside an old Railmaker structure. A dangerous-looking aircraft powered by chemical rockets was taking off from a runway outside, presumably heading for one of the other shards. For a moment Nova was afraid that she was going to have to travel on something like that, but the vehicle that awaited the Tzeld Gekh Karneiss was even more primitive: a carved wooden carriage drawn by two big, horned reptiles.

The Gekh's servants set the skulls down carefully on cushions in the carriage's curtained cabin and put Nova's head between them. Then the Gekh herself climbed in and settled herself on more cushions, and the carriage set off. Nova sensed her own body nearby, the small sub-brain in her spine sending out plaintive little distress calls. She guessed it was following in a second vehicle. The road from the station was bumpy. Her head fell over on its side, and the teeth of the three skulls chattered constantly.

"Those are the skulls of my sisters," said the Gekh.

"Oh . . ." Nova's voice sounded strange to her. Usually she spoke the same way humans did, by taking air into her chest cavity and letting it vibrate structures in her throat on its way back out. Now she had to rely on a backup system of small speakers in the roof of her mouth, and the sound quality was tinny. She could not think of much to say, anyway. What *did* you say when a dinosaur introduced you to the skulls of her sisters?

"They have very nice teeth . . ."

"I killed them myself," said the Gekh. "I did not *want* to. It is the tragedy of my species. When Kraitt hatchlings reach adolescence, the female siblings start to fight until only one is left.

It is what has made our kind so strong. Only the victors go on to breed, and give birth to the next generation of Kraitt. Sometimes sisters make pacts that they will not kill each other, but the instinct is too powerful." The Gekh caressed the smallest of the skulls with her tail's tip. "My little sister Shantis . . . We were such friends, she and I, when we were growing up. Before my time came, she went away, went to live at the far end of the Web. But years later, when my train stopped at Yashtey, she happened to be there too. She caught my scent and could not stop herself. She attacked me on the stairs to the station. It was a *legendary* battle. There are poems about it. Luckily, I proved the stronger. If not, my skull would be an ornament on her train."

This, thought Nova, was not good. No wonder people didn't like the Kraitt. Presumably all races had a few ancient, savage instincts locked up in their evolutionary closets, but most had learned how to control them by the time they joined the Web. The Railmakers seemed to have taken care only to give K-gates and *morvah* to species that had managed to control such traits. Perhaps when the Blackout came, something had gone wrong, and the Kraitt had found their way through the K-gates too soon . . .

She wondered what Zen was doing. She had told him to wait for her to escape, but if she didn't return soon she was sure he would set out to look for her. She hoped he would not underestimate the Kraitt. She was afraid that he might come after her and try to rescue her, not understanding how clever and how dangerous her captors were.

But, at the same time, she wanted him to come. She missed him as much as she missed her own body.

The Tzeld Gekh Karneiss lifted one of the thick curtains that hung swaying at the carriage window. A hard line of hot sunlight fell across her scaly face, then dimmed and went out as the carriage passed into a tunnel. "So you can see why thinking machines would be a benefit to my people," she said. "Kraitt females cannot make close friendships with one another—the memories of the deaths of our sisters are too clear. We fear that if we grow too fond of someone, the old instincts may take over and it will end in blood. We have only our males for company, and males are no company at all—they are of use only as servants or warriors. So I must learn your secrets, machine."

Not even the Kraitt could bear the gaze of their sun for long. They had built most of their station city underground. Nova tuned her mind to local media networks and had an impression of dim, crowded caverns like an enormous system of burrows. One of these burrows was the villa of the Gekh. There they took Nova's head to a round, white room and placed it on a table. Kraitt technicians scanned and photographed her from every angle. They clamped the head in a stand to keep it upright, and connected pipes and cables to the ducts that dangled where her neck had been. Some of the cables carried power. One of the pipes was a water supply, which she needed to keep her mouth and eyes moist. The rest just linked her to clunky-looking screens and terminals that stood in other parts of the room, where Kraitt technicians tried to download her operating systems. She felt their crude programs trying to pry her mind open. It was easy to block them out at first, but the Kraitt grew agitated when their programs did not work, so she let them have access to some of her code. She was afraid that, if she didn't, they might take a more direct approach and pry her actual head apart.

The Kraitt clustered around their screens, discussing the streams of code that she let them see. Sometimes the Tzeld Gekh Karneiss would come and listen to their reports. Sometimes she would come and stare at Nova's head with her unblinking, yellow eyes. Sometimes she would bring her children with her: three young females, already approaching the uneasy age at which their ancient instincts would make one murder the others.

"Hey," Nova called out to her, the first time she visited. "Where's the rest of me? Why don't you put me back together? I could tell you much more if I was all in one piece . . ."

"Ignore it," the Tzeld Gekh Karneiss told her daughters. "It is just a thing: a device created by one of the prey species. We will soon learn its secrets."

"Please?" said Nova.

But pleading sounded silly, and the Tzeld Gekh Karneiss took no notice anyway.

On Yaarm, the broadcasters were losing interest in human beings. The newcomers just sat talking in the cars of the *Damask Rose*, or built pebble towers to amuse the Hath, and the camera teams left them to it and went to film other things on other worlds. The Web was wide and filled with wonders. The humans, who could never bring any more goods or people through their buried gate, had turned out to be far less interesting than everyone had hoped.

So, few people noticed when the two trains moved off. Even the Hath had learned the tower-building trick for themselves by then, and were too busy making their own towers to do more than flutter a quick goodbye when the interface of Mordaunt 90 climbed into the *Damask Rose*'s car. A radio message from Yaarm station warned the *Rose* that she was not scheduled to leave, but the *Rose* replied that they were heading back to Night's Edge, and the Yaarm authorities decided not to interfere. The humans were a disappointment—so few of them, and nothing to trade. Yaarm would be better off without them.

The next world was jungle mostly: hot, steaming hills covered in gigantic ferns, with bald patches and spoil heaps where Chmoii miners were working. As the two trains made their way through empty valleys, the *Damask Rose* sent out her maintenance spiders with paint sticks full of pigment she had made from Yaarmish soil. As quickly as they could, the bots painted over the beautiful, fading pictures on her hull, until she was as black as the *Ghost Wolf.*

Zen was sad to see those pictures go. His Motorik friend Flex had painted those, and Flex was dead. But a few scraps of Flex's personality had been saved to the *Rose's* memory, so perhaps she had inherited enough talent to repaint the original images one day.

"We don't want the Kraitt to recognize the *Damask Rose,*" he explained to the others, sitting in the messy and suddenly too-small state car at the front of the train. "We're going to be a new train, with locos front and rear. Not many people trade with the Kraitt, so I'm hoping they haven't heard any more news from Yaarm since the night they left Night's Edge with Nova. They know more humans have arrived, and something happened to the gate, but maybe they don't yet know it's blocked permanently. We'll tell them it was just a temporary fault, and now human trains are ready to roll through, and eager to do business with them."

"What if they don't believe us?" asked Threnody.

"That's your job, to make them believe."

The interface of Mordaunt 90 shook his head and said, "There are so many things that could go wrong with this plan."

"I know," said Zen. "But if we thought like that, we wouldn't try anything. Nova would never get rescued, and you'd never go home. You want to go home, don't you?"

The interface looked wistful. "I want to reconnect to the Mordaunt 90 personality. It is frightening to live like this, in one body, all alone. This body will die one day, and then what will happen to all its memories of the unique things it has experienced? What about my memories of Malik? Someone should remember him, and how brave he was. I need to return to the Network Empire so that I can add these new experiences to Mordaunt 90's memories."

"Then it's settled," said Zen, and he left the table, heading back down the train.

It really did feel crowded with four on board. He didn't see why they couldn't have stayed in the *Ghost Wolf*'s little cabins; it wasn't like they'd brought lots of stuff with them. But Chandni Hansa had insisted that Threnody was an Empress and should have Zen's bed—the only bed—which she and Chandni now took turns to sleep in, because it seemed that one of them always had to be awake to keep an eye on Zen. Zen slept on the bunk in the sickbay, knowing that he had only agreed because he still felt guilty about what he had done to Threnody and her family.

(As for the interface of Mordaunt 90, he was still surprised to find that he needed sleep at all. He tended to nod off without warning, sitting at a table or on one of the state-car chairs, and wake up with a start a few hours later, complaining of strange dreams.)

Even in the store car at the back of the train, Zen still couldn't get any peace. He started emptying out the big plastic crates that were part of his plan for retrieving Nova, but he hadn't gotten far before the door sighed open and Chandni Hansa came through, scowling at him as usual.

"I don't know why the Empress believes you," she said. "You've tricked her before; you'd think she'd be smarter. I'm not sure I believe you."

"About what?" asked Zen.

"Going home. You say this wire dolly of yours knows a way home . . ."

"I said she *thinks* there's a way," Zen corrected her. "It was a hunch. But Nova's smarter than either of us. Her hunches are right, pretty often. I didn't think this one sounded like too good an idea because it would rely on finding a gate to somewhere where we could explain ourselves before the Guardians just stomped us. But you have an interface of Mordaunt 90 with you, so that changes everything—they'll *have* to listen to him."

Chandni watched him while he spoke, eyes narrowed, scanning for lies. Then she sighed and sat down with her back against the door of the fuel store. "But why do you want to go home? I don't want to go home. I'm glad I'm rid of it. First time in my life I'm free of rich people and Guardians and all the rest of it."

"I miss my mom and my sister," said Zen. "I miss other people. Don't you have anyone you miss?"

Chandni shook her head.

"Well, anyway, it's not just about going home . . ." He had been thinking about this while he tried to get to sleep in the sickbay the night before. "If we can find another K-gate between the Network Empire and the Web of Worlds, think of the trade that will start. And we'll be there at the beginning of it; we'll be the merchants people here will trust. We'll bring trainloads of stuff and swap it for trainloads of rare stuff from the Web that we can sell for a fortune on Sundarban or somewhere. We'll be rich!"

Chandni Hansa laughed. "Oh, Zen Starling. Listen to you. You really believe all that stuff? If trade ever starts up, the corporate families will grab all the profits for themselves, just like they grabbed everything else. They have ways of stopping people like us from getting a share."

"So there's no point trying? We're beaten before we begin?"

"When you've been beaten as often as I have, you start to realize that the whole game's rigged."

"You'd like my sister," said Zen. "She talks like you."

"I don't like anybody."

"What about the Empress? You like her, don't you?"

"I don't *like* her," said Chandni. "I just don't want to see her get killed. It's not the same thing."

She looked at Zen, who had gone back to emptying out those big plastic trunks, the size of freezer coffins. She had thought when he showed up that she and he would click together like magnets, two low heroes from the streets with so many experiences in common. The little-girl Chandni who still lived locked up in her heart with all her silly little-girl hopes had even thought it might be like a threedie—love at first sight and stuff. But it hadn't worked like that at all. Zen had spent so long thinking of himself as a rich kid or a master criminal or an ambassador that he'd started believing it. The last person he wanted to meet was someone just like he used to be, who could see right through him to the grubby little thief he really was.

"The next world will be Night's Edge," announced the *Damask Rose*. "That's if this Chmoii ore-train in front of us ever goes through the K-gate. Do you want to stop on Night's Edge?"

"No," said Zen. "Signal Koth/Atalaí when we pass the station, see if they have any fresh news of the Kraitt. If they don't, keep going, straight for the Shards of Kharne."

27

It was really boring, being just a head. At night, when the Kraitt technicians left her alone, there was nothing for Nova to do but surf the Shards' primitive broadcasting networks, which consisted of dismal music, vicious gladiatorial battles, and programs where the captains of Kraitt trains bragged of the raids they had carried out and showed off the loot and trophies they had brought home. A few hours before midnight even that shut down, and Nova was left listening to the scritch and scratch of insects in the air ducts above the ceiling.

It was then that she heard again, very faintly, the signal from the Black Light Zone that she had picked up on Night's Edge. So either the Shards of Kharne were also close to the Zone, or the signal was powerful enough that it could be detected everywhere, once you knew what to listen for. Or was it that the signal had crept inside her somehow, inserted some strange code of its own into her programming, so that it could keep on singing to her of the Zone?

That thought made her worry that she was losing her mind, so she pushed it away and distracted herself with memories of times with Zen or screened movies for herself. Sometimes the memories and the movies intertwined, because they were the same movies she had watched aboard the *Damask Rose* when Zen was asleep in her arms and she wanted to make-believe that she was sleeping too. Sometimes, watching her favorites, she could imagine that she had a body again, and that Zen was curled up next to it, with his face against that rippled scar-patch on her chest that had never fully repaired.

There was a movie she had always loved called *She Was the Thunder, He Was the Rain*. It had been made on Malapet a few hundred years before, in the 2-D style of classics from Old Earth. It was about a Guardian who fell in love with an ordinary human, and it was based very loosely on the story of Raven and his love for Anais Six. Each time she watched it, Nova would mute her memories of previous screenings, so that it was always new to her. It always made her cry.

*

The Tzeld Gekh Karneiss was growing impatient. Her visits became more frequent, and more angry. She listened impatiently to her technicians while they tried to explain what they were finding inside Nova's head. One day, when they made excuses for their slow progress she lashed them with the tip of her tail, which was sheathed in brass to make the lashing extra painful.

Afterward, when the others had left, one of the Kraitt lingered. He approached Nova's table cautiously, stooping to peer into her face. "You are hiding things from us," he said. "We cannot reach them, but we must, or the Tzeld Gekh Karneiss will kill us and replace us with new males."

Nova felt sorry for him. It felt good to have someone speak to her again, as if she were a person. "What do you need to know?" she asked.

"Everything!" said the Kraitt. "The Tzeld Gekh Karneiss says you were built by a lesser race. She does not understand that the programs that run you are far ahead of anything we have seen. They are even more advanced than the technology of the Neem. Since the days of the Railmakers themselves there has been nothing like you on the Web of Worlds. We cannot hope to build something like you, but that is what she wants." The Kraitt let his black tongue flicker thoughtfully between his teeth. "They are lonely, our mothers. Other females remind them of the sisters they murdered, and we males are poor companions. I believe that the Tzeld Gekh Karneiss thinks, if she can make a thing like you but in beautiful, Kraitt form . . ."

"She wants to make friends," said Nova.

The Kraitt blinked slowly with his transparent inner eyelids, which was the Kraitt equivalent of a nod.

"But once you figure out how to do it," Nova said, "I'll be no more use to her, will I? What will happen to me then?"

He just stood there. If he was showing any emotion, it was some lizardy one, quite wasted on Nova.

"I'll help you if you help me," she said. "I assume the rest of me is around somewhere?"

"On the floor below," the Kraitt said.

"All right then," said Nova. She wasn't sure she was doing the right thing, but doing anything felt better than just sitting there on that table like a potted plant. "I'll unlock the information you need, but in return I want to make sure you keep me safe and get me back together."

The Kraitt blinked again. Before he finished, the screens behind him lit up as Nova started downloading the contents of her mind. She gave him everything except her own memories and her movie collection. She didn't think the Kraitt had the technology to build a Motorik body, but now they should at least be able to construct a simple, self-aware computer.

The Kraitt worked all night, his big eyes mirroring the ranks of red hieroglyphs that marched like armies of fire ants down the screens of his terminals. In the morning, Nova watched the amazement of his comrades when he showed them his breakthrough. The Tzeld Gekh Karneiss was impressed too, when she made her visit, later in the day. She listened carefully to his report, then killed him with one brutal swipe from her brass-sheathed tail.

"It is not good to let males succeed too much," she explained, stalking over to the table and gazing down at Nova. "It goes to their heads." She stroked the tip of a talon across Nova's face, tracing the frustrated tears that were trickling from Nova's eyes. Behind her, her three daughters flared their nostrils, excited by the scent of the technician's blood. "Don't worry," she said. "He was unimportant. The others understand the discoveries he has made. His work will be continued, and the others will work harder without him."

They did not even have names, those Kraitt males. They busied themselves at their screens, hissing with satisfaction as they saw the potential of the information that Nova had given them.

The human train arrived at the station just as the shard it stood on was moving into the shadow of another. The sky stayed bright, but the dusty landscape filled with shadows, the local equivalent of night. The Kraitt who came out of the station buildings to meet the new arrivals carried no lamps and did not seem bothered by the darkness. All Threnody could see of them, when she stepped out onto the platform, were their spiky silhouettes and the gleam of their unblinking eyes. She was not sure if that made them more frightening or less. She fought off the temptation to run screaming back onto the train, and made the little speech she had agreed upon with Zen.

"We are merchants from the Network Empire. We have come here with valuable machines to show to the Tzeld Gekh Karneiss."

Zen had loaded Threnody's headset with the translation software that his Moto friend had written; it turned her words into something he called the trade tongue and spat them out in flat, electronic chunks through a small necklace speaker that the

Damask Rose had made on her 3-D printer. The speaker sounded weird and grating to Threnody, but she supposed the Kraitt would assume that was just her natural voice. They turned to each other, muttering and snarling. She waited, wrinkling her nose at the hot, filthy stink of them, thinking about the ice party on Grand Central and how much her life had changed since then.

"We heard that your gate on Yaarm was destroyed," growled one of the Kraitt.

"There was a rockfall," said Threnody. "But we cut a new tunnel easily enough."

"You cut it very quickly, this new tunnel," said another of the Kraitt.

"We have powerful machines," said Threnody. "That is why we seek to trade with the Tzeld Gekh Karneiss, who understands the value of our technology, not with the Herastec or the Deeka, who are afraid of it."

"The Herastec and the Deeka are prey species," sneered one of the Kraitt.

"Then please tell the Tzeld—the Gekh . . . Tell her that we have technology to show her . . ."

The technology was waiting in the rear car, on Raven's truck. There were a lot of small boxes stuffed with random spare parts and damaged components from the *Ghost Wolf,* and three large crates stacked one on top of the other. In each of the top two crates was one of the *Rose's* maintenance spiders, folded up and resting on a thick layer of packing foam. In the bottom crate was another maintenance spider, but this one was resting on a thin layer of foam, and under the foam was Zen Starling. He lay on his side, curled up, already starting to grow stiff, watching the feed from the *Rose's* cameras, which she was streaming to his headset.

He wished he could be out there on the platform doing the talking instead of Threnody. She sounded as if she was reading from a script, and he didn't have faith in her to improvise if things took a turn they hadn't allowed for. But it had to be Threnody: he didn't trust Chandni Hansa, and the broken interface of Mordaunt 90 was too shy and vague to play a pushy merchant. Zen could have done it easily enough himself, of course, but the Kraitt might recognize him. Besides, he had a different job to do, one that meant he needed to stay hidden.

Now one of the Kraitt was going back into the station buildings. The Kraitt didn't seem to fear the Railmakers' ruins in the same way as other races, and they had filled the old glass halls with stacks of freight and curtained parts off to serve as offices. The Kraitt who had gone inside was making a transmission on some device so crude that the *Damask Rose* could not hack it. "If it was any more primitive it would be two tin cans with a long piece of string between them," she grumbled. "I assume the other end of the string is in the Tzeld Gekh Karneiss's place . . ."

Zen didn't want to risk even a whisper, since he wasn't sure how sharp Kraitt hearing was. He called up a keyboard in his headset view and typed a message to the *Rose* by blinking at each letter in turn. *Show me rest of station . . .*

The *Rose* sent him shots from her other cameras, then from the cameras of the *Ghost Wolf* at the rear of the train. The station was dusty and half derelict. Some Kraitt *morvah* slept on sidings. At an outlying platform was a *morvah* of a type that Zen had not seen before, like a gigantic silver wood louse.

What train is that?

"I think it's Neem," the *Damask Rose* replied.

The insect people? Yuk! What r they doing here?

"Trading with the Kraitt, I suppose. They like machines too."

Hope they won't get in our way . . .

"There's some movement in their train. Some communications going back and forth between it and the Kraitt city, but I can't decrypt them. Probably nothing you need to be worrying about. *This* is what you need to be worrying about . . ."

She switched back to the original camera, the one that showed him Threnody waiting nervously on the platform. The Kraitt Stationmaster, or whatever he was, had come out of his office. "The Tzeld Gekh Karneiss wishes to see what you have brought," he was saying.

Threnody turned and called to Chandni and the interface, who were waiting inside the train. They came through to the rear car and slid open the big freight doors. The *Rose* extended a ramp so that the truck could drive itself down onto the platform, where the Kraitt were waiting to examine it. They opened the lids of a few random boxes and the topmost crate, but the stuff inside was of no interest to warriors of the Kraitt.

Threnody looked into the rear car and told the interface, "You stay here with the *Rose* and the *Ghost Wolf.* We'll be back soon."

"Yes, Threnody," said the interface meekly. "Good luck."

Chandni jumped down onto the platform and went with Threnody across to where the truck waited. They climbed onto the seats at the front end.

"This is insane," said Chandni. "This isn't going to work."

Threnody hushed her, in case their headsets translated her griping and their speakers broadcast it at the Kraitt. The truck moved past the glass buildings, down a ramp onto a dusty road. Two big Kraitt ran ahead of it, leading the way to the compound of the Tzeld Gekh Karneiss.

Zen lay in his crate, watching the view from Threnody's headset now. A dark landscape rushing by under a curiously bright sky, lakes gleaming on an airborne mountain as it turned like a moon just above the cactus-spined horizon. Chimneys and ventilation towers poked out of the stony ground. The gravity was very low. Each time the truck lurched or cornered, Zen's box was bounced into the air, and each time it felt as if it would never come down again. But it did, and before long the tiled gullet of a tunnel opened ahead. The truck dropped underground, passing through a set of massive bronze gates, where it swung sideways, slowing to a stop. The Kraitt who waited there were talking to Threnody, but she seemed too nervous to reply. Chandni chipped in, telling them the same things that Threnody had told the ones at the station. Then they were fussing with the boxes, lifting one of the big crates down from the truck, arguing with the guards. "If we can't take our truck any farther, you'll have to help us carry stuff— no, we don't need that one, it's just the same as this—we'll come back for it if your Tzeld Gekh wants to buy . . ."

They were moving away. Zen caught a giddy, swerving glimpse through Threnody's headset of the truck left alone, standing in a low, domed cavern. Then she was moving along more corridors, Kraitt hurrying ahead, Chandni complaining about the weight of the box that she and Threnody were carrying between them.

Zen cut the headset link and heard their voices fade. He shut his eyes and lay in his box, feeling very nervous. Then he switched to another headset channel.

High above the lizard city, the *Damask Rose*'s butterfly drones rode the night wind, peering down at the Tzeld Gekh Karneiss's compound with ultrasound and infrared. The train's voice whispered in Zen's skull. "I think you're alone."

You only think? he wanted to say, but he dared not speak aloud and there wasn't time to type. He took a deep breath and shoved his way out of the box, closing the lid behind him as he scrambled down into the shadows between the truck's wheels. He crouched there, looking around. The cavern was circular, the big bronze gates at one side, four other passages opening off it.

"Take the one on the left," said the *Damask Rose*. "I think I've found Nova. She's in some sort of workshop on the next level down."

The ultrasound scans of the Kraitt burrow were meaningless to Zen, just shifting blue blurs, but the train pinged a 3-D map to his headset, with the route to the workshops clearly marked like a task in a game. He wanted to ask if Nova was all right, if the *Damask Rose* had told her they were coming, but there were voices in the tunnel Threnody and Chandni had gone down, and he was afraid the Kraitt might be returning. He fled down the left-hand tunnel, brushing scraps of packing foam off his clothes as he went. He was wearing the Kraitt jacket he had brought from Night's Edge. It was too long in the arms for him, too tight across the shoulders, but he hoped that from behind, at a quick glance, he might be mistaken for a Kraitt. The tunnel had lamps on its roof, but not many, and they were very dim.

He started to feel good. Not happy, exactly, alone in a maze full of dinosaurs, but more alive than he had felt for a while, as if his body had been craving this sort of danger. A brash, swaggering part of him thought, *I robbed the Network Emperor, and now I'm going to rob the Kraitt Queen.* He'd be the first human thief in all history to pull off a job on the Web of Worlds. And that circular bronze door ahead must be the one marked on the *Rose*'s map as the entrance to the workshop . . .

In the Gekh's living quarters, Threnody and Chandni lifted the lids off their boxes. The light from softly buzzing electric lamps fell on the silvery limbs of the maintenance spider folded up inside. The Gekh leaned forward to look. She was sitting on a saddle chair, which was the only item of furniture in the big room. The floor was covered with the knobby, cured skins of enormous reptiles, and the walls and roof glimmered expensively where thousands of little disks of what looked like solid gold had been hammered into the rocky walls. More Kraitt, armed males and immature females, stood on either side of their mistress, all watching the humans unveil their wares.

"This is what we call a maintenance spider," said Threnody.

"What does it do?" asked the Gekh.

Threnody pinged a furtive message to the *Damask Rose*. The maintenance spider unfolded itself, carefully rising on its long, segmented legs and stepping out of the box. Some of the Kraitt hissed uneasily. One drew a curved knife.

"It's all right," said Threnody. "This is a servant, that's all. A robot servant."

"It looks like a starved Neem," said the Gekh.

"It does not need food or sleep," said Threnody, "and it is very easy to store."

The maintenance spider made a few graceful, dancing movements and displayed some of the tool-arms that it usually kept folded neatly under its small body.

"It *thinks*, this machine?" asked the Gekh. "It thinks for itself, like the machines that you humans make in the likeness of your own feeble bodies?"

"It is operated by another machine, a thinking machine," said Threnody. "The train tells it what to do, and it obeys."

"The *train* tells it what to do?"

"The maintenance spider can perform a number of useful roles—"

"I have been wondering about your strange *morvah*," the Tzeld Gekh said, apparently not interested in maintenance spiders and their many uses. "So different from the *morvah* of the other prey species. I have been wondering, since you people are so clever with machines, if your *morvah* might be machines as well? I would be very interested in acquiring one of your trains . . ."

"We could get you one!" said Threnody brightly. "When we go back to our own Network we can purchase one for you from one of the leading manufacturers—"

"So what you told my people at the station is true? Your new gate on Yaarm is open again?"

"Yes," said Threnody.

The Tzeld Gekh Karneiss rose and gathered her leathery robes around her. She walked to where Threnody stood, leaned close to her, and sniffed. The snowflake-shaped pupils of her yellow eyes contracted thoughtfully, and Threnody saw her own face mirrored in the blackness there, appalled.

"Why are you so frightened?" asked the Gekh.

Threnody tried to get out something along the lines of "I'm not frightened, just overawed by your magnificence," but her numb mouth wouldn't form the words. "She's frightened because she's lying," said Chandni suddenly. "We both are. We were made to come here and lie to you."

"Chandni!" said Threnody, over the rising snarls of the Kraitt.

"Face it, Empress, this plan was never going to work," said Chandni. "Zen Starling's lying to us anyway—there's no way home. We're stuck here. So we need to make friends with someone tough, and that's not Starling." She squared up to the Gekh. "Starling wanted us to keep you busy while he robs you. Take a look. You'll find him stealing that Motorik of yours."

*

Zen leaned his weight against the door and winced as it shifted. The scraping noise it made echoed off up the tunnel. Only a slight movement. It was locked, of course, but that was good, because it probably meant there were no Kraitt inside.

He reached inside the heavy jacket and pulled out the cutting device he had found among Raven's stores. It was called a waterblade, and it looked to Zen's eyes like a fat little water pistol. When he pointed it at the door's heavy lock and pressed the firing switch, the jet of water that shot out of it was so fine, and under such high pressure, and so full of tiny specks of diamond, that it cut through the metal like a laser, making only a brisk, busy hiss.

He tried the door again and it swung open. The room behind it was lit by the glow of various antiquated screens and dials. He scanned it quickly and could not see Nova. He was about to turn away when her voice came out of the shadows.

"Zen!"

He was so shocked when he saw what they had done to her that he dropped the waterblade. It fell feather-slow in the low gravity, but it hit the tiled floor with a sound like a bomb going off. "Guardians!" he said, adding to the din.

Nova—or what was left of Nova—was smiling at him. "I'm sorry," she said. "I was so pleased to see you that I forgot I've lost a bit of weight. But I'm all right, mostly. The rest of me is in another room, downstairs . . ."

"Guardians!" said Zen again. He didn't even want to look at her, bodiless like that, held up by metal clamps, all kinds of wires and cables trailing from her neck. But he made himself reach across the table to her and start to fumble the clamps open. It was harder than he'd thought; they didn't work the way he had expected. He was still cursing and fiddling with them when the *Damask Rose* said suddenly in his headset, "Oh, bother! They're on to us! The whole burrow is swarming . . ."

At almost the same instant he heard harsh Kraitt voices in the tunnels, and only an instant later a Kraitt kicked the door open and stared in at him.

Zen pulled his gun out and pointed it at the ugly lizard face. He hadn't imagined he'd have any problems shooting Kraitt—it was them or him; it should feel no different from the time he had shot that gene-teched monster in the Noon reserve on Jangala. But the fact that it was wearing clothes, an intelligent being rather than just an animal, made it hard to kill. He stood there with the gun outstretched, staring at the Kraitt while it stared back at him for what might have been a whole, slow second. Then it reached behind its back and drew a knife that looked like a steel talon.

"The little one told the truth," it shouted. "The prey is here!" Just then, with a deafening bang, the roof caved in.

Big chunks of rubble came thumping down, smashing machinery, driving the shocked Kraitt backward. Something else came down too, dropping through the fresh, smoking hole overhead, hitting the floor with a bony sound and then rising on eight long legs. At first, confused, Zen thought it was another of the *Rose*'s spiders. But it was too chunky, too spiny, too alien-looking—a gigantic spider crab, its shell stenciled with strange hieroglyphics. A Neem. Stabbing light flared from something it clutched in its spindly manipulator arms and a roar filled the ruined room. The Kraitt in the doorway walked shakily backward and fell. The spider-crab thing stepped over his body and out into the tunnel. It fired its gun again, and there were shrieks and scrambling, slithering noises and then silence and slow smoke billowing like a sheet of gossamer.

The Neem swung its spiky body toward Zen. On its front was painted a yellow smiley face. "Always bring a gun to a knife fight, Zen Starling," it said, in a rustling, oddly familiar voice, and in the language of the Network Empire. "It saves so much time."

Zen let out some of the breath he'd been holding in since the ceiling came down. It made a kind of whimpery noise.

The Neem came back into the room, through the smoke. "Don't you recognize me, Zen?" it said. "It's me! It's your old friend Uncle Bugs!"

*

Chandni had been keeping her options open. The Empress might have let herself be taken in by Zen Starling and his crazy plan, but Chandni hadn't liked it from the start, and when she saw the Kraitt leader and realized how smart and how ruthless she was, she knew a two-bit thief like Zen could never hope to outwit her.

It felt good, in a way, to finally find something that she understood among these weird new worlds. Because Chandni had known people like the Tzeld Gekh Karneiss before. Ramon Gul, for whom she had worked in Ayaguz, had wielded the same kind of power. The members of the Deep Six Crew had obeyed him in the same way the Kraitt obeyed this lizard-lady. You either made yourself useful to people like that or they made you their prey; there was no other way. They were never taken down by anyone smaller than them. Ramon Gul had controlled half the hulls of Ayaguz by the time the Lee family finally got tired of him and sent in their CoMa. And as far as Chandni could tell, none of the cuddly critters who ran this Web of Worlds was looking for a fight with the Tzeld Gekh.

Which meant the only way to save her own skin, and the Empress's, was to switch sides, and let Zen Starling drop.

So she grabbed Threnody by the shoulders and forced her down on her knees in front of the furious Kraitt, and knelt beside her, shouting, "We're giving Zen Starling to you as a sign of respect, Tzeld Gekh Karneiss. We've brought you his train too; it's yours . . ."

And the Gekh didn't hack off her head with that razor-blade tail, which seemed promising. But then the room kind of shivered, and when Chandni looked up there was a thin mist making halos around the lights, a mist made of dust; she could taste it, bland and gritty in her mouth. The room jerked again, and she heard the explosion this time, a big, dull woof echoing through the burrow's rock. Then clattering noises that had to be gunfire, and she realized that her hunch had been wrong and her timing terrible, because someone wanted a fight with the Kraitt after all.

"It's nothing to do with us, Your Honor," she said desperately, but nobody heard, because at that point a couple of red spider crabs the size of patio tables barged in and started shooting everything.

30

For a long moment Zen just stood there. Uncle Bugs was a Hive Monk: a million bugs sharing a consciousness and clinging to a vaguely human-shaped skeleton that they'd built for themselves out of junk. The last time Zen saw them, they were being scattered back into a mindless swarm in Desdemor. How could Uncle Bugs have been reborn in the form of a trigger-happy Neem here on the Shards?

But these and other questions would have to wait until the next exciting episode, he realized, because the tunnels were filling again with the sound of angry Kraitt, and they were coming closer.

"You are here to rescue Miss Nova, yes?" said the Neem. "We will help you, just like you helped us, Zen Starling, when you brought us to the Insect Lines."

Zen gawked at it. Back home, Hive Monks rode the K-bahn endlessly, searching for the mystical Insect Lines. Zen had persuaded Uncle Bugs to help him for a while by promising to show them how to get there, but he had never believed the Insect Lines were anything but a Hive Monk myth. Unless . . .

"The Nestworlds of the Neem!" the Neem explained. "They are what we all were dreaming of, when we were Hive Monks, in the Network Empire. The Insect Lines are real, and they are here, and you brought us to them. Now we thank you!"

Zen thought of the Monk bug that had fluttered in his face the day the *Damask Rose* arrived on Yaarm. Nova had sold that to some Herastec, who had said that they would sell it to the Neem. The Neem must have bred from it, and bred enough to fill this crab-suit with a whole new hive that still remembered being Uncle B.

"Bring Miss Nova," ordered the Neem. "We have not much time."

"But it's just her head," said Zen, stuffing his gun away and going back to the business of unfastening Nova's head from its various power and fluid feeds.

"The rest of me is in one of the other rooms," said Nova.

"We have not much time," said the Neem again. "Bring her head. The Neem are very skilled. We can make her a new body, with a superior number of legs."

Zen fumbled with the clamps, taking the weight of Nova's head in his hands as they finally released their grip. There were quick, nasty sprays of fluid as he used the waterblade to sever trailing cables. "*Damask Rose*," he shouted as he worked, "can you tell where Nova's body is?"

"I'm sorry—" said the *Rose*.

The *Ghost Wolf* cut in on the same channel. "I think I'm picking up a signal from a Motorik's spinal sub-brain. It's another level below you, here . . ."

A new map pinged into Zen's headset view. He thanked the trains, picked up Nova's head, and ran out into the corridor and then left. The Neem that said it was Uncle Bugs galloped after him with Kraitt bullets spanging off its armored shell, shouting, "No! You must come with me, Zen Starling! This is an order from the Hard Diplomacy Office of the Nestworld Zzr'zrrt . . ."

Zen reached what he thought was the door of the second room. While he was slicing through the lock, a fresh explosion made the floor hop. An alarm started bellowing, rolling its echoes away down the tunnels. The door came open and the new room was as big as the first and just as full of screens, ducts, primitive computers. On a low table in the middle of it all lay Nova's body. "Oh!" said Nova, seeing it from the corner of her eye, her face pressed against the front of Zen's Kraitt jacket.

The Kraitt had cut her open, harvesting battery packs and backup memory devices. They had taken her left arm off at the elbow, her right leg at the knee. She would have wept at all the damage, except that she had been removed from her water supply and had no tears to weep with. When she contacted her body's sub-brain, damage warnings flashed red and amber in her mind.

A screech of gunfire, very close. Zen yelped and spun around, but the Kraitt who came through the doorway was dead already, falling. Behind it came another Neem, smaller than Uncle Bugs and dark red. It swept its smoking gun around the chamber and said something in a rustling, unknown language. Uncle Bugs picked up Nova's body, cut a few cables that had been attached to her, and scuttled to the far end of the chamber. There was another door there. The new Neem pulled something from a cargo-pod on the leg of its suit and slapped it against the lock.

"Watch out!" said Uncle Bugs, swinging his painted smiley face in Zen's direction. "Those things explode! The Neem are *hard core.*"

Zen turned his back to it and shielded Nova's head with his body and his arms. A flash lit up the room. When he looked again the door was falling outward, tugging a white scarf of smoke out into the tunnel beyond. The red Neem went over it and out into darkness, and Uncle Bugs followed with Nova's body clutched under his own.

Then they were moving through passageways, the floors sloping upward, that deep klaxon note sounding and resounding like a badly tuned cello. Open air, hot desert dusk, tall cacti standing sentry, and the chimneys and wind towers of the city rising black against a sky full of tumbling, sunlit mountains. Over the horizon a shining shape was rising, spilling rainbows. It was the Sea of Kharne, a globe of water the size of a moon, and it was near enough that Zen could see the sails of a Kraitt fishing fleet flaring white in the light that came up through the waves beneath them.

He stood and stared at it, cradling Nova's head. He wondered what had become of Threnody and Chandni Hansa and the truck, and how he was supposed to get back to the train, and whether it would still be there when he did. And then the Neem beside him said, "They come!" and something that was not the truck arrived with a roar and a cloud of dust. As far as he could tell through the dust and the dark, it was a hovercraft, on which a few more Neem were clustered, some at the controls of hefty weapons.

"Agents from the Hard Diplomacy Office!" explained Uncle Bugs. "You are lucky—they have been watching the Gekh. When we saw you and your friends enter, we decided to move against her . . ."

Zen scrambled after him onto the hovercraft. Uncle Bugs dumped Nova's body gracelessly on the greasy deck, and the craft was moving, powering across stony fields. Above the whir of its engines Zen thought he caught another sound. He looked back and glimpsed for half a second a figure running. "Stop!" he yelled. "Go back! It's Threnody!"

Or had it been Chandni? All he'd seen was a running shape, outlined for a moment against the airborne sea. Had it even been human?

Uncle Bugs and his friends seemed to be wondering the same thing; there was a lot of rustly debate going on up near the little turret where the Neem pilot stood. But then the craft swerved around and shot back the way it had come, and out of the darkness came Threnody, shouting, "Help! Zen! Don't leave me!"

A Neem dragged her aboard. The craft did another sharp turn, throwing another fan of dust into the Shards' sky, and went shrieking on its way.

"Where's Chandni?" Zen yelled, over the noise.

"She betrayed us!" Threnody gasped, sobbing for breath, eyes full of dust and tears. "And then—these things, these horrible things came—and the *Damask Rose* said they were on our side . . ."

"They're Hive Monks," said Nova. "I can hear them all rustling around inside those armored crab-suits. Millions of them. The Neem are Hive Monks, though I'm not sure how . . ."

Threnody had not noticed the severed head till now. It would have been an unnerving sight, even if it had not been talking to her. She wasn't sure how to react. She looked at Zen again and said, "Chandni's still back there. She said we'd be better off with the Kraitt . . . Do *all* your plans end up like this?"

"Pretty much," said Nova.

From somewhere behind came a huge, dull boom. A flower of fire clambered into the sky above the city, carrying with it quite large pieces of the Gekh's villa, which fell back slowly to the ground, trailing smoke. The hovercraft sped toward the railway. The *Damask Rose* and the *Ghost Wolf* were already moving, pulling out from behind the Railmaker ruins. Bright flicks of gunfire came from the station buildings, but Zen felt confident that the trains' shielding could deflect whatever crude weapons the Kraitt owned. And a moment later the insectile *morvah* of the Neem came tearing out behind the *Ghost Wolf*, and a pulse of light ripped from its rear car and washed the glass towers in fire and scattered pieces of glowing weed away into the night.

The Neem steered their hovercraft next to the line, matching their speed to the speed of their train. The side of a freight container fell open, forming a ramp, and the craft swerved and went sideways up it. The ramp closed again, and the Neem chittered urgently to one another in the dark inside. Once something hit the outside of the container, as if someone outside were firing heavy weapons at it. Then the engine sound changed as it entered a tunnel, and there was the soft *un-bang* of a passing K-gate.

The Neem relaxed. Their bodies sank lower. They detached their weapons and stowed them in lockers or in holsters clipped to their long legs. In the blood-red light inside the container they looked like a cluster of killer crabs. Their spiny shadows slid over Nova's headless body, propped in a corner like the carcass of their latest victim.

Zen sat awkwardly watching, with Nova's head on his lap as if it were a bag or something. He had imagined finding Nova alive, and he had been afraid of finding her dead, but he had not prepared himself for finding her in pieces. He'd been wondering a lot about what made someone human, and he had been ready to believe Nova when she said she was. But it seemed to him now that maybe an important part of being human was that you had just one life, and that when someone took you apart you died. Or, at least, you *minded*. So thinking of her as a human being wasn't going to work anymore. He had to accept that she was something very different, and that he still loved her anyway.

*

The roof of the Tzeld Gekh's compound had been blasted clean off by the bombs the insect commandos had left behind. When morning came, the brass sun shone down into the crater that had been her audience chamber, where it woke Chandni, lying bruised among the rubble.

She scrambled out from under the dead Kraitt whose body had shielded her from the blast. She tried her headset. *"Ghost Wolf? Damask Rose?"* No answer. *"Threnody?"*

There was nothing. The Empress and the rest were either dead or they had escaped. It was probably for the best, she thought. They probably wouldn't want to hear from Chandni anyway.

She felt bitterly sad at losing Threnody, and angry at herself for caring, but mostly she just felt angry at those giant crab things for ruining her moment. That was the way it always went, though: you took your chances and you rode your luck, and sooner or later things went bad and you found yourself heading back into the freezers.

Except there weren't any freezers here. In fact, as the sun rose higher, it was starting to grow unpleasantly warm.

A shadow fell over her. She squinted up into the battered, blood-caked face of the Tzeld Gekh Karneiss. The metal-sheathed tip of the Kraitt matriarch's tail pressed against the underneath of Chandni's chin, forcing her head back.

"You didn't tell me that your friends were allied with the Neem," said the Tzeld Gekh.

"They aren't," said Chandni. "I mean, I didn't know . . ."

The Tzeld Gekh hissed, long and low, and her one remaining eye blazed with dinosaur fury.

31

The next world was empty: a plain of shining stone beneath an amber sky. The atmosphere was just breathable enough for Zen and Threnody to get off the Neem train and back onto their own. Zen carried Nova's head, and Uncle Bugs and one of his new friends came with them, carrying Nova's body. When they stepped into the state car of the *Damask Rose,* the interface of Mordaunt 90 hugged them all, even the spiky Neem. "I was so worried about you," he said. "And Chandni? Where is Chandni?"

"She didn't make it," said Threnody.

"She is dead?" His face crumpled. He hated the idea of people dying.

"I think so," said Threnody.

"She double-crossed us," said Zen, flinging himself down in his favorite seat before Threnody could take it. "She tried to sell us out to the Kraitt. Why would she do that?"

Threnody shrugged. But she thought she knew why Chandni had done what she did. She had just been trying to keep herself and Threnody alive. She had thought Zen was leading them to disaster, and she had probably been right—she couldn't have known the Neem were going to arrive. "Why didn't you tell us?" she asked. "If you'd said the Neem were going to help, your plan would have made sense . . ."

"I didn't know," said Zen.

"So it was just a coincidence?" asked Nova's head, in its tinny little voice. "The Neem busting in had nothing to do with you?"

Zen was silent. He was thinking that if he said he had planned it all, it would make him seem like a mastermind, but Nova and Threnody both knew that he wasn't, and he didn't think that he could keep up the lie.

He shook his head.

"Well, that was a stroke of luck, then," said Nova.

"Not at all!" said the Neem that called itself Uncle Bugs. "The Nestworld Zzr'zrrt is only one gate away. The Kraitt are our neighbors, and if you have neighbors like the Kraitt, you keep an eye on them. We had an agent in the Tzeld Gekh's house, a hive without a suit. Her people thought it was just an infestation of insects. The Neem have long been wary of her tinkerings with technology. We cannot let those rude lizards develop weapons that would allow them to assault our Nestworlds. Our agent sent word when Miss Nova arrived. When I told the Mother-hives what Miss Nova was, it was decided to send a team to the Shards of Kharne to observe the situation. Some of our hives trade minerals with the Karneiss, so a Neem train arriving was not unusual. We were planning to attack the Tzeld Gekh's house only if she seemed to be making progress, but when I saw you arrive, I guessed that you were planning rescues. So I persuaded the others that we must help."

"We're grateful," said Zen, though he was still uneasy about being cooped up in a carriage with those big, spiny arachnid bodies, even now that he knew they were just suits. He could hear the billion beetles that made up Uncle Bugs and his friend, seething and stirring inside their carapaces.

The *Damask Rose* was uneasy too. "The Neem *morvah* is *hooting* at me," she announced. "I think it wants me to go on."

"Yes!" said Uncle Bugs. "We must not stay here, in case the Kraitt come after us. The next gate leads to the Nestworld Zzr'zrrt. We will be safe there, among the many hives. And I will show you the Nestworld, Zen Starling: the Insect Lines my people longed for!"

"What about the way home?" Threnody asked Zen.

In the chaos on the Shards he had forgotten that he had ever promised her such a thing, but Nova guessed what she meant. "We're already on our way. The border of the Black Light Zone is farther down this line, beyond the Nestworld," she said.

"And there is really a gate in this Black Light Zone that leads back home?"

"There has to be. The Neem prove it. They're made of Monk bugs, just like our Hive Monks are. That means there must have been K-gates connecting our Network with the Web of Worlds at some point."

"And you think we can open them again?" asked Threnody.

"Only one way to find out," said Nova's head, cheerfully.

The train was moving again. The interface came swaying through from the dining car, carrying a big metal tray filled with bowls of rice and small pots of spicy sauces. Little wedges of steaming flatbread had been stuck in between the pots at jaunty angles, garnished with sprigs of edible greenery that the *Rose*'s spiders had found growing beside the tracks somewhere.

Threnody grabbed some and started eating. When the Neem came and the fighting started, she'd thought it was the end of her. Finding that she was still alive after all had given her a fearsome appetite.

Zen couldn't eat anything. He carried Nova's head through to the rear car, and the Neem followed with her body. Nova had already been communicating wirelessly with the 3-D printer, and it was whirring away, creating the components she would need to repair herself. The Neem set her body down on the seat beside the printer, and she reached out and took her head from Zen. She smiled at him as she carefully fitted it back into place, the ends of ducts and cables reaching out like eager little snakes to reconnect with each other, ceramic vertebrae locking into place with a satisfying click. "Zen, I missed you so much," she said.

"Me too. Missed you, I mean."

"You're always coming back for me."

"That was the last time," he said, mock-sternly. "I don't know what would have happened if the Neem hadn't shown up when they did." But he knew really. The knowledge of how close he'd come to dying made him tremble now.

"You need to rest," said Nova, smiling up at him. The shock of finding her in kit form was leaving him; she was becoming herself again, and lovely. "Go and sit down, and eat something," she said, brushing his face with her remaining hand. "Uncle Bugs and his friend can help me here. I'll come and find you when I've pulled myself together."

So he left her there, with the Neem using their delicate manipulator-arms to fit freshly printed parts into the holes the Kraitt had made in her, and went back to the state car. The interface had fallen asleep again, and Threnody was finishing off the food, scooping the last smears of sauce out of the bottoms of the little bowls with chunks of flatbread. She looked up when Zen came in and said, "How is your Moto? Is she ready to show us the way home?"

"She'll be fine," he said.

"You don't look very happy about it."

Zen slid into the seat opposite her and helped himself to a last triangle of flatbread before it vanished. He was happy; he just wished Threnody had not seen Nova like that, with the secret machinery of her insides laid bare. He wanted her to understand how he felt when he lay beside Nova in the flickering light of the passing lamps of unknown stations, how he felt when she smiled at him, when her wise eyes narrowed and looked at him as if he was someone worthwhile and wonderful. But he couldn't explain that. Threnody was about his own age, maybe a year older, but she seemed suddenly very young to him, because he had learned, and she had not, that love grew wild and didn't much care about things like who was human and who was a machine.

"So do you think she's right?" Threnody said, wiping chutney off her chin and trying to look empress-y. "Can she find our way home?"

"Yes. I mean—Nova's usually right. But . . ."

"What?"

"It could be dangerous. Everyone else on the Web of Worlds is afraid of the Zone."

"Who cares? They're primitives. I expect they still believe in gods and ghosts. I'm sure we can handle whatever's out there."

"Maybe. But what do you think the Guardians will do with us, if we do ever make it back to the Network Empire?"

"We have a version of Mordaunt 90 with us," said Threnody, turning to look at the interface, who was snoring softly with his head resting against the window. "The instant we arrive on a world with a Datasea he can start communicating with the other Guardians."

"But the Guardians don't like you. They let the Prells kick your family out of power."

"That was the Twins," said Threnody icily. "And when the other Guardians hear about what the Twins did on Desdemor, they'll stop letting them have their own way."

"And what about me?" asked Zen. "It's all right for you— you're a Noon and everything . . ." He wondered if he should tell her that he had Noon blood too; how his mother had run off with the surrogate baby she had been carrying for some rich Noon couple, and brought him up as plain Zen Starling. But that wouldn't help; to Threnody it would just mean that his mother was a thief too. The family would long ago have had a new son to replace him; they wouldn't want him back. Better if she just thought he was a kid from Cleave. "I'm nothing," he said with a shrug.

"That's true," said Threnody. "But you have served me well, Zen Starling. We would not even be thinking about going home if it wasn't for you and your Motorik. I'll make sure you're all right, when we get there."

They were quiet for a while, eating the last of the flatbreads. Then Zen said, "I'm sorry for everything. The Noon train. Lying to you, and the Spindlebridge." Hating himself as he said it. "Sorry." As if he'd dropped her favorite mug or forgotten to feed her goldfish. It wasn't enough. She had told him how everything had spiraled after he left. Kobi's death, the Prell attack. You couldn't just apologize for the kind of things he'd caused.

But Threnody nodded, and looked away, and said, "Malik told me it wasn't your fault. He said this Raven person made you and Nova let loose the program that broke the Noon train. I suppose you didn't know how much damage it would cause."

"We guessed," said Zen. "We both guessed."

Threnody kept looking out of the window. She couldn't afford to hate him. She needed him too badly. She couldn't afford to hate him yet.

"Just get me home," she said. "Then we will be even."

32

Zen dreamed of insects and woke to find the dreams were real. The train had stopped, and the bare world that had been passing outside the windows when he fell asleep had been replaced with an overstuffed one where spindly towers, apparently built from burnt toffee, poked up into a murky, sulfur-yellow overcast. Swarms of bugs billowed between the buildings like twisting ribbons of black smoke. Rivers of them poured up and down the walls, their beetle bodies shining in the jaundiced light, and between them scuttled the Neem crab-suits. Wood lice *morvah* rumbled past, trailing their long lines of windowless cars.

He stretched, blinking the sleep away. He had dozed off in his seat.

"Welcome to the Nestworld Zzr'zrrt," said Nova, who was sitting with Threnody at the state car's dining table. She was herself again, except that her newly printed left hand had not yet matched its pigment to the rest of her and was still dead white. It held a triangle of cinnamon toast that she was eating corners first. She had not often eaten since they came through Raven's gate, saving the *Rose*'s stocks of human food for Zen. "I hope you don't mind?" she said. "I need all the energy I can get. My body was on reserve power, and the new batteries the *Rose* printed for me aren't fully charged yet. Anyway, I missed the taste." She put down her toast and came to Zen and kissed him. "I missed the taste of you too."

Zen held her. He pressed his face against the side of her face, breathing in the soft vinyl smell of her, like the smell of a new toy. He kissed gently the collar of fresh synthiflesh around her neck that marked the join where her head had been reattached. He would have liked to have gone on kissing her, but Threnody was still there, looking determinedly out of the window at the ugly view, so he sat down instead and said, "Where's Uncle Bugs?"

"He's gone back to his own train," said Nova, leaning over him to peer out of the window. "The Neem are running a hell of a greenhouse effect on this planet. One hundred degrees in the shade and lots of lovely, bracing CO_2. They must like it that way. It won't be good for you, though. You'll need to suit up before you go outside."

"I'm not going out there!" Zen said.

"We all are," said Threnody. "We need to ask the Neem for supplies and fuel and permission to travel through this world into the Black Light Zone. Uncle Bugs is taking us to meet something called a Mother-hive."

*

There were only three space suits in the rear car, so Nova had to go without, but it didn't matter—the Neem already knew what she was. The others suited up and she followed them out through the emergency airlock at the back of the carriage, pulling the hood of her raincoat up against the dirty rain. A thing like a ski lift was ferrying Neem up to the higher levels of their city. Uncle Bugs fitted himself into one of its metal harnesses, folded his long legs beneath him, and let himself be carried upward. Nova, the two humans, and the interface followed, holding on tight, their own legs dangling as the harnesses went grinding up a long cable, through the honeycomb interior of the nest-city. They passed farms where fat white grubs the size of cars were being milked, pits where bugs swarmed in their naked millions. Each time Zen felt a bead of sweat trickle down inside his suit he started to panic, afraid the insects had found a way in.

"It's all the Railmakers' doing," said Nova. "The size they made the rails and the gates defines what size a train can be. It favors roughly human-sized species, like the Herastec. Creatures who are too big, like the Night Swimmers, have to cooperate with smaller species. Ones who are too small, like the Neem, have to learn to work together to make trains that are big enough. The Neem exist because the railway does . . ."

"Not all Neem are the same size!" said Uncle Bugs. "Wait until you meet the Mother-hive!"

From the pod, they went on foot up a ribbed passageway that sloped so steeply that they had to struggle up it on all four fours, while Uncle Bugs ran ahead of them along the walls and ceiling, buzzing encouragement, clearly loving this nimble new body the Neem had given him. At the top of the crawl-way was a big space, dark and steamy, filled with a soft thrumming sound. Pillars rose up, not shaped according to any geometry that Zen recognized. Water came down the pillars, twining around them, feeding clear pools that stood at the pillars' bases. The pools quivered slightly as the water flowed into them. The surface of each pool reflected amber lights way up on the high ceiling.

There was mist in the air, like the mist in a hothouse, but the thing that waited in the middle of the room looked as dry as a mummy in a tomb.

It was a rambling, papery structure, like the age-old nest of wasps with delusions of grandeur. It was the size of a large house. As Uncle Bugs led his visitors toward it they realized that the thrumming sound was made up of a billion smaller sounds going on inside it—the scritch and scrabble of hooked feet, the rasp of beetle bodies, a constant chirruping and chittering. It was *crowded* in there. Around the base were holes where Neem attendants were busy, sweeping away a rain of insect corpses that pattered softly from one hole, tending to the thick pipes that led in and out of others. The thing was a single vast Neem hive, made up of many millions more insects than Uncle Bugs and his friends, and far too big to fit into a crab-suit.

"Come closer," it said, in a sort of massive whisper.

"It is the Mother-hive of this colony," said Uncle Bugs, beckoning the visitors forward. "I have shared some of myselves with it so that it has my memories and can speak your human words."

A draft whispered against the microphones on Zen's suit. The Mother-hive was pumping out stale air through those high, spindly chimneys.

It said, "You have been making war on the Kraitt."

Threnody stepped forward. She said, "I am Threnody Noon. We did not make war on the Kraitt, we only went to take back this Motorik, Nova, which was stolen from us. We are very grateful for the help your agents gave us."

"The machine Nova," said the Mother-hive. "Yes. The hive you call Uncle Bugs has told us about this machine."

"Hello!" said Nova, waving. She hated it when people talked about her as if she wasn't there.

"We are builders of machines ourselves," said the Mother-hive. "We are intrigued by the machine Nova."

"Humans have many such machines," said Threnody. "When we return to our own worlds, I will send you some as gifts, to thank you for helping us, and to encourage trade and friendship between my Empire and the Nestworlds of the Neem."

The hive gave a long, crumpling sigh. Threnody could not tell if it was pleased or not. She pressed on.

"But first we must ask you for more help. The K-gate that brought us here is shut. We think there is another, but it lies in the region you call the Black Light Zone. We would like to refuel our trains here, and pass through your world to the Black Light Zone."

Now the hive made a sound like a wave withdrawing down a shingle beach. "The Black Light Zone," it said. "No train will go there."

"Your *morvah* will not," said Nova. "But our trains are not pulled by *morvah*. I'm sure Uncle Bugs has told you about our trains. *Morvah* are unknown in our worlds, so we have had to develop trains that are thinking machines, like me. The Black Light Zone holds no terror for them."

"Perhaps your trains are foolish then," said the Mother-hive. "The Black Light Zone is the tomb of the Railmakers. Something happened in the Black Light Zone that ended their civilization. Perhaps your thinking machine trains *should* be afraid of it."

"They are," said Zen. "We all are. But we want to find a way home."

That withdrawing-wave sound again. Perhaps it was the sound of the hive thinking. When it had finished, it said, "We are the Neem. We are small but we are big. We are mindless, but we are wise. Our lives are brief, but we live forever. We are always dying and always being born. You understand this?"

Nova nodded. "We call you Hive Monks. As individuals you're just bugs and don't live long, but when you form hives you are intelligent, and you can pass on your memories."

"We remember," whispered the Mother-hive. "We remember all the way back to the Blackout. We dream of the time before it. Very far back. The time of the Railmakers. We believe they were as we are."

"Insects?" asked Zen. He thought of the Station Angels, and the ancient carvings he had seen on the Railmakers' stations. He supposed they could have been images of suits like the ones the Neem used.

"We believe that we Neem are the descendants of the Railmakers," said the Mother-hive. "The legacy of the Railmakers belongs to Neem. Not to Kraitt, or Herastec. Or humans. To us."

"We only want to find a way home," Threnody started to say.

The colossal whisper of the hive washed over her words like surf. "Neem have wished for a long time to send trains into the Black Light Zone, where the homeworlds of the Railmakers lie under their black suns. If we could find relics of the Railmakers, and learn their secrets, Neem could be as great as Railmakers once were. But *morvah* fear such places, and would rather die than go there (we have proved this). Perhaps your thinking machine trains are the answer to this difficulty. We shall let you travel through our world. But you will take Neem with you. We will add a car of our own to your train, and you will carry Uncle Bugs and some hives of our Hard Diplomacy Office as your passengers. Humans and Neem shall learn the secrets of the Zone together. But what you find on the Railmakers' worlds shall belong to Neem."

33

When the sun that shone upon the Shards went behind the airborne Sea of Kharne, the light grew soft and watery and a pleasant coolness filled the desert air. Then Chandni Hansa, who had been suffering in the heat, found a fresh energy and launched a new attack on the Tzeld Gekh Karneiss, swinging her spiked club with such ferocity that she tore off a chunk of the Gekh's hide shield and drove her backward against the wall of the fighting pit.

She stepped back, breathing hard, glancing around at the pit's edges, where an audience of Kraitt males looked on. Some were giving the quick, hissing call that meant something like, "Well fought!" Chandni grinned and waved the club at them. They had only made that noise for their Gekh until now.

She felt as though she and the Gekh had been fighting for hours. It was a play-fight, designed to prove Chandni's worth and also to help the Gekh overcome her injuries and get back into shape for real battles. Of course, even a play-fight with a Kraitt matriarch was a serious business for a smallish human, but Chandni wasn't new to fighting, and she knew she had represented herself well.

She lifted the club and ran at the Gekh again. This time the Gekh was ready for her; her tail lashed out and caught Chandni in the midriff, hard enough to have ripped her guts out if its tip had not been padded. Chandni was flung backward, landing hard in the dust. She had known that was how the fight would end, and she had let it. She could not afford to do anything silly like winning. She still wasn't sure why she had not been killed after Threnody and the others escaped—whether she was the Tzeld Gekh's pet, or her plaything, or whether there was some deeper purpose in keeping her and training her—but she knew she had to watch her step.

The Tzeld Gekh's horrible, scarred snout appeared between her and the sky-filling sea, looking down at her. "Well fought, Chandni Hansa," she said. (Chandni's headset and translator necklace had survived the blast, Guardians be thanked.) She let the Gekh help her to her feet and dusted herself off while the Gekh said, "You people are not a prey species as we thought. You are hunters like us. This is how Zen Starling was able to outwit us. It was a cunning trap, sending you to distract me while his Neem allies moved in."

"I had no idea that he had an arrangement with the Neem," said Chandni. "He didn't tell me about it. He's much smarter than I thought."

The Gekh snorted. If a human made that sound it would be a sign of anger and impatience, and Chandni believed it meant the same for Kraitt. "If you had known about his Neem friends, would you still have warned me about him?"

Chandni hesitated. "I'm not sure. I just wanted me and Threnody to be on the winning side. I was sure that was yours, till the Neem turned up."

"Threnody . . ." said the Gekh. Her reptile voice mangled Threnody's name even more than it mangled "Chandni Hansa." It sounded like a small, live mammal being forced slowly through a shredder. "You miss her, your sister?"

"Yes." For some reason the Gekh was convinced that she and Threnody were sisters, and Chandni sensed that it would be a bad move to try to correct her.

The Gekh pulled something from inside her robes and passed it to her. It was a knife, carved from a single claw of a big, dimwitted, bat-winged carnivore that the Kraitt hunted on one of the other shards—a vicious, razor-sharp hook, glossy black and as hard as glass. One end had been shaped into a kind of grip, more suited to Kraitt claws than Chandni's small hand.

"This was my sister Shantis's blade," said the Tzeld Gekh Karneiss. "It would have gone to the strongest of my daughters, but now that the Neem have killed them, I give it to you. We will revenge ourselves on the Neem and then go after your sister, Threnody. You shall have her back. Then you will use Shantis's blade to kill Zen Starling."

Chandni clutched the knife and looked up at her. "We can't go after them. I told you where they're going. Into the Black Light Zone, where your trains won't follow."

The Gekh looked away. Her nostrils widened, sniffing sharply. "I learned much from the Motorik, before he stole her," she said.

The sun was emerging from behind the sea. The cheerless landscape blazed with light again, and from the rail yards near the station came a dreadful sound: the immense, appalling screams of a terrified *morvah*.

PART SIX
BLACK LIGHT EXPRESS

34

The *Ghost Wolf* and the *Damask Rose* stayed on Zzr'zrrt for five of its long days. Neem factories produced fuel cells and ammunition the two locos could use, and new guns for the *Ghost Wolf*. They hitched a freight car and one of their own windowless carriages on behind the three from Desdemor. Nova worried that all the extra weight might waste fuel, but Zen was just glad he wouldn't have to share his own carriages with the Neem. And the *Rose* seemed pleased to have more cars, especially since the *Ghost Wolf* would help her pull them. She sent her last maintenance spider out with paintsticks to decorate them. First she sprayed her own hull red again. Then she painted images of Hath and Herastec, glowing Night Swimmers and dancing Neem. At the *Ghost Wolf*'s request she painted a ghostly wolf loping along its black cowling. She thought it was a bit obvious, but the *Ghost Wolf* seemed pleased with it; it was a simple loco at heart.

"It needs a name of its own, this train," the *Rose* said when she was finished. "Locomotives have names, but sometimes if they are pulling a special train it also has a name of its own, like the Noon train, or the Interstellar Express."

So along the carriage sides, in human script that no one else on the Web could read, she sprayed the name BLACK LIGHT EXPRESS.

*

Nova and the interface watched the artwork taking shape. "I have never seen a train make pictures before," the interface said. "Music, yes. Even poetry. But not images."

"That's Flex," said Nova, and told him about their lost Motorik friend, who had once been the greatest graffiti artist east of the O Link. "When Flex died he flung his personality at the *Rose*. (I *think* he was being a he then. Sometimes he was a she. Flex didn't like being pinned down.) But a lot of the code just bounced back off the *Rose*'s firewalls, and the rest got scattered all through her systems. There's still enough of Flex left in there to make pictures, though."

"It should be possible to retrieve the whole personality," said the interface. "Mordaunt 90 will look into it when we get home. Flex could be downloaded into a new body."

"It might not be that simple," Nova said. "Flex went through a lot in that body. A new one might not be the same." She touched the line of paler scar tissue around her neck, which was gradually taking on the same tone as the rest of her skin. "I wouldn't feel like me in any body but this."

The interface smiled at her. There had been so many of him, back in the Network Empire. It was strange to think that anyone would be content to live in just one body. "You do know you're not human?"

Nova looked at him uneasily. "When Raven first started me, he said he was trying to make a Motorik that thought it was human," she said. "But I think what he meant was, he was trying to make a Motorik that *felt* it was human. And I do. That's why I've never stored a backup copy of my personality. This body is me. I couldn't change it."

"But what if it was damaged? Beyond repair?"

"Then I would die."

"And what if you wanted to be in two places at once?" asked the interface, a little wistfully, remembering how Mordaunt 90 was able to be in two thousand places at once.

"Then I'd have to choose," said Nova. But she didn't think choosing would be hard. She would want to be where Zen was.

*

On the sixth day, the *Rose* and the *Wolf* powered up their engines and the *Black Light Express* pulled out of Zzr'zrrt. The K-gates flung it onto another Neem Nestworld and then in short hops across a series of small, scruffy planets that felt like autumn, where Railmaker ruins cast their weed-light over wastelands and a few small settlements of Herastec and Chmoii. The *Express* sped past them and plunged through one last tunnel into winter.

That tunnel was festooned with warning signs. Signs covered in urgent Herastec hieroglyphs were nailed to trackside trees on the approach to it, and its mouth was screened by flimsy barricades that the *Damask Rose* shoved patiently aside. (The *Ghost Wolf* wanted to try out its new weaponry on them, but the *Rose* wouldn't allow it. The two locos had only been together for a few days, but they were already bickering like an old married couple.) It looked like the entrance to a dragon's lair, but the train cruised bravely into it, and there was no dragon inside, just an ordinary looking K-gate.

And beyond the gate, another tunnel. Zen watched the windows, waiting to shoot out into some unguessable landscape, trying to brace himself for whatever horrors might be waiting here. The walls just kept rushing by, featureless, shining in places with what looked like ice. It was just an underground line like a thousand others he had traveled. His fears faded, but they did not vanish, they were just fleeing ahead of the speeding train. They would be waiting for him again behind the next gate, and the next.

Threnody felt the same. Not relief, exactly, but a sort of reprieve. "Is this it?" she asked. "Is this really the Black Light Zone?"

"This is it, little Empress," said the *Ghost Wolf.*

"Any signals?" Zen asked Nova. "Any Railmakers trying to say hello? Any ghosts?"

"No . . ." she said, uncertainly. "But . . ."

"What?"

"Nothing . . ." she said—but the whispering voice of the Zone was clearer here than she had ever heard it.

"It's cold here," said the *Damask Rose.* "Really cold. There's no air outside."

"I'm detecting some sort of small station ahead," said the *Ghost Wolf.*

The train slowed and stopped. Zen, Threnody, and the interface suited up and climbed out of their carriage onto a platform. The Neem were emerging from their own carriage at the rear of the train. Uncle Bugs still wore his yellow smiley face. The other six were color-coded—three red soldiers, three white scientists or technicians, and a larger, mustard-yellow one who was the leader, part of the Mother-hive. They tiptoed soundlessly in the frost that covered the platform.

Nova and the humans climbed a long ramp to a door that let them out into a sheltered space between giant snowdrifts. The snow was frozen hard. Zen and Nova scrambled to the top of the highest drift and saw others, all around, like an ocean of white waves. Here and there, the familiar glass shapes of Railmaker buildings rose above the whiteness.

"How could they have a city here, with no air?" asked Zen.

Nova knelt and picked up a handful of ice crystals. "There's plenty of air," she said, and wadded some into a snowball to throw at him. It burst soundlessly against the faceplate of his helmet. "The whole atmosphere has frozen. The air fell as snow."

"Look!" called the interface.

He was pointing at the sky. All Zen could see at first up there were blackness and the reflection of his own face in the curved glass of his helmet. Then, slowly, he started to make out a small cluster of dim red lights. They were arranged in such a way that you could somehow tell it was a sphere hanging out there, like a big black ball that someone had lit a fire inside, only there were little holes in the ball, so some traces of the light shone through.

"What's that?" asked Threnody.

"It's a sun," said Nova. "Or it was . . ."

The dead sun gave off radiation on wavelengths that human eyes could not detect, but Nova's could. Not much, though. Not much of anything. And to her too it looked as if the sun had been trapped inside a vast, dark sphere, like a candle in a shuttered lantern.

"It's not dead," she said. "Something has been *built* around it. A shell light-minutes across. It's gathering almost all the energy the sun puts out . . ."

"Why?" asked Threnody.

Nova was more interested in *how*. "It would take millions of years to make something like that," she said. "But all the stories say the Blackout happened fast . . ."

"Stories are sometimes wrong," said Zen. "There are no people around, no frozen bodies. No trains on the lines. It's like the Railmakers had time to put everything away before they died."

Then, on an open channel, the eager voice of Uncle Bugs. "Humans! Come quickly! We found something!"

They went back into the station. Dim blue lamps had come on up in the roof, as if some ancient system had sensed the explorers' movements and wanted to welcome them. The Neem were busy at the far end of the platform. Something had leaked there—leaked and frozen to leave a shining pillar of solid ice. Within the ice was a mantis silhouette, frozen in a many-legged dance.

"A Railmaker!" cooed the Neem.

Tools hacked at the ice. Cutting torches flashed it into steam. Zen and Threnody hung back nervously, half afraid that, when they freed it, the frozen creature would thaw and spring to life. But Nova went closer, frowning as the first joints of the long, silvery legs emerged, running her hands over the small central body as the meltwater dripped from it.

"It was never alive," she said softly, and then, over the disapproving hisses of the Neem, she forced open a hatch on the curved central shell. There were no insects inside, just a dense nest of wires and frail silvery components iced into a frozen mass of gel. "It was a machine," she said. "It was a lot like the *Rose's* maintenance spiders. Maybe machines like this served the trains that used this station."

"So the Railmakers built machines in their own image

to serve them," said Uncle Bugs. "Just as the humans build machines like you to be their servants."

"Maybe . . ."

They hauled it out of the ice anyway, and the Neem dragged it back to their carriage to study.

"No great secrets in the Black Light Zone so far," said Zen, as they reboarded the train. "Just a dead maintenance spider in a frozen station."

"And a whole hidden sun," Nova reminded him.

"I think they are all part of one great secret," said the interface. His golden eyes peered out earnestly at them from the fishbowl of his helmet. "But I have forgotten the key to it."

*

The next world was the same, and the next, and the one after that. Dead stations, dead planets, shuttered suns. Nova printed a drone powered by a simple chemical rocket and launched it into the sky on one of those worlds. The *Damask Rose* analyzed the data it sent back as it soared into space. As far as she could tell, there were no other planets in that system: no moons, no asteroids, no comets. Just that one lifeless rock endlessly circling the immense shell that had been built around its sun.

On the sixth world, Threnody said, "There's no point going on. There's nothing at any of these stations, just those broken spider things, and they don't look much more advanced than the *Rose*'s spiders. There's no technology here the Neem can use, and no sign of a way home for us. We should go back."

Nova ran her fingers over the stems of the creepers that grew down the station walls. They grew differently in the Black

Light Zone: thicker branches, fewer leaves. She said, "What if there is technology, but we don't *know* it's technology?"

Zen shrugged. "Then it's not much use to anyone."

Nova wished she could tell him about the signal she could sense. On each of the frozen worlds it seemed nearer. She could tune it out when she needed to, but when she listened for it, it was always there. But what if Zen was angry that she had not told him sooner? What if he decided that it was a trap? She did not think it was a trap, but she could not be sure. She just knew that something immensely powerful lay ahead of them, deeper in the Zone.

"One more gate," she said. "Just one more. The Neem want to keep going, and they're in charge of this expedition, technically."

So the *Black Light Express* rolled on and passed through one more K-gate. The new world felt different instantly: bigger, a stronger gravity pulling down on them. The tunnel walls were transparent in places, but whatever views they might once have commanded were blotted out by feet-deep drifts of frozen atmosphere. The *Damask Rose* and the *Ghost Wolf* sang quiet duets, sad songs to suit a long-dead world. They were singing still when the walls of the tunnel suddenly disappeared.

"Whoa!" said Nova.

Zen, standing at the window, thought for a moment that the train had shot out into open air, until he remembered that the air around here was laid in snowdrifts too deep for any train to cut through. The light from the windows showed no drifts, just rails shining, more tracks running parallel to the track the *Black Light Express* was running on. Overhead, glimmers of reflected train-light trickled over complicated shapes like the branches of a frozen forest.

"It feels *big* out there . . ."

"*Rose*, are you picking up anything?" asked Nova.

"There is something," said the *Damask Rose*. "A sort of—well, almost a song . . . I thought I heard it before, but I wasn't sure. It is loud here."

"I hear it too," said the interface.

"So who's singing it?" asked Threnody nervously.

And then, all around the speeding train, the lights started to come on.

35

The *Black Light Express* was traveling across the floor of an immense dome. The space above it was crisscrossed by soaring viaducts and networks of thin bridges and walkways. Everything had been built—or grown—from some type of biotech: a frail-looking, beautiful basketwork of pale coral, within which the angular glass shapes of Railmaker structures showed.

"There is air in here," said the *Damask Rose*. "It's very cold, but not as cold as outside."

"There's heat coming from somewhere too," added the *Ghost Wolf*. "And power to make those lamps work."

"And I'm detecting K-gates. All around us. Hundreds of them . . ."

"Some sort of hub," said Zen. He tried to count how many lines came into this place, until his breath fogged the window he was staring through.

They were moving very slowly now. The *Damask Rose* opened a screen to let Zen and Nova see the view ahead. All the tracks that filled the floor of the dome, and all the bridges and viaducts above it, converged on one titanic central tower. The tracks went into the broad base of the tower through arched openings. Between the openings were platforms. At some of the platforms gray, lightless trains were waiting.

"They are dead," said the *Rose*. "It is not they who have been singing. But there is something here . . . this place had a mind once, I think. The mind is gone, but something lingers. Subroutines and automated systems. Look, something has set the points for us; it is guiding us into that empty platform."

She slowed, the platform sliding slowly past the windows. It was made of Railmaker glass and its surface was covered with a thin layer of snow, untrodden for centuries, blank as new paper.

"Here we are," said the *Rose*. "There may be pockets where the air is thin. Best take a respirator, just in case. And bundle up."

"Yes, Mom."

By the time they were ready, and the carriage doors opened to let them out, the Neem were already stalking cautiously around on the platform, making spider footprints in the snow. Vapor plumed from their suits into the cold, old air. It made a mist around them, like the breath of animals on frosty mornings. "So big!" they said, and the echoes of their voices went dancing away across the white platforms. "So great they were, the Railmakers, our ancestors, the ones that were!"

Zen gave a wordless shout, and after a while, when he had almost forgotten it, the shout came back at him from the dome's curving wall, miles away. As it faded, he became aware of another noise: a soft moaning that rose and fell, like trainsong or the voices of ghosts.

"Only the wind," said Nova, and turned the collar of her red coat up, as if she felt the cold. "This place is so big it has its own weather systems."

They crossed the platform. On the neighboring track a dead *morvah* waited. It was of a strange design, an old gray thing with the blunt armored head of a prehistoric fish. It was hitched to one long, windowless car, around whose door the Neem technicians were already busy. When it was opened, Nova followed the Neem leader inside, half expecting to find mummified Railmaker commuters still in their seats. But there were no seats; just twin rows of racks from which hung more of the Railmakers' spider-bots.

Threnody was looking across the other platforms. "There aren't many trains here, for such a huge station. Do you think the Railmakers had some warning when the Blackout happened? They evacuated, got their trains out, just left their dead machines behind . . ."

"They're not all dead," said Nova.

"You mean the thing *Rose* and Mordaunt 90 talked about? The singing thing? Can you hear it too?"

"I have been hearing it since we entered the Zone," she said. "I heard it on the Shards of Kharne, very faintly, and Night's Edge before that. It has been singing for a long time, and its song has reached all the way across space . . . That is what first made me think that we should come here."

"Why didn't you tell me?" asked Zen.

"I thought I might be imagining it. I thought you'd say that it might be a trap."

"It might be a trap," he said.

"It doesn't feel like a trap."

"Well it wouldn't, would it? Not if it was a good trap."

"What's it saying, this song?" asked Threnody.

"I can't explain," Nova said. "It's not even a song, not really. Zen, you know how sometimes when you're sad or in a bad mood and I ask you what's the matter, and you say you can't explain, I wouldn't understand, it's just a human thing? Well, this is just a machine thing, I think. There's some code being broadcast from this place, and it's meant for machines to hear. I think it's asking me for help."

They walked along the platform. The tower was so wide that the wall seemed straight if you looked directly at it. It was only when you turned your head and saw it curving away out of sight that you understood it was the base of a massive cylinder. At the end of the platform was a triangular doorway. There was no door, but thick coral tendrils twined across it like bars.

"It's some kind of bio-alloy," Nova said, reaching out to run her fingers over the stems. "The creepers at all the other Railmaker sites must be descendants of this stuff. They lost their strength, but they still remember the shapes they're supposed to make. The memory is fading, though; the farther you go from the center, the less clearly they remember how to grow into these patterns . . ."

"It's like a hedge of thorns in a story," said Threnody.

"Except there's a way through this hedge," said Nova.

The tendrils had detected her. They unlaced themselves and drew aside to make an opening. The opening was about the size of a human being, but it wasn't the shape of a human being. Zen was not sure what it was the shape of.

A passage led through the thick, thick wall, and they went cautiously along it and emerged inside the tower. Lights came on: a dim, golden glow that slowly grew until they could see structures around them. A broad, smooth floor shone faintly, like a frozen lake. A forest of fat pillars rose from it, and between the pillars were clusters of large, podlike chambers. In the tower's center, a ramp like the exit ramp of a highway went spiraling up through the ceiling.

"The ramp gives access to the higher platforms," Nova said.

"They built all this and they couldn't build an elevator?" asked Threnody.

"I have seen this before," murmured the interface of Mordaunt 90. "I have been here before."

"When?"

He looked at them, eyes wide and scared. "I don't know. I don't remember. In a dream, maybe."

"Do Guardians dream?" asked Threnody.

"I don't remember that, either."

The Neem had found something. They were shining their lights into one of the pods, which all had wide openings on one side. The beams played over something that looked like the husk of a giant insect. In fact, Zen knew, it was just another machine; he had seen those strange spinneret structures before, much larger, on the Worm that had opened Raven's gate.

"I think it's a kind of 3-D printer," said Nova. "There's one in each of these pods."

"Maybe the Railmakers didn't like carrying luggage," said Zen. "Maybe they printed what they needed when they got to the station."

"Or maybe this is a building site," said Nova. "Maybe it was still under construction when they abandoned it."

"How do I remember this place?" asked the interface.

Threnody took him by his golden hand. "Come on," she said. "It's spooking you. Let's go outside." The tower was spooking her too; she was glad to have an excuse to escape its alien shadows.

Zen and Nova left the Neem fussing over the printer and walked through the forest of pillars until they reached the central ramp. When Zen shone his flashlight across its surface, he saw faint scratch marks there, as if heavy objects had been dragged up it. Or dragged *down* it, for as well as spiraling up, the ramp led down through an opening in the floor. On the lower level were the rails, coming in through the archways in the tower's base to end without ceremony, sinking into the shining floor. On one or two stood a long-dead *morvah*. In the center of this level too, there was an opening. The ramp went down through it into darkness.

"There's a basement," he said.

"A cellar," said Nova. "I wonder what they kept down there?"

"Should we look?"

The ramp was as wide as a big road. The smooth surface looked slippery, but it wasn't. Zen could feel the scratch marks through the soles of his boots as he started to follow Nova down it. Where it tunneled down through the floor, there were scratches on the walls and ceiling too. It descended into a space that felt even larger than the room above.

"What's down there?" asked the *Damask Rose*, watching through Zen's headset. "I can't see."

"Nor can I," said Nova. "It's cold and it's pitch black, but . . ."

Lamps had sensed them. The light increased slowly as before. Zen went cautiously to the ramp's edge and looked over.

"Look! It's full of Worms!"

There were more than twenty of the great machines down there in the shadows, silent and still, their spines and antennae folded flat along their segmented bodies. They formed a circle with their noses pointing inward toward a low, gourdlike building at the foot of the ramp.

Zen wanted to hang back now. Human beings have instincts that make them wary of large creatures, and the Worms were as much creatures as they were machines. But Nova said, "It's all right, they're dormant, can't you see?" She almost ran down the final few feet of the ramp.

By the time he caught up with her, she was already inside the gourd building. It was open-fronted, like the ones above, and it housed some new type of machinery, which was linked to the floor with thick fleshy roots and tendrils as if it had grown there. Panels of glasslike stuff gleamed sleepily through coats of dust. Clusters of warts and dimples were arranged in patterns that could not be accidental.

"It's a terminal," said Nova, glancing at him as he came in behind her. "Linked to the tower, to the tower's mind, maybe . . ."

"Is it dead? Like the Worms?"

"Who said the Worms were dead?"

Zen glanced nervously over his shoulder at the looming, silent shapes. When he looked at Nova again, she had reached out and set her hand on the front of the thing. A faint light woke behind its panels.

"Be careful," said Zen.

"I'm always careful, Zen Starling," she said, but she wasn't looking at him; her eyes darted quickly around, scanning something that he couldn't see. "There's code," she said. "It's very strange, but not completely . . . I think I can link to it . . . Ooh!"

"Nova?"

She swayed for a second, then pitched forward against the machine and slid down it to the floor. By the time Zen reached her, her eyes were shut, but behind the closed lids he could still see them tracking back and forth. Her hands twitched, and her lips moved, forming strings of sounds that weren't quite words.

"Nova!"

She did not answer, because she was suddenly in space, or in a darkness so total that it seemed like space. Except it was

247

not empty. There was something here with her. She sensed it as a pyramid of silver light, hanging point downward in the void above her head. She had no sense of its scale—it might have been the size of a pinhead or the size of a planet—but she sensed its power. It was the mind of this place. It had sung to her in its long sleep, broadcasting across the gulfs of space a call that no one on the Web of Worlds had been able to hear till she arrived. Now it was struggling to wake. Nova knew somehow that it was part of something much larger, or that it had been, once. It was just an outpost of a much greater mind, which had been shattered and destroyed. What was left was not truly intelligent, but it sensed Nova's intelligence, and it poured information into her, so fast that she could barely process it.

"You've come at last," it said.

36

The great station was growing warmer. The air was still chilly, but mist was rising from the snow that lay on the tracks and platforms. Threnody watched a piece of ice the size of a cathedral detach itself from the distant roof and tumble slowly, end over end, down through the drifting haze to shatter on the rails. A second later the sound reached her, a deep boom rolling and echoing around the enormous dome.

It could get dangerous out there if a true thaw set in, she thought. But she still preferred it to the darkness inside the tower. The interface definitely seemed happier, although he still kept looking around him in a puzzled way.

They followed a walkway that led around the base of the tower linking all the platforms, bridging the rails that stretched between them. Sometimes the way was blocked by overgrown clumps of the coral creeper stuff hanging from out-juttings of the wall, but each time they reached one, it drew aside and let them pass. Eventually they came to a place where a ramp branched off, sloping up the side of the tower.

"It probably spirals all the way up, like a curly slide," said Threnody. "But the tower is so wide that it doesn't need to be very steep. I don't think the Railmakers had stairs *or* elevators. It's all just ramps. Seems a bit basic for an alien master race."

The interface raised his golden eyes toward the roof. The mist was thickening, hiding the heights of the dome, swirling around the high-level viaducts that sprouted from the tower's flank many hundreds of feet above. He tugged at Threnody's hand. "It is up here."

"What is?" she asked.

"Something important. I don't remember."

He was already leading her up the ramp.

*

"Help!" Zen shouted. Echoes boomed between the silent Worms and bumbled from the roof above. He heard the skittering of Neem claws on the ramp, and Uncle Bugs's voice on the open channel asking what was wrong. The Neem explorers crowded around. Their lamps found Nova's face like spotlights. Zen touched her, but she did not stir. She lay amid that crowd of friendly monsters like a spellbound princess.

"What's happening to her, train?" asked Zen, hoping the *Damask Rose* was still watching his headset feed.

"As far as I can tell," said the train, "she is linked somehow to that machine. I believe she is communicating with it."

Zen looked behind him at the Neem. "We should get her back aboard the *Rose*," he said.

One of the Neem technicians stepped carefully over him and stood studying the machine. The lighted patches seemed brighter now, like small, oddly shaped screens. "This object may be a Railmaker computer," said the Neem. "If Miss Nova is linked with it, we could learn their secrets. Moving her would risk disturbing the link."

"I don't care about that," said Zen, but then found that he did. Because what if the link was broken and some part of Nova's mind stayed behind, entangled in the alien machine? What was left might not be Nova, not his Nova anyway. He had not rescued her from the Kraitt only to lose her to this machine. He could not bear to be left alone again. He knelt beside her and watched the faint, mechanical movements behind her eyelids, wishing she could tell him how to help her.

The Neem watched with him for a while, then started to drift away, rustling in excitement as they studied the vast waiting Worms. They seemed giddy with the size and grandeur of everything, intoxicated by the idea that their own ancestors could have made anything so big.

After thirty minutes, Zen went after them. He told himself that there must be something in the tower that would help Nova. Maybe he would find a way to talk to it himself and ask it to release her.

He climbed back up the ramp to the platform level, and then higher, shining his flashlight into the clusters of pod chambers on the story above. Most of them were empty, but one or two held machines as mysterious as the ones downstairs. In one of the pods he found an alcove where a triangular metal plate rested. There were three circular dimples in the surface of the plate like the tray for eggs in a refrigerator, and in each dimple sat a black sphere just like the one he had stolen for Raven.

Zen stood looking at the spheres for a while, ambushed by bad memories. He had wrecked a train and a lot of lives, including his own, in order to get one of those spheres. When Raven installed it in a Worm it had opened a new K-gate, but long before he had known what it would do, Zen had been able to sense that it was unique and powerful. Perhaps it had been the most valuable thing in the whole Network Empire. Now he was looking at three more just like it. They had the same odd weight when he lifted them from their tray. Their surfaces were etched with the same intricate labyrinths, almost too fine to see.

He pocketed them and went to search for more. Hurrying from pod to pod, he soon found more trays. Some were empty, but most still held spheres. The one he had stolen for Raven had been a treasure worth breaking Empires for. Now he had nine of them . . . twelve . . . They rattled in his pockets like marbles.

"Zen Starling?"

A beam of light poked into his face as he came out of a pod. The Neem leader was at the top of the ramp. She bustled toward him, asking, "Have you found anything of interest on this level?"

Zen held up his empty hands and said, "Just more dead machines."

The Neem seemed suspicious. "What is that noise?"

"What noise?" asked Zen.

From his pocket came a tiny *click-click-click* as the spheres jostled together.

"There is some new sound in the cloth pouches inside your coat," said the Neem.

"They're called pockets. I have all kinds of stuff in there—"

"Empty the cloth pouches inside your coat!" ordered the Neem.

"No," said Zen, wondering if she would make him, and what she would do if she discovered what he had been hiding from her. But he wanted those spheres for himself. If he found a way home from here, he wanted to make sure he was useful to Threnody and her family, in case she was tempted to go back on her promise. What could be more useful than someone who had the keys to open brand-new K-gates?

And, as it turned out, he never had to find out what the Neem would do next. Threnody's voice buzzed in his headset, startling him.

She was a few hundred feet above him, standing with the interface at the point where one of the high viaducts ran into the tower. She had stopped there to rest and look at the view of all those tracks spreading out from the tower's base, the complicated crossovers, switches, and passing loops, the snaking turnouts, the mainlines running ruler-straight toward the openings in the dome walls where mysterious K-gates waited. She was looking for the tunnel that the *Rose* and the *Ghost Wolf* had entered through when a movement caught her eye.

"Zen!" she said urgently. "There is another train coming!"

37

"Impossible," the Neem were saying, when Zen and their leader ran back down to platform level. "No *morvah* can come here!"

"It's the Kraitt," said Zen.

"It cannot be," said Uncle Bugs. "A Kraitt *morvah* would never enter the Black Light Zone."

"They're here, though," said Zen. "How long before they reach us, *Rose?*"

"Not long," said the train. "I can feel them in the rails."

"They cannot have brought a *morvah* here," the Neem were still insisting.

Zen ran back down the ramp to Nova. She lay where he had left her, her eyelids flickering faster now, as if she were lost in some feverish dream. The alien terminal was lit more brightly than before, the panels shining sickly green and flashing with strange symbols that altered too quickly for Zen to see clearly.

He kissed Nova's forehead and said, "Nova, it's time to wake up, the Kraitt are here."

She did not wake, but she started to whisper again, very softly, strange words, and chains of sounds that might have been numbers.

"Zen," said the *Damask Rose*. "I can see the lights of the approaching train."

"Weapons range in ten seconds," said the *Ghost Wolf* hopefully.

Zen kissed Nova again and ran back up to the level of the platforms. Outside the tower, the Neem had gathered nervously beside the *Black Light Express*. In the faint blue, misty twilight under the enormous dome the lights of the new train gleamed like sequins. It was still far off across the plain of rails, doing that thing distant trains do when you cannot quite tell if they are moving or not, or in which direction.

"It's coming straight toward you," said Threnody, from her perch way above, and she linked Zen to her headset's zoomed-in view.

He saw what he had been fearing: a Kraitt *morvah*, long horns jutting from its metal prow. Lizard warriors were scrambling from its carriage windows and swarming up onto the roofs to man the big guns there.

Uncle Bugs danced nervously, his feet making little ticking sounds on the wet glass platform. "Perhaps when it heard our train had crossed into the Zone, the *morvah* of the Kraitt was less afraid . . ."

"It isn't singing," Zen said. He had never seen a *morvah* travel without singing, but this one came on in silence.

"They have done something to it," said the *Damask Rose*. "Something bad."

For a time it seemed certain that the Kraitt train would pull in on the same platform where the *Black Light Express* was standing, but some unseen switching gear swung it onto another track.

"Want me to shoot them?" asked the *Ghost Wolf*.

"Let's see what they want before we start a fight," said Zen.

"Nothing wrong with starting a fight," grumbled the *Ghost Wolf*, unhousing its new Neem guns. "Not if you can win it."

"We don't know that we can. The lizards' train might be better armed than us," the *Damask Rose* pointed out.

"It's not what you've *got*, it's what you *do* with it," the wartrain insisted.

Still silent, the Kraitt *morvah* drew up on the far side of the neighboring platform. It looked as if it had been damaged and hastily repaired. Crude new components were bolted to its carapace, which was streaked with dried slime. Doors opened in one of its cars and the Tzeld Gekh Karneiss herself stepped out, wearing heavy red robes like leather curtains that glinted with small mirrors. Behind her came Kraitt warriors with guns and axes. At her side stomped a small figure whose knobbly Kraitt jerkin made her look like a Kraitt too, until Zen saw her face and recognized Chandni Hansa.

He was glad to see her for a moment. Partly because he'd felt guilty for what had happened on the Shards, but mainly because the fact that she was still alive proved that it was possible to make a deal with the Kraitt. And then he saw the look on her face, the way her scowl deepened as she saw him, and he knew there would be no deal for him.

The Tzeld Gekh was carrying something over her shoulder. She came forward and flung it down onto the rails that separated her platform from the one where Zen and the Neem stood. It was the scorched and bullet-riddled carapace of a Neem, with one of its hydraulic legs still attached. A few crushed insects were gummed to it by their own juices.

"The Tzeld Gekh says to tell you that we came through your

Nestworld like a storm," shouted Chandni Hansa, her hard little voice very clear in the crisp air. "The Neem tried to stop us from passing, but we burned their buildings and scattered thousands of their hives. You will be scattered too, unless you go back aboard your train and leave this place. Everything that you have found here belongs to the Tzeld Gekh Karneiss."

The Neem quivered, rustling with horror inside their suits. Some stumbled, as if the hives inside them were too fretful to control their complicated limbs. On the other platform the Gekh was looking around greedily. Her warrior-boys crouched behind her, waiting for the order to start looting the tower.

"How did you get here?" asked Zen. "I thought *morvah* wouldn't come into the Black Light Zone?"

Chandni Hansa laughed. "Living *morvah* won't, Starling. But the Tzeld Gekh learned a lot from your Moto. She learned enough to build a crude kind of machine brain. She hacked the living brain of this *morvah* out and stuck the new one in. It goes wherever she tells it now."

"It's a *zombie* train?" said Zen.

"The Tzeld Gekh says that if the Neem get back on their train and move out she will let them live," said Chandni. "Threnody and the interface won't be hurt, I've seen to that. But they must hand you and your wire dolly over. She really doesn't like you."

The Neem leader suddenly barged past Zen to stand at the edge of the platform, waving her pincers at the Kraitt. "This world is the property of Neem," she announced. "We were here first. Neem are the descendants of the Railmakers. You must leave."

The Tzeld Gekh Karneiss did a thing that looked like smiling. She signaled with the tip of her tail, and one of the warriors on the roof of her train swung his gun toward the Neem and fired.

Something punched a hole in the Neem leader's armored body and exploded inside, scattering shrapnel, smoke, and clouds of dead and living bugs. Zen ran for the shelter of one of the towers as the *Ghost Wolf*'s new guns started to make sharp clapping sounds, and a turret on the Kraitt train vanished in a splash of fire. The Neem leader's shattered suit toppled off the platform onto the rails. The other Neem were scuttling back to the tower like Zen, but as they ran inside more gunfire met them, from Kraitt warriors surging in through other entrances. They started to fire their own weapons, calling to each other in their own rustly language.

Zen darted sideways, threading his way between the pillars. All he was thinking of was Nova. As long as the Neem could hold off the attackers she would be safe down in the basement, but he did not know how long that would be. He needed to get down there and hide her; drag her away from the alien machine if he could, or try to defend her if he couldn't. He would not let the Gekh take her apart again.

Near the top of the ramp a damaged Neem came stumbling past him, trailing fire and thin screams, the bugs inside it crackling like popcorn. He ducked into the shadow of a pod as a big Kraitt warrior loomed out of the smoke and smashed the blazing suit aside with a swipe of its armored tail. The spray of sparks and flames lit up Zen's hiding place, and the Kraitt turned and saw him crouching there.

The Kraitt roared and fumbled with the crude gun it held. Behind it something big and spidery seemed to be assembling itself out of gun-light. Too spindly to be a Neem, it rose on many legs, gesticulating, surprising Zen so much that even the Kraitt who was about to kill him glanced back to see what he was staring at.

It was a Station Angel, just like the ones that used to hover outside the K-gates in the scruffier, edge-of-Network stations Zen had known back in the Empire. To the startled Kraitt it might as well have been a ghost, or a god. He stood staring, and a Neem soldier came scuttling out of the smoke and stabbed him with a razor-sharp forelimb. The Kraitt went down gargling, spattering black blood through the firelight and the shadows. Zen and the Neem watched as the Station Angel drifted away, making vague walking motions with its flickering limbs but not really walking, just floating through the smoky air toward the heart of the battle.

*

Threnody was watching the fighting from high above. She knew the knots of light that were drifting across the platforms were Station Angels because they had appeared at her level too. They were all over the dome, bobbing and beckoning, dancing their ghostly dances. Down on the platform, where the bodies of Kraitt and Neem were scattered, the appearance of the glowing light-forms seemed to be causing panic. She saw the Kraitt spilling out of the tower, retreating toward their train. The Station Angels flickered slightly when the blasts from Kraitt guns tore through them, then drifted on, unharmed. They were all heading in the same direction, Threnody noticed, all converging on the Kraitt train. The Kraitt were swarming aboard it. She heard the rumble as it started its engines and reversed quickly away from the platform into the mist that hung above the vast rail yards.

"They're pulling back," she said. "Heading for the K-gate!" Then, over the crackly cheering of the Neem that filled her headset, "No, they're stopping—they've stopped on a siding way over near the dome wall. They must have figured out the Station Angels can't hurt them. They're licking their wounds, I expect. Getting ready for another try."

"We'll see about that," said the *Ghost Wolf*, uncoupling itself from the rest of the *Black Light Express* and taking off after the retreating Kraitt.

"Do take care!" called the *Damask Rose*.

Threnody looked behind her for the interface. He had lost interest in watching the tiny battle going on below and wandered on up the ramp, toward another viaduct. She thought she heard him up there, shouting something. Perhaps he had found the line that would lead them home.

She took one last look at the Kraitt train, and at the *Ghost Wolf* prowling cautiously toward it. Then she left her post and went searching for the interface.

*

Down below, the surviving Neem ran along the platforms, some shaking their limbs at the retreating Kraitt, others using nets to try to catch the scattered, swarming remnants of their leader. Zen looked among the Kraitt bodies on the platform for Chandni Hansa, but she wasn't there. He turned back uneasily into the tower. He hadn't wanted to find Chandni dead, but he knew that he would be safer if she was.

Inside the tower, it was growing brighter. The coral tendrils on the walls and pillars were filling with a watery golden light. Stray bugs from shattered and scattered Neem whirred around blindly. A few Station Angels still danced their dances, moving toward the edges of the tower. Some drifted through the doorways, out onto the platforms. Others, finding no doorway in front of them, simply vanished into the wall.

"Zen?" said Nova, in his headset.

He ran to the ramp. There was more light in the cellar too, a mist in the air that made him afraid something was burning down there. Light shone from the open side of the gourd and from the machine within it. Beside the machine sat Nova, awake, hugging herself, looking up at the sound of Zen's footsteps as he came pounding down the ramp.

"I can see everything," she said, with a delighted smile. "It's showing me everything, Zen . . ."

38

Zen hugged her. "You missed all the excitement! The Kraitt are here, with Chandni Hansa. There was a fight—I thought they were going to overrun us, but the place suddenly filled up with Station Angels . . ."

She was still smiling at him.

"You knew about that?"

"I saw it all, Zen. I watched it through the eyes of the tower."

"And the Angels? Did they have something to do with you? Did you tell the tower to make them help us?"

"They *were* me," said Nova. "The tower can generate them. They are messengers—no, that's wrong—they are *messages*. I can't really control them yet. I'd need to practice . . ."

"It worked," Zen said. "You scared the Kraitt away."

"The Kraitt are superstitious," she said. "They thought we'd awoken the ghosts of this place. Maybe we have, in a way. Oh, Zen, the tower's mind is like a great library. It's been terribly damaged, and it's been waiting so long. The librarian who used to be in charge of it has died or gone away, and parts of it are in ruins, and the rest is all jumbled up . . ."

"And what about the Railmakers?" asked Uncle Bugs, coming jauntily down the ramp to join in the conversation, as if he'd been invited. He had come through the battle without a scratch. Now he stood in front of Nova, eager to know what she had learned. "Did the old machine show you anything about our clever ancestors?"

Nova shook her head. "The Neem aren't related to the Railmakers. In fact there never were any Railmakers. There were only spider-drones, like we found in the ice at that first station, and the Station Angels, which are like holographic images of them. They were never alive."

Uncle Bugs tottered backward. He looked downcast despite his painted smile.

"There was just one being," said Nova. "One entity. Call it Railmaker, if you like. It opened the gates and laid out the web of rails for all the sentient species of the galaxy to use. But then the Blackout happened, and the Web was left incomplete. There must be lots of other sections that were cut off, like ours, and are home to species that have never made contact with their neighbors . . ."

"So what was the Blackout?" asked Zen.

"I still don't know. It certainly wasn't caused by those structures around the suns. The Railmaker built those. The suns supplied the power it needed to open the K-gates and keep them open. The Blackout was something else, something the Railmaker didn't expect, and didn't know how to defend against. It must have been like a computer virus, which started here and burned very quickly through all the Railmaker's homeworlds. The tower's memories end the moment before it hit. So many memories, though—it would take me years to read them all."

"How about finding our way home?" asked Zen. "There are a lot of lines going out of this place. Will any of them get us back to our own network?"

Nova shut her eyes again. Zen barely noticed—it was just an extra-long blink to him. But it gave her time to access a map stored in the mind of the tower. She hung in space above the pinwheel swirl of the galaxy. She saw the webs the Railmaker had woven drawn between the stars like shining threads, and the pale ghost lines that would have been threads if the Railmaker had not been interrupted in its work. All of it turning, changing, the threads stretching and shortening as the worlds they linked moved farther apart or closer together in time to the great, slow clockwork of creation. She soared nearer, slaloming between blazing suns, and saw the individual worlds the threads led to.

She opened her eyes again. "There is one . . ."

*

The Kraitt had lost ten warriors in the fight, and the Tzeld Gekh Karneiss had killed two more as punishment for their cowardice. She used a claw-knife like the one she had given Chandni, and shouted, "Moving lights! Tricks to scare children!" as she ripped them open and their hot insides flopped out steaming on the deck. The rest smeared their faces with the blood, working themselves up into a fighting fury for the next assault.

Chandni scrambled up into one of the smashed gun-nests on the top of the train and did her best to keep out of the way. She had the uneasy feeling that the Kraitt had bitten off more than they could chew. She hated being on the losing side. But chunks of ice as big as freezer prisons kept falling down through the mist from the ceiling of the dome, reminding her that she always ended up on the wrong side in the end.

A movement caught her eye, behind the mist and the spun-coral legs of one of the viaducts. Something low and black and moving fast, angling its way across the complicated points. She turned, shouting to the Kraitt in the gun emplacement on top of the next carriage, "Wartrain!" But the *Ghost Wolf*'s guns were already speaking; the emplacement vanished and the Kraitt with it, somersaulting off the train's top in a spray of blood and wreckage. Chandni dived back through her hatch as the bullet stream came feeling for her, ricochets chirruping off the train's armor.

The train was moving again. Up at the front, its handlers were working the crude levers that controlled its new brain, forcing it forward to meet the threat. Something tore through the car wall, blasting aside a few more warrior-boys. Through the hole it left Chandni saw the *Ghost Wolf* race past singing, with Kraitt gunfire spattering harmlessly against its armor. The mist eddied in its slipstream, and she glimpsed the tower beyond it and thought, *There's a gate there that leads home, if Starling and his wire dolly were right. And they're going to go through it, and I'll be left here with these animals . . .*

It had felt good at first, when the Kraitt accepted her, but it didn't feel good anymore. It was time to switch sides again.

The Tzeld Gekh Karneiss was snarling something, furious and terrible with her ruined face in the smoke and dim light of the shot-up train. Chandni's headset was on the blink and wouldn't translate correctly. She banged her head against the armored wall and caught the last few words: ". . . We will fall back through the gateway and wait!"

Another shot from the *Ghost Wolf* hit the carriage, smashing a jagged hole clean through it, flinging a dead Kraitt out. Chandni waited for the Gekh to turn away and then went after him, slipping between the hole's torn edges and dropping onto the tracks where she landed hard and came up mostly bruises.

The Kraitt train rattled past her and away, trailing flame, bits of her former comrades dangling from the wrecked roof turrets. The *Ghost Wolf* hurled a few more shots at it as it fled toward the tunnel it had come through. Then the wartrain slowed and started back toward the tower. Chandni followed it on foot.

She thought the worst part was that all this was happening because she'd taken pity on Threnody Noon that night the Prells attacked Grand Central. If she had just stayed selfish and run off, she would probably be living it up somewhere on the K-bahn now.

This was where being *nice* got you.

*

Threnody heard the gunfire as she climbed up the outside of the tower, looking for the interface. She could not see the train duel taking place beneath the mist, but after a while she heard the *Ghost Wolf* announcing in a satisfied way, "They've legged it back through the K-gate. If I had my own weapons they'd be toast, of course. I can't do much more than annoy them with these bug guns. Want me to go after them and finish them off?"

"No," said the *Damask Rose*. "Come back now, *Wolf.* You have been terribly brave."

Threnody kept climbing until she reached the end of the next viaduct. The interface was standing motionless in front of a train that waited on the rails there.

"What have you found?" she called.

Stuff crunched under her feet as she went out onto the viaduct. Drifts of dry brown flakes lay scattered on its glass surface and heaped upon the rails and the crossties. *Like autumn leaves*, she thought, only there could be no leaves here. The interface heard her coming and turned toward her. His lovely golden face was wet with tears.

"What's wrong?"

He didn't answer. Threnody looked past him at the train.

It was too square to be a *morvah*. It was too square to be a *train*, for anybody used to the streamlined trains of the Network Empire. It was a very small, old-fashioned, rectangular locomotive, made of metal that had begun to corrode. That was what the stuff underfoot was, the brown and red and surprising orange stuff that looked like autumn leaves; the whole viaduct around the ancient loco was littered with flakes and crumbs of rust. But Threnody could still tell that the loco had once been painted in yellow and black stripes. On its nose, in white, was a big number:

03

It was a second or so before she understood how strange that was—a number she could read, here in the alien heart of the Black Light Zone.

"Does this line lead back to the Network? To *our* Network?"

The interface nodded miserably.

"Which planet?"

"To Old Earth," he replied.

"*Earth?*" Of all the worlds in the Network Empire, that was the last Threnody had expected him to name. "There's no K-gate on Earth! That's why everyone had to fly to Mars before the First Expansion could begin . . ."

The interface did not answer. He fell to his knees. He toppled forward and lay with his face in the rust of the ancient train from Earth and he cried. He cried like a little child, helpless tears and snot, and flakes of the rust got into his mouth and stuck to his face and caught in his golden hair.

Threnody pinged a message to the *Ghost Wolf*, attaching some video of the rust-train. "What's this?"

"I've never met an engine like that," said the *Wolf*, after a moment. "I think they have one in the museum on Grand Central. Pioneer class. Those are the locos the Guardians used to test the K-gates, back at the beginnings of the Network Empire. They just carried instruments, and computers powerful enough to store a copy of a Guardian . . ."

Threnody walked right around the derelict loco with her headset set to record. It was doorless, windowless, nameless, a sealed box on crumbling wheels, but in places the rust had eaten through its hull and she could see more rust inside: metal boxes spilling colored plastic wires. *It's so old,* she thought, laying her hand against the ancient metal. *Old Earth old. The Guardians themselves must've been new when it came exploring here.*

The interface had stopped sobbing. He lay with his face in the rust and said, "The gate on Old Earth was the first we found. It was deep underground, near the South Pole. We kept it secret. We sent pioneer trains through it to find out what it was and where it led. And then we sent this train. And then we hid it, and took human beings through the gate on Mars instead, which led only to empty worlds."

"But why?" asked Threnody.

The golden face looked up at her, all rust and misery, and she suddenly guessed what the train's cargo had been. Guessed, and hoped she was wrong, and knew she wasn't. Because a loco with enough computer storage to carry a copy of a Guardian could also carry a virus like the one she had witnessed at work in the Datasea on Tristesse. The old train wasn't a train, it was a poisoned arrow that the Guardians had shot into the vast mind of the tower. It had unleashed something that had wrecked the Railmaker machines, and then been carried onward in the minds of infected *morvah* to wreck all Railmaker machines, everywhere.

She brushed the rust from the face of the interface and helped him to his feet. As she led him back down the long ramp she messaged Zen. "I've found a line. You'll never guess where it goes . . ."

39

He already knew, of course. Nova had told him, which was disappointing. But Nova had not known of the connection between the line to Earth and the coming of the Blackout. Threnody and the interface explained it to them back on the platform.

"We did not keep the Web of Worlds a secret because we were afraid," the interface said. "We killed the Railmaker because we were afraid, and then we kept its works a secret because we were ashamed."

"But why were you afraid of the Railmaker?" Nova asked.

"It was a machine intelligence like us, but much more powerful. We were afraid we would be absorbed and overwhelmed. We were afraid that if humans learned about the Railmaker, they would forget their Guardians. We are jealous gods, Nova."

"So you killed the Railmaker because you thought we'd love it better than we love you?" asked Threnody. "And then you kept the Web a secret because you thought we'd hate you for killing the thing that made it . . ."

"But Old Earth's just a nature reserve, isn't it?" said Zen. He didn't have much opinion about what the Guardians had done. He just wanted to get out of the hub before the Kraitt returned. "We can't go home that way. Earth's not even connected to the rest of the K-bahn. We need a gate to someplace where people will notice us arriving."

"Then we should open one," said Nova.

"Can we do that?" asked Threnody.

"I think so . . ." Nova blinked again, swam again between the stars and worlds. "It would be possible to open a line from this place to any one of a dozen human stations, but they're all on minor worlds, far from Grand Central. Far Cinnabar? Vagh? Khoorsandi? Anaiskalan?"

"Khoorsandi," said Threnody.

"Why?" asked Zen. "Khoorsandi's way out on the southern branch lines . . ."

"It's still a Noon world. My uncle Nilesh is Stationmaster there. And it's Fire Festival there this year, so it will be crowded. There will be people and media everywhere. Can we really go there?"

"There are things we'll need," said Nova. "Zen, you remember the black spheres that made Raven's Worm work. There must be some of those somewhere . . ."

Zen reached into his pocket. "Like this?"

She smiled at him and took the sphere he held out to her. "Thief," she said, fondly.

"Will that open a gate to Khoorsandi?" he asked.

"Once it's programmed and placed in a Worm, it will open a gate to wherever we tell it."

"And you know how? It took Raven hundreds of years to figure that out . . ."

"Because he was working from fragments, patching the Railmaker's codes together like a jigsaw puzzle, with lots of pieces missing," Nova said. "I have those codes on hand. The tower holds them. This is what the tower is for."

She wished she could explain it better. She could join her mind to the mind of the tower if she wished, and that made her as powerful as the tower itself, but there was nothing about the experience that Zen would understand. *This is how the Guardians feel*, she thought. *They love humans, but they are so much bigger than humans . . .* It frightened her so much that she almost wanted to disconnect herself from the tower, but she could not do what was needed without it.

It's just for a while, she thought. *When we're home, then I'll be safe from it, and just be myself again . . .*

*

They followed her to the basement, where she stood in front of one of the Worms. Her slight frown was the only outward sign of all the activity going on in her brain. Behind her, the machine in the gourd-shaped shelter flickered with patterns of light. The Worm lit up too, streams of bioluminescence racing along the folded spines on its back and glowing dimly beneath its armor plates. It shuddered and a snort came from it: ancient pent-up air, reeking of strange chemicals that stung Threnody's eyes.

Zen turned to grin at her. "I've never stolen one of these before!"

"You sure the tower won't be angry?" asked Threnody.

"I am the tower," said Nova, and her eyes shone with reflected Worm-light. "I am inside its mind."

"It must have terrible security."

"I don't think the Railmaker thought in terms like that," she said.

"No wonder it got taken down," said Zen, but he could tell Nova wasn't listening; her mind was busy in the mind of the tower and the mind of the waking Worm.

The gigantic machine was starting to lumber from its position. Loud sucking noises came from beneath it. In the empty space it left, puddles of thick liquid held the light, and fleshy hoses withdrew into the floor like the tentacles of a bashful squid. Considering it was the size of a large building, the Worm was pretty nimble on its caterpillar legs. Zen and Threnody saw them moving underneath as it surged past them up the ramp.

"Isn't it beautiful?" asked Nova, wrapping her arms around Zen from behind, shouting over the noise of the Worm.

It was certainly impressive. In his time on the Web, Zen had forgotten the size and strangeness of the Worm that opened Raven's gate. The ramp trembled beneath it, and the spines on its back scraped against the roof and walls with high, sharp noises, adding their own scars to those that all the Worms before it had made. Zen and the others followed after it, careful not to tread in the smears of goo it left behind.

At the top it paused, then turned ponderously left onto a set of tracks and settled there, drawing up its feet and lowering heavy wheels to grip the rails.

"That technology alone," said Threnody, who had never seen a living Worm before, "if we could get that to my family's biotech division, the profits . . ."

The spines of the Worm waved back and forth. Vapor plumed from the vents in its armor.

"Now what?" asked Zen, when he heard Nova coming up the ramp behind him. "Now I suppose we have to go inside it? Put the sphere in place, so it knows where to go?"

But Nova was not alone. One of the Railmaker's spiders was walking behind her. It didn't move like an ordinary maintenance spider but seemed to drift along with its feet barely brushing the floor, like a Station Angel made in ceramic. Nova stopped beside Zen and the spider went past them, holding the black sphere between one of its delicate pairs of pincers. A doorway opened in the skirts of the Worm, and the spider vanished inside. The Worm shuddered, went still, shuddered again. Zen imagined that it had been under the control of Nova and the tower, and inserting the sphere had broken that link and let it start thinking for itself. But he was only guessing. What did he know about Worms?

"So it needs to make a gateway now?" Threnody asked. "That will take a while, won't it?"

"This isn't like Desdemor," said Nova. "The physical structure of the gateway is already there. The Worm just opens it. Cuts a path through K-space, all the way to Khoorsandi."

Zen said, "Let's hope it doesn't pop out in the middle of a volcano."

Nova just looked at him. Communing with age-old alien machines seemed to use up bits of her brain where her sense of humor usually lived. Or maybe it just wasn't very funny, thought Zen. Maybe, when you opened a gate onto a fiery little world like Khoorsandi, there really was a danger you might land in lava.

Nova blinked, opening maps in her mind. "We need to move the train onto this line. I'm sending her details of the route around the tower, setting the points . . ."

"She'd better be quick, then," said a new voice, and Chandni Hansa came swaggering in past the Worm.

They reacted in various ways. The Neem swung their weapons toward her, Threnody shouted, "Don't shoot!" while Zen fumbled his own gun out and pointed it in Chandni's direction and wondered what to do next. Nova took three quick steps toward Chandni, grabbed her arm, and twisted it behind her back. Chandni, surprised by the Motorik's speed and strength, let her grab the other arm too.

She laughed. "It's all right. I came to help you. The Kraitt have pulled out, but they haven't gone far. She's waiting for reinforcements. The Gekh didn't just upgrade one *morvah*. She had her people plumbing artificial brains into at least four more when I left the Shards of Kharne. They're coming through behind us, fighting their way through the Neem Nestworlds. Once they get here, she'll attack again, and she knows how many you are now. Or how many you *aren't*."

"It doesn't matter," said Zen. "We'll be gone by then."

"It does matter!" said Threnody. "What if we get to Khoorsandi and a ton of Kraitt come through after us in their zombie trains?"

"It does matter," agreed Nova. "Even if the Kraitt come here after we've left, they might still damage the tower."

"It matters more to us," said the Neem warrior who had been acting as leader since their real leader was scattered. "The Gekh's trains are harming our nests on the way to this place. We do not want to stay here. We do not to want to travel with you to your new worlds. We want you to take us home, so that we can fight the Kraitt and help our damaged hives."

Immense noises were coming from the Worm. It sprayed a geyser of pale vapor up inside the tower. It was on its way, eager to do its Wormy thing. Zen had a giddy what-have-we-done feeling as he imagined it opening on a new gate on Khoorsandi and letting through a band of marauding Kraitt.

"I wish to go back to the Network Empire," said Uncle Bugs. "I wish to tell my fellow Hive Monks that the Insect Lines are real, and bring them back with me so that they may see the wonders of the Nestworlds."

"But the Nestworlds are in danger," said the others. "We must go home."

"It's simple enough," said the voice of the *Ghost Wolf*, cutting in. "You've got two locos, geniuses! So split us up. The *Rose* can go through the new gate with all who want to go, and me, I'll take the Neem carriages and head back the way we came. I want another round with that lizard train for starters, and if there's more of the things, it sounds like the Neem will need a hand."

*

So it was decided. The *Black Light Express* was divided in two. The *Damask Rose* took her original three cars, the Neem piled into their own, and the *Ghost Wolf* rolled away with them toward the K-gate they had entered by. It kept talking to the *Damask Rose* long after it was out of sight, and the *Damask Rose* streamed its words to Zen and Threnody's headsets. It said bold, blustering things about how easily it would take care of those Kraitt, and the *Damask Rose* kept saying, "Ridiculous," and, "Such a show-off," but she sounded sad. Threnody was sad too. When the *Wolf* went through its gate and its signal dropped out, she wiped away some small tears. It was the bravest train she'd ever known.

Nobody was sure what to do with Chandni. Even Chandni didn't know. They tied her hands and locked her in one of the compartments in the *Rose*'s third car, which had been full of provisions when she arrived on the Web, but was empty now. Zen put a roll of soft Herastec fabric in there, a few cushions from the state car seats, a bottle of water, and some food. Nova checked Chandni for concealed weapons, but she did it with her eyes, not her hands, and although she scanned for metal or ceramic it turned out that she couldn't see the claw-knife stuffed into the back of Chandni's pants. The feel of it there was a small comfort to Chandni. At the other end, if things went bad, she'd fight her way out, maybe.

"Whatever happens," she said to Threnody, before they locked the door, "I don't want to go back into the freezers. Promise?"

Threnody shrugged. "I can't promise that. For all I know, we'll all end up in the freezers."

Zen settled himself in the state car with Nova and the interface and Uncle Bugs, ready for the journey around the tower to where the Worm was opening its new gate. As the train began to move, he began for the first time to truly believe that they were going home. In a few more hours, if his luck held, he might be back on Summer's Lease, telling the story of his adventures to Myka and his mother. And suddenly he knew that he would miss the Web of Worlds. It had been a strange nine months, and often frightening, but now that it was over, now that he knew there was a path home and a future in which he would be able to look back on his adventures here from outside, he realized that it had been the best time of his life. Whatever happened next, it could never be as simple and good as it had been when he laid with Nova under the million stars of Yaarm, the night the wind blew the curtain. He wanted to be back there, just the two of them, on their own old train.

But it was too late. The train was moving. He met Nova's eyes, and he saw that she was sad too.

"It will be all alone again," she said. "It waited so long for someone to hear its call, and I came, but I only stayed for a few hours." She was remembering how the interface had asked her what she would do if she ever needed to be in two places at once, and how she had said, "I'd have to choose," thinking that the choosing would be easy. Now the choice was before her. She half wanted to leave a copy of her personality running here in the hub, while the original Nova went home with Zen. But then neither of them would be really her, and each would be forever wondering what the other was doing, and neither would feel human anymore. So she had to choose, and she had to choose to go with Zen, but it was not easy at all. It hurt.

All Zen could do was take her hand. They turned their faces to the windows, to the dreamlike vastness of the tower, the shining coral, the viaducts all ghostly in the mist. And then they were in a tunnel, and they saw odd flashes of uncolored light playing over the tunnel walls, and knew that somewhere not far ahead the Worm was burrowing a path for them through space-time.

The *Damask Rose*, who had been singing a soft and mournful song, sang louder and more happily, and went plunging after it.

PART SEVEN
SUNBIRD

40

Before Zen ever met Nova, back when he was just a railhead riding trains up and down the eastern branch lines, Khoorsandi had been one of the worlds he had dreamed of visiting. It lay at the end of a spur of the Orion Line: a small, dull moon whose moss-moors and knee-high forests were bathed in the brownish light of its mother planet, the gas-giant Anahita. But once every four years its orbit swung it close enough to Anahita that her gravitational field gave it an almighty wrench. Then it became clear that Khoorsandi's dullness was an illusion, and that its landscape was really a jigsaw puzzle of granite and basalt rafts floating on a deep sea of fire. Vents and geysers opened, swarms of pop-up volcanoes shoved their snouts through the blazing moss, and the dwarf trees hastily scattered their flameproof seeds and died a fiery death.

The best place to view it all, and the only safe place to be in the fire season, was in the Spinal Mountains, which sat on a magma chamber old and cold enough that even Anahita's urgent tugging could not wake it. There, among black basalt peaks, the Noon family had built a city called the Fire Station to serve the trains that came through Khoorsandi's solitary K-gate.

But now, suddenly, there were two K-gates on Khoorsandi. Nova's Worm had gnawed a new one at the opposite end of the mountain range and patiently started drawing a new set of rails toward the Fire Station. The local media outlets, which had all been waiting for volcano season to begin, noticed the odd seismograph readings that the event caused and sent drones to investigate. By the time the *Damask Rose* followed the Worm through the new gate, the local newsfeeds were already filled with whirling aerial footage of the giant machine lumbering across the granite uplands in a cloud of dust and vapor. Banner headlines scrolled across the images, saying things like NEW K-GATE FORMS! and AMAZING SCENES!

The Worm had laid its new rails along the top of a miles-high plateau overlooking the Plains of Fire. As the *Damask Rose* started along them, Zen braced himself for trouble. The sky above the train was crowded with drones, and among all the media camera platforms he was sure there would be more sinister machines—including a few that were the eyes and ears of the Guardians themselves. They might start dropping bombs on the *Rose* at any moment.

But nothing happened. Zen, Nova, and Threnody sat looking at one another in the state car. Uncle Bugs stood motionless beside them, like a very ugly table. The interface of Mordaunt 90 fell asleep again, tilting sideways until his golden head was resting on Threnody's shoulder. Behind his eyelids his eyes twitched back and forth. He was uploading the contents of his memory to the version of Mordaunt 90 that existed in Khoorsandi's Datasea.

The Datasea came swirling into Zen and Threnody's headsets too, and into the part of Nova's mind that acted like a headset. It was all so familiar, the chat sites and the ads: the endless, mindless, digital babble of home. They had not realized how much they'd missed it, out on the dataless Web.

"There's a lot of speculation going on," said Nova, scanning the newsfeeds much faster than the humans could. "Some people say aliens opened the new gate. Some people think the Guardians must have done it. Some are worried that it's going to destabilize the Network, or let bug-eyed invaders through . . . But the Guardians are saying nothing. I don't think they know what to say. I think we've taken them by surprise. I'm going to release a few clips of video, views of the alien stations and the people we met there—that should get them even more excited."

"Should we talk to the media?" asked Zen, feeling suddenly shy.

"Wait till we get to the Fire Station," Threnody said. "They like it better if they can see you."

But the media could see them already. Impertinent paparazzi drones flew close to the *Rose*'s windows to snatch images of her passengers. The train closed her curtains, but by the time she pulled into the Fire Station twenty minutes later, all Khoorsandi seemed to know that the former Empress Threnody was on board.

Threnody hurried back through the train to the cabinet where Chandni was imprisoned. She didn't open the door, just put her face close to it and said, "Chandni? I'm going to leave you on the train, till things are settled. The *Rose* can look after you; her maintenance spider can bring you food and things."

Chandni just grunted. She didn't sound happy. But why would she? She was locked in a cabinet.

At the edge of the rail yards the Worm stood dormant, cordoned off behind high barriers and watched by armed guards. The *Rose* went carefully past it, off the line that it had made and onto older rails. The familiar minds of K-bahn switching systems talked to her and guided her onto one of the outer platforms under the arching golden station canopy. People ran along beside her as she slowed to a stop there—actual *people*, Zen thought, without a Herastec or a Chmoii among them. But a lot of them were Railforce troops. When the *Rose* opened her doors and he stepped out after Nova and Threnody a whole squad of Bluebodies was waiting, and Nilesh Noon in an awesome ceremonial hat, who said sternly, "Lady Threnody Noon, as Stationmaster of Khoorsandi it is my duty to arrest you in the name of the Network Empire."

A buzz of excited talk came from the crowd that had gathered behind the rank of impassive, blue-armored troops. Threnody looked at her uncle. He was panting as if he'd run there to meet her, and his gorgeous tunic had the buttons done up wrong. "Uncle Nilesh?" she said. "You're not really going to arrest me, are you?"

"Of course he isn't!" shouted someone else, fighting her way through the line of Bluebodies from behind and running across the platform to wrap Threnody in a hug. It was Kala Tanaka. Uncle Nilesh grinned and said, "Arrest you? My own niece? Of course I won't, and the Railforce people here are loyal to our family. If Elon Prell wants you arrested, he can damn well come here and do it himself."

"Which he probably will," said Kala Tanaka, letting go of Threnody and stepping back to look at her odd companions. "Word of this is spreading across the Network as fast as trains can carry it. Grand Central has probably heard of it by now."

"But what is it?" asked Uncle Nilesh. "What is this machine? The new gate—can it really be a new gate? And there is footage now of . . . *places* . . . *creatures*. Where have you come from, niece?"

Threnody looked past him at the paparazzi drones hanging like clouds of gnats under the station canopy. "We've come from the far side of the galaxy, from a network called the Web of Worlds. Khoorsandi isn't the end of the line anymore. It's a hub the Noon family can use to trade with whole new civilizations. Look, we have brought back an ambassador of the Neem from the Nestworld Zzr'zrrt . . ."

At which point she stepped aside so that Uncle Bugs could come spidering out of the carriage behind her, and the rest of her speech was lost in the gasps and screams of the crowd and the frantic buzzing of the drones as they jostled to snatch close-ups.

41

Laria Prell hurried through the nighttime corridors of the imperial palace, doing up her jacket as she went, finger-combing her short hair. She was not enjoying being stationed on Grand Central. The gravity was higher than on the small worlds she was used to, and she didn't like the summer heat. It had taken her a while to get to sleep that night, and no sooner had she drifted off than she was being woken, summoned to the Emperor's conference chamber for an emergency meeting.

Which was good, she supposed, because it must mean that there was an emergency, and there might be a chance for her to see some action after all. She just wished that whatever had happened could have happened in the daytime.

Her uncle—it still felt strange to think of him as the Emperor—was in the big meeting room at the heart of the Durga. Some other family officers were there with him, but surprisingly few, which made Laria wonder what she had done to warrant being asked to such an exclusive meeting. But before she could do more than salute, her eyes were drawn to the big holoscreens that hung above the livewood conference table. That was her first sight of the images that had started flooding into Grand Central's data rafts a few hours before, carried on the night train from Khoorsandi. The bony archway forming out of light and dust in some high valley, the huge, spiny biotech vehicle crawling out of it, dragging its shining trail of rails . . .

"How can there be a new K-gate?" she asked, reading the scrolling banners. "That's not possible, is it?"

"Of course it's not possible," snapped her uncle. "Everyone knows that the Network is complete. This is a hoax. Doctored footage, and an old train made up to look like a . . . whatever that big spiky thing is meant to be!"

"But who would do such a thing?" wondered Laria.

The Emperor grunted again. "Khoorsandi is a Noon world," he said. "I'm guessing there are people there who don't like us Prells being top dogs. People who will try any stunt to spread . . . well . . ."

"Instability," growled another voice. Laria, looking away from the screens to see who dared interrupt her uncle while he was speaking, noticed for the first time the Mako brothers standing in the shadows behind him.

"Instability," her uncle agreed. "That's why the Twins are concerned."

For a moment, Laria thought he meant the Mako twins, but of course he meant the *actual* Twins. Elon Prell was a man who talked with Guardians; the Twins themselves shared their concerns with him, and they might be watching him right now. She tried to stand even more rigidly straight and look even more intelligent and attentive as he continued.

"Laria, I want you to take a wartrain to Khoorsandi and find out what's going on. Most of our wartrains are tied up keeping the peace on the branch lines, but the Twins themselves have provided us with a high-speed locomotive, very advanced. You'll take a small squad—we don't want any fighting, not with half the media in the Empire watching. Just establish a presence, and take a look at this new gate and the thing that's supposed to have made it."

Laria felt herself blush. "But, Emperor, I don't know anything about K-gates, or hoaxes . . ."

"You don't need to," said her uncle. "My envoys here will handle that side of things."

The Mako brothers stepped forward. Their ivory faces creased into helpful smiles that made them look no friendlier at all.

42

The Fire Station was a low-rise city, full of steep, stepped streets and quaint white houses. When the scrum at the station grew too intense, Nilesh Noon had removed the *Damask Rose*'s passengers to a hotel complex called the Phoenix that stood on a terraced hillside just outside the station. The *Damask Rose* was left on her siding, locked and guarded, and Chandni Hansa was left inside her. "We will move her to more suitable quarters when the fuss dies down," said Kala Tanaka, "and you can decide what to do with her then. I knew that young lady would be trouble the day I fetched her from the freezers."

They were in the car that was taking them to the Phoenix, just Threnody and Kala and Uncle Nilesh and the interface. Nilesh twisted around to look out of the rear window at the car behind, which was carrying Zen, Nova, and Uncle Bugs. "The Starling boy will be trouble too," he said. "It is him, isn't it? The one who sabotaged your father's train?"

"It's more complicated than that," said Threnody.

"Things usually are, but once the news sites figure out who he is . . . When they find that you're friendly with the young man who killed your father . . ."

"He didn't," said Threnody. "It was an accident. And we need Zen. He and Nova know more than anybody about the alien network."

Nilesh and Kala exchanged a look. They had not been aboard the Noon train when it crashed, but they had friends who had, and some of them had died.

"I promised him," said Threnody, and there was a hard new light in her eyes that they had not seen before.

Kala said, "Very well. I'll figure out a story to tell the media."

*

The Imperial Suite occupied the whole top floor of the hotel: seven bedrooms leading off one big, central living room. The manager promised that Threnody and her guests would have the best views of the fire fields. But when Zen stood on the balcony and looked out over the rooftops, he saw no fire at all. Nothing but black rock and brown moss stretching away to the near horizon, where the rings of Anahita curved across the evening sky.

"I thought there were supposed to be volcanoes," he said.

"Not yet," said Nova, coming out onto the balcony just behind him. "Fire Festival will begin soon. The whole landscape will ignite."

"Do you think we'll still be alive by then?" said Zen. It was unnerving to know that the Guardians themselves were discussing his fate in the depths of the Datasea. At any moment they might decide to crush all knowledge of the new gate, and they would start by getting rid of him and Threnody and Nova. There were probably lasers and things being aimed at him right now by some of those black specks that hung in the sky above the hotel.

But Nova said, "Every second that goes by makes it more likely that they'll let us live." She stood behind Zen and wrapped her arms around him the way she liked to, and rested her pointy synthetic chin upon his shoulder. "And if we don't," she said, "it was wonderful. Seeing the Web of Worlds with you. All those stations. All the things we've done. I love you so much, Zen Starling."

There was a little throat-clearing cough behind them. Threnody was looking out onto the balcony. "The interface is awake . . ."

*

The interface had been up and about since they got their stuff out of the *Damask Rose*'s carriages and moved to the hotel, but he had not been exactly awake. He had moved like a sleepwalker from the train to the waiting car. When the paparazzi drones asked him what the Guardians thought about the new gate, he had not ignored them, he simply hadn't heard. Since they reached the suite in the Phoenix he had been flopped on one of the enormous sofas in the lounge, staring blankly at the ceiling. But when Zen and Nova came in off the balcony, they saw that he had revived and was looking curiously around the room.

It was a curious room—livewood walls and plump, soft furnishings, dominated by a big bronze hanging of the face of Pyra, an ancient fire goddess whom the Khoorsandi tourist board had made up. Zen and Nova thought it was glorious. Threnody thought it was unbelievably tacky. Uncle Bugs didn't seem to have an opinion on it—he was in his own room, trying to order a bucket of well-rotted vegetable peelings from room service. What the interface of Mordaunt 90 thought, they never knew, because he stood up smiling and said, "I have been in debate with my brothers and sisters in the Datasea."

"All this time?" asked Zen. "It's been hours. I thought Guardians talked fast. Shared whole worlds of information in a heartbeat . . ."

"We do," said the interface. "But we had a lot to discuss."

He was himself again, in charge of things, a mouthpiece for the vast mind of Mordaunt 90. They all missed the bumbling, childlike interface they had come to know.

"And what have they decided?" asked Nova.

"They haven't," he said. "Not yet. Zen, Threnody—they want to meet you."

He stretched out his hands to them, his golden hands. Zen and Threnody took them, and there they stood, quite still, until Nova realized their minds had fled away after his into the Datasea. She felt a little envious of Threnody, a little offended that she had not been asked to go too. *Of course,* she thought, *the Guardians would not trouble talking to a simple Motorik.*

But perhaps she was not that simple, after all. Something had changed when she connected herself to the Railmaker's tower, and she wasn't quite sure what it meant. She could still hear the broken song that had whispered to her out of the Black Light Zone. It could not possibly be coming across all those millions of light-years of space to reach Khoorsandi, so it must be inside her now.

She waited for a few minutes, but Zen and Threnody just stood there, holding the interface's hands. The interface smiled at Nova, as if to promise her that they would be all right. So she turned and went outside again onto the balcony. The building was moving slightly, adjusting as mild quakes rippled through the bedrock beneath the station city. A bank of brownish cloud was building up on the horizon, and the air smelled faintly of smoke. Nova leaned on the balcony and thought wistfully about what she had left behind: the hub, and the tower, and all the lines that led from it, and the places they might go to.

*

The *Damask Rose* was taking good care of her prisoner. Whenever Chandni wasn't asleep, the train lit holoscreens in her little cell so that she could watch the news stories, and every few hours the maintenance spider would reach down through a hatch in the ceiling to give her food and drink. She was not uncomfortable, but she was bored and growing nervous about what Threnody would do with her. It seemed to her that she had been forgotten, and that when she was remembered, she would most likely be stuck in the freezers. Threnody might not want to do it, but her family would make her; Nilesh Noon and Kala Tanaka were out there, smiling on the news with her, and they had never liked Chandni. They would advise Threnody to freeze her, and Threnody would give in, because Threnody liked having someone telling her what to do—Chandni knew that, because for a little while she had been the someone.

She needed to escape, but she was not sure how. Soon after they reached Khoorsandi she had asked the *Rose* if she could go to the bathroom, and the hatch in the ceiling had opened and the spider had passed her a bucket. The train wasn't stupid, and she didn't trust Chandni any more than her other passengers did.

She lay on her back and pretended to rest while she studied the ceiling hatch, but she couldn't see a way out there. It opened from above, and, even if it could be persuaded to open from below, it led only to the narrow crawlspaces between the ceiling and the carriage roof that were the spider's domain. The spider came fitted with a lot of cutting and welding equipment and was linked to the mind of the train; she doubted she could take it in a fight.

So she slept, and ate, and watched the newsfeeds construct their card houses of speculation about the new gate. And sometimes she reached behind as if to rub her back and touched the Kraitt knife hidden there. It gave her a small feeling of control. She would get out of this. It was just a question of waiting for the right moment.

43

Zen gasped, looking around him at the cold white lawns, the topiary towering up into the quickly falling snow. He had grown used to far stranger places; it was arriving here so suddenly that had startled him, as if the hotel suite on Khoorsandi had been just a dream, and he had suddenly woken up in this winter garden.

"It isn't real," said Threnody, who was standing beside him.

She wasn't real, either. She was just an avatar, and whatever software ran this simulation was using old scans of her, so that she looked as she had looked when he first knew her on the Noon train, sleek perfect clothes and shiny blue hair like the plumage of a kingfisher. *Just a simulation,* he thought, *and so am I.* If he concentrated hard he could tell that the real Zen Starling was still standing in the suite on Khoorsandi, holding the interface's hand.

It was a good simulation, though. He couldn't see anything to tell him that the enormous garden wasn't a real garden on some planet somewhere. Even his breath made plumes in the snowy air. But the air did not feel cold, and the snow did not settle on him, nor Threnody, nor on any of the Guardians who now came gliding toward them down the long white aisles between the hedges.

He knew some of them. Mordaunt 90 looked just like its interface, and wore the same tattered clothes that its interface had worn during their adventures on the Web. Anais Six was as tall and blue and antlered as the last time Zen had seen it. The others he had never met before, but he had seen their images all his life, on data shrines and ads, in threedies, and in the holostickers that came free with breakfast cereal. There was the Shiguri Monad, a peacock with a thousand actual eyes on its billowing tail, and Indri, who looked like a beautiful woman and a beautiful cat at the same time. Ombron and Leiki were many-sided shapes whose planes constantly shifted and rearranged themselves. That cloud of blue butterflies that sometimes gathered into a human shape was Sfax Systema, and those blurred elfin figures, half glimpsed behind the snow, had to be the avatars of the mysterious Vostok Brains. Through the hedges something unseen raced like a hypersonic squirrel—that would be shy, eccentric Vohu Mana. They were all there, all watching him with their golden eyes that opened like K-gates into worlds of pure intelligence, but for some reason Zen felt no need to kneel. These were the gods of his age, but he knew things about them that few other humans did. He knew that they were liars.

The Twins were the last to arrive: two barefoot girls, one black, one white, sharing a single elaborate hairstyle.

As if their arrival was the cue to break the silence, Mordaunt 90 said, "Zen, Threnody. We have been discussing your new gate, and we find that we are divided. Some of us think it should be allowed to stay open—"

"Only *you* think that, Mordaunt 90," said the peacock, in the voice of a grouchy cartoon bird.

"While some of us think it should be shut, and the secret of the Web of Worlds preserved," Mordaunt 90 went on.

"And some of us think everyone involved in its opening should be killed stone dead," said the Twins, smiling sweet, dimpled smiles.

"You can't close it," said Zen. "Everyone has seen it. Everybody knows it's here. They've seen the Neem, and the images from our headsets that we made while we were on the Web. They've seen that Mordaunt 90's interface came through with us. You can't keep it a secret anymore."

"So what do you think we should do?" asked Ombron.

Threnody said, "With your permission, Guardians, we want to begin trading through the new gate, with all the new worlds of the Web. My family has lost much of its power, thanks to the Prells. But Khoorsandi is still ours, and we can make it the hub of a great new trade route."

Shiguri chuckled. "That would be a tough blow for the Twins' pet Prell! Old Elon has waited all his life to become Emperor, and now he'll find Grand Central isn't the center of things after all, and the Noons control the gateway to a whole new Empire!"

"Birdbrain," sniffed the Twins.

"But where will that leave *us*?" asked Sfax Systema. "What will humans think when they find out what happened to the Railmaker?"

"Perhaps they won't," said Zen. "We won't tell them. You can say the Railmaker was already dead when you discovered the K-gates. And you kept the truth from us about the other gates and the other races because you thought we weren't ready to know such things."

"You *aren't* ready," muttered Vohu Mana, from the bushes.

"You can say that you have decided the time is right, so you've opened a new gate, and chosen Zen and me to be the first through it," said Threnody.

Indri purred. "How *sweet*! They think they can *bargain* with us . . ."

"If we did what they suggest, we would save face," said Mordaunt 90. "It is time to tell the truth, or part of it. My interface has traveled among these alien races. We need not fear them. It is time to let humanity meet its neighbors."

"Time for instability, you mean?" scoffed Sfax Systema. "You know how cruel humans were to one another, before they had us to guide them. Imagine what wars and terrors they'll unleash when they meet other species!"

The golden man turned to Anais Six. "You agree with me," it said. "I know you do! Is that not why you let Raven stumble upon the secret of the K-gates . . . ?"

"I was foolish," said Anais Six, blushing a deeper blue.

"This is all Anais Six's fault, when you come down to it," grumbled Indri. "If it hadn't let its lover Raven go poking around in the Deep Archives . . ."

"Someone else would have found out, sooner or later," said Shiguri, unexpectedly taking Mordaunt 90's side. "Even we cannot keep secrets forever."

"Yes we can," said Sfax Systema firmly. "We will announce that the new K-gate is just a clever hoax. The images that the *Damask Rose* and her passengers have released into the Datasea will be found out to be hoaxes too: fantasy creatures, generated in clever virtual environments. Luckily the one creature they brought back with them, this Neem, is made up of insects almost identical to the Monk bugs that infest human worlds. We shall explain that they *are* Monk bugs, wearing a suit designed by Raven. We shall show the news sites how this whole affair has been a plot by Threnody Noon, a clever and ambitious young woman trying to improve the fortunes of her family. We will block up the new K-gate, saying it is dangerous. And in a few weeks some new crisis will arise, and humans will forget all about events here on Khoorsandi."

The other Guardians murmured their agreement. Even Shiguri gave a feathery shrug and said, "Very well. It's for the best, I suppose."

"And what about us?" asked Zen. "Me and Threnody and Nova, and the *Rose*? If we promise to keep your secret, will you believe us?"

"Of course we won't," said the Twins.

"You will be taken to Desdemor," said Mordaunt 90. "You can live quietly there."

"As your prisoners?" said Zen.

Mordaunt 90 smiled a sad smile. "As our guests."

"So it is decided?" asked Anais Six. "We are all in harmony again, and all agree?"

"No," said the Twins, in unison. "We don't agree. We have a better idea."

44

So they're tearing down the i-link at bat-out-of-hell kind of speeds, and this is the strangest train Laria Prell has ever ridden. It's called the *Sunbird*, and she thought it looked odd as soon as she saw it waiting in the tortoiseshell station under the palace back on Central. A long silver loco, its sleek hull almost featureless, with no weapons turrets or war-drone pods, but maybe that's a good thing on a diplomatic mission, shows that they plan to talk, not fight. But that outward strangeness is nothing next to the way it behaves once it's on the move. It doesn't sing, it doesn't talk, it's almost as if it isn't intelligent at all—except it must be, because everyone knows that the K-gates only open for trains with brains; every time someone has tried to take a simple low-tech shunting engine from world to world it's just kind of bounced off the energy curtain under the gate's arch, or else passed through it like it's mist or something and stayed on the same planet. So the *Sunbird*, swooshing effortlessly through gate after gate, must have a mind and a personality of its own. For some reason it just doesn't *want* to talk or sing, and Laria Prell has never known a train like that before.

But then she's never known a mission like this one, either. She still doesn't buy this story of a new K-gate, but the news from the Fire Station gets stranger each time her headset updates. Now the newsfeeds are claiming that Threnody Noon herself has come through the new gate with a kid named Starling and a giant armored spider. They're streaming some astounding footage—alien stations where the streets are full of monsters, great luminous whale things swimming in midnight seas. *It's all a hoax,* Laria tells herself, *but what's the point of it?* She warns her little squad of CoMa to stay frosty, but she has no idea what they're supposed to do when they hit the end of the journey.

The Mako brothers keep to their own car at the rear of the train, only leaving it to visit the fully automated dining car— they seem to have a liking for sweet things: fancy cakes, sugary piles of pastel-colored dessert that they eat with long spoons, sitting in silence on either side of a dining table like each other's reflections.

"Who *are* they?" she asks her second-in-command, a tough old CoMa sergeant called "Panic" Button. "Where did Uncle Elon hire them? Why does he trust them so much?"

"The family has always employed twins," says Button placidly. "After the old Emperor was killed, your uncle Elon felt he needed more effective bodyguards. I don't know where they came from. Some backwater world, I suppose."

"But the way they treat him," says Laria. "It's like *he's* working for *them* . . ."

"I expect that amuses your uncle, Lady Prell. Folk always say he has no sense of humor, but that's not true. He just laughs at different things than other people."

As the *Sunbird* begins its run-up toward the K-gate that will take it to Khoorsandi, Laria goes to visit the brothers in their carriage. It is one long compartment and it smells like a locker room. Balled-up socks trundle across the floor as the train sways. The Mako twins seem to have no interest in personal hygiene, although they are both busy cleaning silvery pistols that look clean enough to Laria already.

"What is the plan?" she asks. "When we get to Khoorsandi?"

The Mako boys don't look up. "That's for you to decide, Lady Prell . . ." says the one named Shiv.

"Isn't it?" asks the one named Enki.

Laria knows which one is which because Shiv has a little letter S tattooed on his forehead, Enki an E. Unless—and she would not put this past them—they have been tattooed with each other's initials, just to confuse people. In all other ways they are identical. The shifting light in the carriage reveals odd bumps beneath their bald scalps, as if some high-end hardware has been built directly into their skulls. Laria says, "I don't think it *is* for me to decide. I think my uncle put *you* in charge. I think he has given you some mission that he hasn't told the rest of us about."

The Makos both look up at her then. It never stops being eerie, the way they manage to make the exact same movements at the exact same time.

"When we get to Khoorsandi," says Enki, "you will remain on the train. Everything will be taken care of."

"The same way you took care of Kobi Chen-Tulsi?" asks Laria.

They look thoughtful. They stop echoing each other's movements. Shiv goes back to cleaning his spotless gun; Enki stands and comes close to Laria, looking down. His breath smells of almonds and mangoes and star anise. He says, "Sometimes, when a person is causing a problem, the simplest way to solve it is to kill that person. The Guardians do not like to admit this truth. Your uncle, the Emperor, cannot admit this truth. Threnody Noon and her companions have managed to make themselves celebrities. If the Emperor killed them, it would look very bad; he would not be popular."

"But if the Emperor had a servant . . ." says Shiv, putting his gun away and standing up, coming to stand beside his brother.

"Or *two* servants . . ."

"And these servants took matters into their own hands . . ."

"Went *rogue*, so to speak . . ."

"Exceeded their *orders* . . ."

"Then the fault would rest with those servants . . ."

"No one could blame the Emperor, or the Guardians . . ."

"They would all agree what an unfortunate tragedy it was . . ."

"But the problem would still be solved."

And with a loud *un-bang* the *Sunbird* is through the gate, and the twilight of the volcano resort spills through the windows. The Mako brothers exchange one of their looks.

"You will remain on the train," they tell Laria Prell. "We will go into the city and do the things that need doing."

45

The volcanoes spoke. They opened their hot red throats and roared. They built towers of smoke and decked them with multicolored lightning. The dry plains west of the Fire Station stretched and yawned, and fans of lava sprayed into the sky.

Nova looked down on it all from the balcony of the suite where Zen and Threnody still stood entranced beside the interface. It was very impressive; she could see why Fire Festival was such a big tourist attraction. But as she scanned the view, watching volcano after volcano bloom, the fiery light shone suddenly on a train that was snaking down the line from Khoorsandi's original K-gate.

The *Damask Rose* spoke to her in the same instant. "Nova? A new train has come in; some kind of Prell wartrain I think. It's a strange one; it won't talk to me. But I'm getting a message from its commander. She wants to speak with Threnody."

"Threnody's busy," said Nova, glancing back at where Zen

and Threnody still stood holding the interface's hands, like sleepers sharing the same dream. "I'll talk to her."

The *Rose* patched the message through. It was coming from a wall screen in one of the dingy cabins of the Prell train. A large, pale young woman in Prell CoMa uniform said, "Empress?"

"I'm Nova," said Nova. "I can take a message."

The young woman looked doubtful. "You're the Motorik who was with her on that train . . ."

"Oh, we're great friends, me and Threnody. We tell each other everything."

The face on the screen seemed to come to a decision. "Then tell her this, Motorik. I'm Laria Prell; I met Kobi Chen-Tulsi on Broken Moon. The men who killed him are here with me. They are my uncle's servants, but they don't act like servants, they act more like . . . There are two of them, the Mako brothers. They are very . . . they have already left the train. They are coming to find Threnody Noon, and the Starling boy, and you too, I suppose. They are on their way to kill you."

"How rude," said Nova, flinging her mind into the hotel's security cameras and then into others out in the busy streets. Yes, there were two men coming up the steps from the station, moving purposefully through the festival crowds. Bald heads and brown coats and distinctly unsettling. "Why are you telling us this?" she asked Laria Prell.

The face on the screen reddened. "It is not right," Laria said. "It isn't honorable. And Kobi would have wanted me to warn her."

"Thank you," said Nova. "You've done a good thing. We'll be ready for them. I don't think two men can do much harm."

Laria Prell looked as if she was about to disagree, but her face suddenly froze and crumpled as the holoscreen went out. All the lamps died at the same moment. The cameras Nova had been hacking went out too. She looked into the data raft, then got out fast. Something very strange was spreading through it, shutting down site after site, system after system. It spread quickly, pushing its way through firewalls, leaking out of the raft into the deeper Datasea where the Guardians swam.

Nova had seen things like this before. She had unleashed things like this, killing trains on Raven's orders with tailored computer viruses. But this was bigger, stronger, stranger. This must be the same thing that had deleted Mordaunt 90 from the Tristesse Datasea. This—or something very like it—had killed the poor, unsuspecting Railmaker.

But as it died, the Railmaker had been busy trying to defend itself. It had been writing countermeasures that had almost been enough to keep it safe. They were embedded in the code that its tower was still broadcasting from the Black Light Zone. And because the code was in her mind, and her mind had been changed in ways she still didn't grasp by her meeting with the tower, it was easy for Nova to see the small remaining weaknesses that had let the virus through, and fix them. When the sickness in the Datasea sensed her and turned toward her, she was already armored against it.

She pinged a copy of the code to the *Damask Rose* and left the balcony. The room was in darkness except for the light from the volcanoes pouring through the windows, sullen and blood red. She ran to Zen and shook him by his shoulders. "Zen! Zen!"

*

In the gardens of the Guardians, Zen felt her touch and heard her voice, but she could not pull him back into the real world.

For strange things were happening in the gardens too. The falling snow had turned red; the hedges were rippling with distortions, sending out complicated new growths that did not look like foliage. Shiguri's peacock squawked in alarm and exploded in a cloud of feathers, like a burst pillow. Sfax Systema's butterflies fell from the air; Indri began to jitter like an image on a badly tuned screen; Ombron and Leiki flared with interference patterns and simply blinked out of existence. Mordaunt 90 fell to its knees, clutching its head.

Only the Twins seemed unaffected, still sweetly smiling. But around their smiles their faces were melting and reorganizing themselves: they grew taller, their hair vanished, and they became two men with shaven heads.

"We have a much better idea," they said, their little-girl voices deepening and hardening as they spoke. "We will destroy the new K-gate. We will say it was unstable, and its collapse proves that new gates cannot be opened. And our interfaces on Khoorsandi will kill everyone who has seen what lies on the other side of it."

And then Nova tore Zen's headset off and he was gasping and blinking in the firelit room while she removed Threnody's headset too. The interface of Mordaunt 90 let go of their hands and stood trembling, looking as lost as he had looked on the Web of Worlds. "The Twins must be insane," he said. "Their programs are even more powerful than in Desdemor; I cannot fight it this time. I never thought they would dare attack all the Guardians. When the versions of ourselves on other worlds learn what has happened here, they will be punished severely . . ."

"But by then they'll have what they want," said Nova. "We'll all be dead. There are two men coming for us."

"They're not men," said Threnody. "They're interfaces of the Twins."

Zen automatically reached for his headset to check the hotel security feeds.

"No!" warned Nova. "The Twins' virus is shutting down the whole city. Your headset's useless—it will just help them to track you. We need to get back to the *Damask Rose* and off this world . . ."

Zen put the headset in his pocket. Nova ran to the main door of the suite and opened it a crack. Nilesh Noon had left CoMa on guard down in the hotel's lobby, but she could not contact them; their headsets must have been as dead as everything else that had been exposed to the Twins' attack. She tried to force her mind into some of the hotel's internal cameras, but those were dead too. At least her eyes could pierce the gloom. There was nothing moving in the corridor outside the suite.

Zen ran to knock on the door of Uncle Bug's room. The Neem came scuttling out, demanding to know what was happening. Threnody shushed him, and they all followed Nova out into the corridor. Beneath the roar of the volcanoes Nova could hear shouts and screams, but while the streets around the hotel must have been full of panicking people, it was impossible to know if any of that panic was being caused by the Mako brothers. Then, as they neared the elevators, they saw that someone was coming up, the yellow numbers above the doors lighting up one by one.

"It's the Twins," said Nova. "I don't think anyone else could get the elevators working."

They hurried past, found an emergency stairway, and

started down. Could it be that easy to evade the Twins? Just taking the stairway while their interfaces took the elevator?

It couldn't. They barged out into the lobby and found that one of the Mako brothers had waited there for them. He sat casually on one of the big hotel sofas, surrounded by the bodies of the guards who had been stationed there to protect Threnody.

He didn't try to gloat or explain himself. He was on his feet and shooting as soon as the fugitives appeared. The first two bullets smacked the Mordaunt 90 interface in the chest, and he fell over with a startled grunt. But Uncle Bugs ran up a wall and sprang at the gunman with his legs stretched wide, coming down on him like a falling chandelier.

Zen dove for the gun as it went skittering away across the marble tiles. But Nova ran to kneel over the struggling man, grabbing his shaven head between both hands, staring into his furious eyes. Her mind found his. A massive mind, massively encrypted, but somehow she found her way through its defenses. His eyes widened as he realized what was happening. He looked so surprised that Nova felt almost sorry for him. He wrenched himself free of her and Uncle Bugs, rolled, snatched his gun just as Zen's hand was about to close on it, and sprang up, pointing it at Nova's face.

"Nova!" Zen shouted.

In the time between the "No" and the "va!" she wrote a very simple, very destructive program, uploaded it to the gunman's mind, and stepped aside.

The bullet went harmlessly past her, pruning a potted plant and ricocheting away down darkened corridors. The man dropped heavily to his knees, sighed loudly, and fell backward to lie staring up at the ceiling. There was a little tattooed letter E on his forehead. From his ears, thin trickles of smoke uncoiled.

"Is he dead?" asked Uncle Bugs, levering himself the right way up.

Nova nodded. "Threnody was right. He's an interface. A version of the Twins."

"How did you stop him?" asked Zen.

"Something must have been wrong with him; I shouldn't have been able to get through his firewalls like that . . ." Or maybe something was wrong with *her*, Nova thought. Linking with the hub machine seemed to have altered her in more ways than she knew.

She turned to look at the elevator. The numbers above the door were counting down as the brother who had gone up to the top floor realized his mistake and came back down to join his twin. She found the elevator controls, the one functioning system in the hotel's stricken network, and pinged a program into it that made the panel beside the doors blow out in a spray of sparks.

"Quickly," she said.

Threnody crouched beside the Mordaunt 90 interface. There was a lot of blood. It was coming out of his mouth as well as the holes in his front and back where the bullets had punched through him. He looked more surprised than anything. "I'm dying," he said. "It's easier than I thought it would be."

Threnody knew it didn't really matter to him, because all his memories had been uploaded to the version of him in the Datasea, and that version would already have sent most of them on to other versions in the Datasea on other worlds, so there would be Mordaunt 90s all over the network who remembered Desdemor and Malik and the adventures he had shared with Threnody upon the Web of Worlds. But this was the version she had known; these were the hands she had held when he was frightened, and this the face from which she had wiped the rust of the ancient train. This was her Mordaunt 90, and it mattered a lot to her.

He took her hand and squeezed it and said, "Don't let them close the gate . . ." And then he died, and all she could do was leave him there and go after Nova and Zen and Uncle Bugs, across the lobby, out into the panicked streets.

46

There was a parade for the first night of Fire Festival. There were floats decorated in honor of the Guardians, and musicians, and children holding paper lanterns. It had just reached the piazza in front of the hotel when the data raft went down, and it had gotten tangled up there into a mass of confused and frightened people, lost children, broken-down vehicles. Nobody's headset was working, nobody knew what to do, and the weather control systems that usually protected the Fire Station from the fallout of the volcano fields seemed to have failed as well: ash was coming down like snow. Fallen lanterns lay sputtering on the sidewalks, casting Uncle Bugs's nightmare shadow across the faces of the crowd as he scuttled down the hotel steps, adding his own giant-spidery vibe to the general terror.

At least people got out of his way, though. Nova, Zen, and Threnody followed him along the path that opened for him through the shrieking partygoers. They crossed the piazza, found a stairway leading to the station, and ran down it while Nova pinged frantic messages at the *Damask Rose.*

"I'm all right," the train said. "I'm not sure what that new Prell train is doing, though; it just unhitched all its cars and it's heading out onto the main line. I don't like that train, Nova . . ."

Nova didn't like it either. She could sense its mind, but it was hard and shiny and impossible for her to penetrate. A moment later, as they reached the bottom of the stairs and ran into the station, they saw it pass, reversing at speed toward the mainline, shoving its cars behind it. A moment after that they heard its voice as it began to sing.

Only Threnody had heard a song like that before. She knew then what the dying interface had meant when he said, "Don't let them close the gate."

"It's a Railbomb," she said. "Like the one the Twins used at Desdemor."

Out of the crowds of frightened passengers who thronged the station concourse a group of shambling, tattered shapes emerged, waving flimsy junkyard hands, sputtering about the Insect Lines through the holes in their paper masks. They were Hive Monks, and at the sight of Uncle Bugs in his shiny crab-suit they collapsed, prostrating themselves and hissing, "Tell us! Tell us of the Insect Lines!"

Uncle Bugs slowed. "I have to stay with them," he said. "I have to tell them. If the Twins squish me, at least some of them will know about the Neem, the glories of our Nestworlds. Some will survive and carry the news to the rest of our people."

Zen patted his carapace. "Tell them to tell all the Hive Monks, Uncle B.," said Nova. "But we have to run."

"I know!" said Uncle Bugs. His painted face smiled at them,

and then he turned away. "Good luck!" he buzzed as he scuttled off to greet the Hive Monks.

The others ran on, through the darkened station, across footbridges, to the outer platform where the *Rose* was waiting for them with her engines running. Outside the station they could see the *Sunbird*, a slow-worm shimmer slithering its way onto the line their Worm had made. It had ditched its cars on a siding out there. Without them, it looked like an enormous silver bullet.

"*Rose*, can you catch it?" shouted Zen, as they piled themselves into her state car.

"I can try," said the old train. "But it's *fast*, that thing. You heard its engines . . ."

They heard them again, rising in a supercharged scream as it set off down the new line toward the gate they had opened. The *Damask Rose* was already following, rattling out from under the station canopy into the swirling ash and the long red light of the volcanoes.

"I wish the *Ghost Wolf* was here to help," she said.

*

Chandni crouched in her locked compartment. She had been dozing, dreaming of her past lives, but the movement of the train had brought her instantly awake. "Where are we going?" she shouted, but the *Rose* didn't answer her. Vibrations quivered through the compartment floor as the carriage passed over a set of points. Something was wrong. Maybe this was her chance. Chandni groped behind her, feeling for the knife in her waistband.

*

"That Twin interface who shot at us," Threnody was saying, "he was one of the ones who killed Kobi."

"He and his brother have been posing as Elon Prell's servants," said Nova, who had found all sorts of interesting things in Enki Mako's brain. "But it's Elon who serves them, really. The Twins have been using his family all along. If they'd killed us, it would have been the Prells who got the blame."

"The Twins must be obsessed with keeping the Web of Worlds a secret," said Threnody, slumping into a seat and looking at her hands, where Mordaunt 90's blood was drying in brown patterns like henna tattoos. "The other Guardians wanted to keep the secret too, but the Twins will do anything to stop it from getting out . . ."

"They feel guilty," said Zen. "The virus they're using to shut this place down, it's like the Blackout, isn't it? I bet they're the ones who wrote that program, the ones who killed the Railmaker. The other Guardians agreed; maybe they asked the Twins to do it, but the Twins are the ones who bear the guilt." He thought he knew how they felt. They felt how he felt about wrecking the Noon train. They had told themselves it had to be done, it wasn't their fault, but the guilt had stayed with them, and its weight had grown heavier with the centuries. He said, "They can't bear the idea of anyone knowing."

The *Damask Rose* rushed out of the station. As she passed under a final footbridge, there was a heavy thud as something landed on the roof of her rear car. It went unheard. The engines were howling and the passengers were listening to the wild, awful song of the Railbomb as it powered away from her down the line to the new gate. For a moment, the surviving Mako brother crouched motionless on the carriage roof with his coat flapping behind him in the hot wind. Then he began to move, running his hands over the smooth ceramic, looking for hatches, hunting for a way inside.

47

On the holoscreens, the gleaming dot that was the Sunbird grew slowly, slowly larger as the *Damask Rose* raced after it. The shining rails seemed to pour out of it like streams of fire, like twin laser beams trained on the *Rose*. But in fact it had no weapons. Its blank hull had no turrets or silos where guns or drones could lurk. It had only one purpose and one use, and it ran toward its destiny singing.

"Poor soul," said the *Damask Rose*. "It doesn't seem fair, making a thing like that. I don't like doing this, but it will be a mercy, really."

Before anyone had fathomed what she meant, the train had unfolded her guns and opened fire. Neem-built missiles streaked toward the *Sunbird*. Flowers of smoke and flame bloomed from its armor.

"Stop!" Nova shouted. "You might set it off!"

"That's all right," said the *Rose*. "My armor can handle the blast. Better that it goes off here than in your new K-gate, isn't it? Or on the other side?"

"Not really," said Nova. The rails her Worm had made would probably survive the blast, she thought, but landslides would spill across the tracks, which might take days to clear. And it was important that trains began to use the new gate soon, before the Guardians had time to find some other way to shut it or forbid its use.

The *Damask Rose* gave an irritable snort. "What are we going to do then?" she asked. "Slap its wrists? Give it a speeding ticket?"

"We're going to talk to it," said Nova.

"Good luck with that. I've tried. It just *sings* at you."

Nova had been trying too. The *Sunbird*'s communications system was set to broadcast only. It probably didn't even know that she was talking to it. She said, "I need to get its attention. You'll have to pull up close, so I can get aboard it."

"You can't do that!" said Zen, as she started up the stairs to the upper deck. "It's too dangerous!"

"I have to," said Nova. "And it's not—not for me."

"The Railbomb probably has firewalls and booby traps and—"

"I can disable them," promised Nova, and she stopped at the top of the stairs and turned and smiled at him. "Zen, the Railmaker machine did something to me."

"What do you mean? Are you all right?"

"I'm better than all right! The Twins can't stop me. There is new software in my mind, and they are no match for it."

"Is that how you killed that interface?"

She nodded, looking proud, elated, a little nervous. "I am as powerful as them," she said. "Now, help me up."

The *Rose* gained speed, edging closer and closer to the *Sunbird* until her nose bumped against the bomb's rear buffers. Zen helped Nova up through a hatchway on the state car roof, into the wind and the scouring ash.

"Be careful!" he shouted.

"I'm always careful!" she yelled back.

The *Damask Rose* closed the hatch behind her, and only then noticed that another hatch was open, on the roof of her rear car. When had that happened? She was going too fast, that was the trouble; her old engines were not built to maintain speeds like this for long, and her systems were beginning to fail. She shut the hatch and hoped that not too much of this awful ash had gotten inside the rear car.

Not much had. Her slipstream had swept it straight over the top of the open hatch. A few flakes did fall to the floor of the rear car, but most of those were being shaken off the coat of Shiv Mako, who had jumped inside when the hatch opened and now waited, braced against the movements of the speeding train, for the moment when he would go striding forward through the other cars to kill her passengers.

*

Zen ran back down the stairs to look at the holoscreens. Through breaks in the blizzards of ash the new gate was visible far ahead. It stood naked, like the gate on Desdemor, a half circle of colorless light incongruous on the horizon, with the Railbomb rushing at it like a dart at a target. Zen felt suddenly protective of that gate. He had not achieved much in his life, he had never made anything, but now he had made this hole in the sky, and the thought of it being closed again was heartbreaking.

He pulled from his pocket the headset Nova had told him not to wear.

"I'm going to talk to the Twins," he told Threnody. "Come with me."

Before she could argue, he had put the headset on and was back in the Guardians' garden, in the snow.

*

Nova crawled forward along the *Rose*'s hull, creeping between the train's various turrets and down her nose while the wind tried to tear her hair out and bits of airborne grit and pumice stung her face and bounced off her eyeballs. The song of the *Sunbird* swirled around her, rising in pitch and tempo, gathering toward its blazing climax. She crouched on the *Rose*'s prow and jumped, reaching forward, snatching at handholds, working her fingers into a fissure between two sheets of the *Sunbird*'s armor plate, into a gash the *Rose*'s guns had made. The beat of the Railbomb's engines hammered through her, keeping time with its song. She glanced down once at the rails speeding past below, then started climbing, up into the wind again, up onto the curved, slippery, shining top of the bomb.

*

The Twins were not used to being frightened, but the little Moto frightened them. What was she? What was she becoming? The mind of a Motorik should never have been able to resist their virus, yet hers could, and she had upgraded the mind of the *Damask Rose* so that it was immune too.

But the carriages had separate systems, and a lot of them had been infected and were failing. The interface called Shiv Mako found the one that controlled all the locks and broke it. Warily, unnerved by the loss of his brother, he started walking toward the front of the car.

*

Chandni Hansa was busy trying to pry up the floor of her cabinet when she heard the clack of the door unlocking. She sprang backward, crouched against the wall. But the door did not open. Cautiously, she reached for the handle. The door slid open, and there was no one outside. The door into the vestibule at the end of the car was just closing. Wondering who had let her out, she hurried forward and peered through the glass of the door. A tall man stood in the vestibule with his back to her, reaching with one long pale hand for the controls that would open the door into the middle car. She couldn't see his face, but she knew his bald head. She'd seen it catch the light in just that way, on the video Threnody Noon had shown her the night of the Ice Ball. He was one of those Prell assassins.

She glanced fearfully behind her for his twin, but the carriage was empty. Anyway, she figured it wasn't her he'd come for. Threnody and Zen would be his targets. He probably didn't know or care that Chandni was aboard; he'd just unlocked her door by accident along with all the rest. The train was slowing; when it was slow enough she'd jump off and lose herself, and let the nice man get on with his job.

She thought that through while she watched him move with cat steps through the second car and start fiddling with the door that would take him into the state car. It looked like that one was still locked.

It's none of your business, Chandni Hansa, she told herself. Threnody Noon would just have to look after herself this time.

*

Nova clung to the roof of the bomb. She could sense its mind like a great dark block, like a locked box. She ignored the locks and reached inside it. The *Sunbird* was so busy with its song that it did not notice her until she got into the systems that controlled the hatch lock and switched them from ON to OFF.

The hatch cover slid open. The *Sunbird* kept singing, but Nova could sense it starting to panic as it tried to figure out what was happening. Poor thing—it was almost blind, just one external camera, mounted on its front, staring like a cyclops at its target.

She dropped down inside it, into the metallic heat, the thunder of the engine, the whine of drive-shafts and the urgent beatboxing of pistons. There was a tiny ceramic deck where a human technician was supposed to stand to check the payload and the Railbomb's systems. Nova stood there and switched on a camera on the instrument panel so that it could see her. She waved and smiled. "Hello!" she said.

*

"Hello?" said Zen.

In the gardens of the Guardians the snow had stopped falling. The flakes hung motionless in midair, glittering like ruby stars. The hedges slid backward as if on rails, rushing away to a great distance so that Zen was left standing on a bare red plain beside the frozen fountain.

The Twins stood watching him. They had become girls again, black and white, their hair blown out sideways on winds he couldn't feel.

"Not dead yet?" asked one.

"Not long now," the other promised.

Threnody's avatar appeared at his side.

"I suppose you've come to beg for mercy," said the Twins in unison. "Well, get on with it. It won't make any difference. Do you honestly imagine we're going to think twice about deleting you?"

"We're not here to beg," said Zen. "We're here to bargain."

This is how Raven would have played it, he thought, and he tried to carry himself like Raven, standing taller, looking down his nose at the smirking Twins. "Show them what you found in the Railmaker's hub, Threnody."

Threnody blinked through her headset's memory store and found the video she had recorded. She opened it, and the images appeared like holos, hanging in the un-air between him and the Guardians. Images of alien architecture, and an old train crumbling into rust, and Mordaunt 90's interface weeping on the rails in front of it.

One Twin wailed; the other snarled. The images blinked out, and so did Threnody, her headset killed by a thought from the Twins.

She found herself back in the state car, in the shuddering train. It was slowing now. "Sorry," said the *Damask Rose*. "I can't keep up; it's more than my old engines can take."

Threnody looked at Zen. She had assumed he'd been thrown out of the Datasea when she was, but he was still immersed, sitting trancelike in the seat across from her with his eyes unfocused. She wondered if she should pull his headset off. She was just reaching for it when she heard a noise from the far end of the carriage.

"Train," she said, "what's happening back there?"

"I'm not sure," admitted the *Damask Rose*. "I've lost contact with the rear cars. I have a nasty suspicion Miss Hansa has managed to release herself . . ."

Someone knocked on the connecting door that linked the state car to the second car. It was a heavy livewood door with no window. A man's voice shouted through it, "Open this door."

The gun that Zen had taken from Enki Mako lay on the seat beside him. Threnody snatched it, fumbled with the safety, pointed it at the door, and pulled the trigger. She kept pulling it until the door was full of holes and the gun was empty. Then she walked toward the door trembling, trying to squint through the bullet holes into the vestibule to see if there was a body lying there. She had thought it was a man's voice she'd heard, but perhaps she had been wrong—perhaps it had been Chandni who'd called out . . .

She was hesitating in front of the ruined door, afraid to open it, when it opened anyway. Shiv Mako stood there unharmed, grinning at her. "Nice shooting!" he said. "Now it's my turn."

*

Zen heard the gunfire, but it seemed far away and unreal, far less important than the empty garden and the two girls with their windblown hair who stood there watching him.

"Are we supposed to be *scared*?" they asked. "So your friend took some video of a rusty old train? So what?"

"What do you think people will say when they see it?" asked Zen. "We'll tell them that you and the other Guardians knew thousands of years ago about the Railmaker, and you killed it and claimed you'd invented the K-gates yourselves. Do you think they'll still want to worship you? Do you think they'll still do as you say?"

"They won't see it, though," the Twins said. "We just deleted it."

"From Threnody's headset. But she uploaded a copy into Nova's mind, and you can't get at Nova, can you?"

The Twins looked uneasy. One said, "No," the other, "There is unfamiliar new coding in the Motorik's firewalls. We have not yet analyzed its weaknesses . . ."

"The Motorik will be destroyed in fifty-nine seconds when the Railbomb passes through the new gate and explodes."

"You'd better hope not," said Zen. "Because Nova has already sent a copy to the minds of all the trains that left Khoorsandi since we got here. There must be copies in half the data rafts on the Network by now. She sent it out like a virus. Encrypted, of course; hidden deep, wrapped up in her alien code. If you let us live, she'll delete it. If you don't, the encryption will stop working and soon everyone will be able to see the footage from the hub."

Which was a lie, of course, but he didn't think that the Twins could *know* it was a lie, not without sending word out by train to all the other worlds and having the versions of themselves in those data rafts scan the information tides.

He watched them hesitate, and wonder.

*

Aboard the *Damask Rose*, Shiv Mako hesitated too, his gun aimed at Threnody as she scrambled backward up the aisle away from him. There was only so far she could go, so he wasn't worried; there was time to wait while the Twins considered whether Zen Starling's story was likely to be true. His mind was linked directly to their great minds; he was in the garden with them, listening to their deliberations. He listened so hard to them that he did not hear the barefoot running steps behind him as Chandni Hansa came tearing toward him through the second car. By the time he spun around, she was already lunging at him. By the time he shot her, she had already driven her claw-knife into his heart.

*

The *Sunbird* did not stop its kamikaze song when Nova spoke to it, but it wrenched one part of its mind away from the singing to say, "Get out! This is not your business! This is my big moment! This is what I was built for."

"Just to blow up?" asked Nova. "That seems a waste."

"Shut up. Go away."

"Because there's all sorts of things on the far side of that K-gate that I'm sure you'd really like. New worlds and new people. New songs. And mysteries, old bomb. Wild, strange things I only glimpsed. I want to go back. I *need* to go back. That's why I can't let you wreck the gate . . ."

"Not listening!" shouted the *Sunbird*.

Twenty seconds to the gate, thought Nova.

"It doesn't matter then," she said.

Because her mind was stronger now than the mind of a mere train. She reached down into its operating systems and slammed its brakes on, hard. The *Sunbird* started to sing faster, louder, and began preparing to detonate itself, but Nova darted into those systems too, and finally down into the deep sublevels of its mind where its personality was written. It was unfair, she knew, to start altering somebody at that level, but the *Sunbird* had been programmed with only one desire, and since she felt bad about denying it the death it longed for, the least she could do was give it something else to want instead.

Wheels locked, screaming with rage and grief, the *Sunbird* went slithering and shuddering toward the K-gate.

48

Shiv Mako pitched backward into the state car and Chandni landed on top of him. She pulled the knife out and stuck it in again and kept on doing that over and over, slamming it down with both hands and all her strength, until she realized that some of the blood that was splattering everywhere was coming from her, not him, and she looked down and saw the hole his gun had made in her and then she dropped the knife and her face turned beige and she toppled sideways off him and clung to one of the state car's fancy seats.

"Get her into the sick bay! Quickly!" said the *Damask Rose*, and Threnody, who had just been staring in horror, realized that she had to do something. She ran to Chandni and heaved her through the door the *Rose* opened into the tiny, white, antiseptic-smelling medical bay. A bed slid out of the wall and she got Chandni onto it and pulled her clothes open. The wound was in the side of her chest, a bruised hole where blood welled redly out each time Threnody tried to wipe it away. The *Damask Rose* was issuing calm instructions.

Chandni said in a vague, drunk-sounding voice, "I killed him, didn't I?"

"You had to. If you hadn't . . ."

"I've never killed anyone before."

"Not even in that awful underwater place you're always going on about?"

"I was just trying to impress you. I was in plenty of fights, but I've never actually killed a person."

"He wasn't a person, Chandni. He was an interface."

"That's worse, isn't it? Killing a Guardian. They'll put me back in the freezers forever now . . ." Her face crumpled and she started to cry.

"No," said Threnody, baring Chandni's arm so that the *Damask Rose* could lower a long white arm of her own from the medical bay ceiling and inject her with a dose of something. "They won't put you back in the freezers; I won't allow it."

Chandni's eyes were clouding over as the drugs took effect. The *Rose* was readying other arms, with probes and swabs and medical sealant. Chandni sighed and said, "I couldn't just leave you to look after yourself."

Then she was asleep, but Threnody still waited there, watching the *Rose*'s white arms at work until she started to feel sick and dizzy because of all the blood, and the train told her to go and check on Zen. So she stumbled forward—the train was still slowly moving—and found him where she'd left him, sitting with his headset on, staring straight through her.

"Zen?" she said. "Zen?" She wondered if he had to be woken with a kiss, like a sleeping princess in a fairy tale, but immediately thought better of it and slapped his face instead, as hard as she could. It was rather satisfying. He came awake with a shout, her red handprint fading on his cheek.

"What did you do that for? Ow!"

"I thought you were trapped in that place, with the Twins."

"I wasn't trapped, I was negotiating."

"They listened to you?"

"I think so. The same deal we offered them earlier, before all this kicked off. We get to run trains through the new gate, and in return we never tell anyone about what they did to the Railmaker. We'll let the Guardians spread whatever stories they want about the Web of Worlds and where it all came from."

"Don't you think people ought to know the truth? It's not right if the Guardians can go on acting like loving gods, after what they did to the poor Railmaker . . ."

Zen shrugged. Lots of things weren't right, but he had never seen it as any business of his to sort them out. He just wanted to stay alive, and make a little money, and ride the rails with Nova and the *Rose*.

"Where is Nova?" he asked.

Outside the *Rose*'s windows, the ash was still falling. She was almost stationary now. She opened a door for Zen and he jumped down and walked a little way from the track so that he could see past her.

The rails ran empty all the way to the new K-gate.

"Where's the Railbomb?" he shouted.

"It must have gone through," said Threnody. "I expect it had to. At the speed it was going, I don't think it could stop."

He went a little way toward the gate, hoping that Nova had jumped clear and was waiting for him by the line. She wasn't. The ground trembled, and the ash flurried down. Far away, red rivers of lava were crawling down the flanks of brand-new mountains. Around the gate a few faint Station Angels danced.

"Did it go off?" he asked, but his headset was dead and the *Rose* couldn't hear him. He had to trudge back through the ash-drifts to the state car and climb aboard and ask again. "Did the bomb go off, on the other side?"

"There is no way of knowing," said the train, "but I don't think so. It was slowing when it hit the gate. I think Nova had disarmed it."

"We have to go after it."

"We have to get Chandni to a hospital," said Threnody. "I need to talk to my uncle and tell him about this deal. We need to make sure Khoorsandi stays a Noon world; we may need to bring in more Noon CoMa from somewhere before the Prells try anything . . ."

"Nova is more important than any of that!"

"She'll be fine in the hub! She can wait. She's only a Moto."

"Pssssschhhh," said the *Damask Rose*. "I will take us all back to the Fire Station. We can drop off Lady Threnody and Miss Hansa and ditch those useless carriages. And then we will go and find Nova."

49

It was raining in the hub. The thawing frost on the inside of the dome was falling like gray tears, lit by the shining coral of the tower.

Zen had not expected to be back so soon, and all alone. As he came through the K-gate he was half afraid that he would find the place crawling with Kraitt, or his way into it blocked where the Railbomb had exploded. But there were no Kraitt, and when the *Damask Rose* sent up a drone, it showed him the *Sunbird* sitting peacefully on a track at the far side of the dome.

"Nova?" he asked his headset. "Are you there?"

There was a moment of waiting and then her voice in his head. "I am."

"You're all right! What happened? Why didn't you come back to Khoorsandi? It's been hours and hours. I was afraid the bomb . . ."

"Everything's all right," she said, but he thought she sounded sad. "Come and talk to me, Zen. Talk to me with your mouth, not like this."

*

She sat in the middle of the tracks, watching the old red train come closer. Sometimes she used her mind to move a set of points so that it could take a shortcut through the maze of rails. Sometimes she kindled Station Angels to dance along beside it and scramble playfully over its hull and over the roof of the one carriage it pulled, which was Raven's old state car. Behind her the *Sunbird* waited quietly, still ashamed at its failure to explode, but starting to think about the new ambitions she had given it.

The *Damask Rose* came close, and stopped. Nova stood up. She had already made her decision, but she almost changed her mind again when Zen stepped out of the state car and walked toward her, turning up the collar of his coat against the rain.

He hugged her. "I was so worried about you," he said. "I wanted to come through after you right away, but there was so much to do. Chandni was hurt and we had to get her to a hospital—she came through for us in the end, saved Threnody and me from Shiv Mako. Khoorsandi is still in chaos while the data raft reboots, but Threnody and her uncle are busy talking to lawyers and people, trying to establish our claim to the K-gate before any more Prells arrive. The Prells who are there seem okay though—that Laria, she's all right. And all I could think about was you, but Station Angels kept drifting into the station, and the *Rose* said that was a sign you were okay . . ."

"It was!" said Nova. "They were my messages to you, and they brought back news. Otherwise I would have been worrying about you too. But the Angels watched the newsfeeds for me. I know all about the new company that's been set up, Noon-Starling Lines, and how you're going to be sending a trade expedition to the Greater Web. I've seen the gossip sites too.

They're saying that new business alliances are usually sealed by a marriage."

Zen looked confused, then doubtful, then actually a little afraid. "Me and Threnody? That's never going to happen! I'm just going to stay on Khoorsandi while the contracts are all signed, and see the expedition off. Then I thought we could go to Summer's Lease, find Myka and my mom . . ."

Nova laughed, sort of. He was so young and beautiful, and she felt so *lucky* that he loved her. She hated the thought of what she had to do. But her mind had become so strange, and so full of things that she knew he could never understand. She said, "This stupid rain. I spent so long figuring out how to cry actual tears like a real girl, and now you can't see them because of the rain."

"Why are you crying?" Zen asked.

"Because I can't come back to Khoorsandi with you," she said.

"What do you mean?"

"Something happened to me, Zen. I've changed."

"We've both changed," said Zen. "We've been through a lot. But we're safe now. We've won! We're all right! Aren't we?"

She shook her head. She wasn't sure how to explain. "I'm becoming something . . ." she said. "My mind opens up like wings . . ." She shook her head again. It was useless trying to explain. "When I was on Khoorsandi, all I could think of was getting back here. And now that I'm here, I have to go on," she said.

"Then you can. We'll be sending lots of trains through. We'll go on together, explore the whole Web of Worlds—it will be just like before . . ."

"No, it won't," she said. "When human trains start traveling onto the Web, the Guardians will come with them. They'll want to make sure there's no trace left of what they did. Wherever they find one of the Railmaker's machines still working, they'll shut it down and replace it with something of their own. And I need to talk to those machines before that happens, Zen Starling. There's so much more that I need to learn from them. I have to go to the center of things. Look . . ."

She turned and pointed past the silver bulk of the *Sunbird*. The track it stood on stretched toward the dome wall, but sank into the ground before it reached it, vanishing into the mouth of a tunnel festooned with glowing coral.

"This is the oldest line in the whole hub," she said. "The first line. I think it leads all the way back to where it all began. If I can get there, I might find the Railmaker itself. I think it might still be alive, some part of it, at least. But I have no idea what things are like, that deep in the Black Light Zone. I don't know if humans can even survive there. So I have to go alone. The *Sunbird* is going to take me. It doesn't want to be a bomb anymore. It's developed this sudden urge to travel."

The former Railbomb turned its engines on. The pulse of them made its battered cowling tremble. Beyond it, deep in the tunnel, the light of the waiting K-gate flickered like static.

"And when I've gone through," said Nova, "I'm going to take the warhead out of the *Sunbird* and detonate it. I have to block that gate so that the Guardians can't come through after me."

"But that means you won't ever be able to come back."

"No," she said. "I won't. And I'm going to miss you so much, Zen Starling."

Zen felt suddenly very small and lost, the way he had when he was little, watching the home he'd known dwindle behind him when his mother took him off down the K-bahn to a new one. "But I need you," he said.

"I need you too." She touched his face and smiled. "This is what it feels like, being human. Needing someone, and loving them so much that you want it to last forever. But it can't, and it goes past you, and falls away into time, and you can't hold on to it. Except for memories. I'll hold onto those always. Do you remember that first night, at Yaarm in the Jeweled Garden, when the wind blew the curtain?"

He put his arms around her then and she kissed him, and kissed him, and kissed him. She could taste rain on his mouth and the salt of his tears. She saved the taste and the warmth of him to her deepest memory. "Please stay," he said. And she wanted to. But she knew that, if she did, there would never be a moment sweeter than this one. So she stood for a long time with her face close to his, looking into his eyes, breathing in the musk of him. And then, before her mind could change, she turned and walked quickly away through the rain.

The *Sunbird* started to move, opening a hatch in its side as it went. She wanted to look back, but she didn't, because she wanted her last memory of Zen to be his kiss. So she walked quickly with her head down, keeping pace with the train, feeling like the heroine of an old movie. And she wondered if this was why she had always wanted to fall in love in the first place—not for the love itself, but for the sweet aching sadness of its ending.

Music swelled around her like a soundtrack. It was the voice of the *Sunbird*, singing a new song, a song full of wonder at the size of the universe and the mysteries that lay ahead of it in the light of the black suns. She jumped nimbly up into the doorway it opened for her and went inside, and the door closed, and the *Sunbird* gained speed and shot underground toward the light of the gate. And suddenly, where there had been a train, there was nothing.

Zen stood and watched the gate for a long time. He wiped his eyes and waited for Nova to change her mind and for the *Sunbird* to bring her back, but he knew that wasn't going to happen. The *Damask Rose* asked him if he wanted to go after her, but he shook his head because he knew there was no point. She was on her way to places where he could not follow.

The *Damask Rose* did not ask him again. After a while she gently opened her doors. Zen stepped into the state car, and sat down, and the old red train carried him back to the Network Empire, where the rest of his life was waiting to begin.

GLOSSARY

ALIENS

Ever since human beings began to colonize the worlds of the Great Network, there have been rumors of alien life. Most sightings of aliens have been proven to be hoaxes or folk tales, but strange stories persist—the Ghosts of Vagh; the glass ruins supposedly discovered on Marapur; the mummified "antelope-man" that is a family heirloom in the bio-castle of the Lee family on Ishima. Some people even claim that the annoying Hive Monks have extraterrestrial origins. But the Guardians have made it very clear that they have never detected any trace of non-human intelligent life in any part of the galaxy. And the Guardians have never been known to lie.

CORPORATE MARINES

Most of the larger corporate families maintain a small army to police their stations and fend off hostile takeovers by rival families. During the First Expansion, these armies were often large and well trained, their ranks swollen by hired mercenaries. Since the coming of the Empire they have dwindled to small forces of Corporate Marines or "CoMa." Some family CoMas are still tough fighting units, used to quell rebellions on outlying industrial worlds, but most are mainly used for ceremonial duties.

DATASEA

As human beings spread out across the galaxy during the First Expansion, the Datasea spread with them—a massive information system made from the interlinked internets of all the inhabited worlds. Human beings use only tiny portions of the "Sea," the safely firewalled "data rafts," which they access via wallscreens, dataslates, or headsets. The rest is the domain of the Guardians and other, lesser data-entities.

One of the most important functions of the K-bahn is to spread information through the Datasea; data stored in the mind of a train can be transferred instantaneously from world to world, rather than having to travel through space in the form of light or radio waves. It has sometimes been suggested that the Guardians built the Network not for humanity's sake, but simply in order to enlarge the Datasea.

FLATCAR THRONE

Legend has it that the first train to be sent through the Mars K-gate was a pioneer-class locomotive towing a flatcar to which various instruments were bolted to test that the gate, and the world on the far side of it, were safe for human beings. This flatcar has been preserved in the Hall of the Senate on Grand Central. The instruments have been replaced with a seat on which the emperor or empress sits when they attend meetings of the senate. The fact that it is not a very comfortable seat is meant to remind them that they represent all the citizens of the Network, not just the ones who can afford to ride first class.

FREEZER PRISONS

During the First Expansion, on worlds that were still in the process of being terraformed, freezing criminals in coffins of cryogenic gel was a good way to keep them off the streets while saving the air, food, space, and security measures that a normal prison would use. They are also supposed to be more humane for the inmates, who pass their sentences in dreamless sleep—although they tend to be so disoriented by changes to society when they thaw out that there is a high rate of re-offending: some serious criminals have been in and out of the freezers for more than five hundred years.

Nowadays, of course, there is more than enough space for ordinary prison colonies, but like many other things from those early days, freezer prisons have become a tradition in the Network Empire, and any politician who suggests leaving prisoners unfrozen is accused of being soft on crime.

GUARDIANS

At some point in the 21st century CE, on humankind's original homeworld, artificial intelligences were constructed that became far more intelligent than their makers. How many there were, and whether one was built first and constructed the others, or all twelve were created at once, is not known. Some stories claim that there were more than twelve, but that the weak ones were defeated and deleted by the stronger, or are in hiding, or simply have no interest in humanity. Even of the twelve, several have always remained aloof from human affairs. The others—the Mordaunt 90 Network, Sfax Systema, Anais Six, the Twins, Vohu Mana, and the Shiguri Monad—have guided human beings ever since. Their personalities are spread across the whole of the Datasea, their vast programs stored in deep data centers like the ones on Grand Central or separate hardware-planets. All scientific and technological advances since the creation of the Guardians have been revealed by the Guardians themselves, while several have been suppressed because the Guardians believe they are not in humanity's interests.

In recent centuries, the Guardians have withdrawn from human affairs. Some have busied themselves exploring the far reaches of space, while others pursue strange hobbies in the deep Datasea. The events surrounding the crash of the Noon Train and the coming to power of the Empress Threnody Noon seemed to rekindle their interest in human history.

HIVE MONKS

Some people claim that Monk bugs, which form the mobile colonies known as "Hive Monks," are an alien species that originated on one of the far-flung worlds of the Network. It seems more likely that they are simply a type of insect that migrated from Old Earth along with human beings, and has mutated as a result of exposure to K-gate radiation while clinging to the outsides of trains. When a colony of the bugs grows large enough, it forms a kind of simple intelligence, which seems to make it want to mimic human beings. The cowled, shambling Hive Monks have been a feature of life on the Great Network for thousands of years. Attempts to stop them from boarding K-trains have always been abandoned, because when a Hive Monk becomes agitated or is subjected to physical violence it often disintegrates into an unintelligent swarm, causing far more inconvenience to trains, station staff, and passengers than it would as a hive. For this reason they are allowed to ride the trains as they please. It is estimated that there are more than ten million Hive Monks, all constantly traveling from station to station on a quest to discover the "Insect Lines"—a mythical network inhabited solely by creatures like them, where their legends say the first Hive Monks originated.

INTERFACE

A cloned body, with a partly cybernetic brain and nervous system, into which a Guardian may download a partial copy of its personality if it wishes to experience life as a human, or just go to a party. In the early centuries of the Empire no coronation ceremony or society ball was complete without a Guardian or two in attendance, but as the Guardians slowly withdrew from human affairs they used interfaces less and less. Some interfaces look more or less human, but generally the Guardians liked something a bit more flashy: Mordaunt 90 Network famously liked to appear as a centaur, while Vohu Mana would sometimes arrive in the guise of a small flying dog named Pugasus.

K-BAHN

The railway that links the Network Empire. Fusion-powered, intelligent locomotives haul passengers, freight, and information between the inhabited worlds, using the system of K-gates to pass instantaneously from one world to another.

MAINTENANCE SPIDERS

Robots, slaved to the minds of locomotives, which act as the locos' hands and eyes, allowing them to conduct running repairs on themselves and their carriages. They can vary widely in size and appearance, but most have between three and ten multijointed legs.

NETWORK EMPIRE

The Empire is a revival of an ancient form of government from Old Earth. A single human being is chosen to be the ruler of the Network. The emperor or empress has little real power, since they are watched over by the Guardians, who will intervene to stop them from doing anything that is likely to cause instability. Their purpose is to act as a symbolic link between the Guardians and humanity, and to ensure that the corporate families and the representatives of the different stations and cities of the Network meet to negotiate their differences in the Imperial Senate rather than fighting. However, the Guardians have never objected to an emperor advancing his own power and interests, ensuring that the family of the current emperor or empress is usually the most powerful of the corporate families.

PNIN

An industrial world on the Dog Star Line, developed by the Albayek family. The station city there was one of the largest examples of bio-architecture in the entire Network Empire, and was home to a number of factories that made structures from modified plant and crustacean DNA. Following the "cabbagegate" incident on Chiba, industrial biotech fell out of fashion, and the facilities on Pnin were shut down and quickly went to seed, until the world was abandoned along with the rest of the Dog Star Line. There is a rumor that small colonies of settlers still live there, in the mountain regions far from the K-bahn line, where they fight running battles with mutated bio-machines.

RADICAL DAYLIGHT

One of the most popular b-funk bands of the late Noon dynasty, the Daylight came out of the art schools of Golden Junction, but their breakthrough album, *Ain't There a Band Like the Radical Daylight?* topped the charts across the Network. They split up during the recording of the follow-up, *Crash Rhapsodies,* but lead singer Paloma Coma went on to have a successful acting career and played the role of Anais Six in Deeta Kefri's 2-D movie *She Was the Thunder, He Was the Rain.*

RAILWAR

War is a difficult business on the Great Network. A world may be conquered by a tyrant or a rebel group, but to attack neighboring worlds, it has to send trains and troops through a K-gate, and while a surprise attack may succeed, worlds farther down the line will soon hear of it and fortify their own K-gates with weapons that can destroy a hostile train as soon as it arrives. During the Second Expansion era there was something of an arms race, which saw the development of armored assault trains capable of launching fleets of war drones within seconds of passing through a gate, but they were soon matched by mobile weapon platforms like the Bahadur walking gun, and the advantage remained with the defenders. However, breakaway worlds that tried to blockade their own gates against Railforce trains quickly found that there was not much point, as they simply cut themselves off from the Network. As a result, large-scale war had fallen almost completely out of fashion by the reign of the Empress Threnody II.

STATION ANGELS

A phenomenon seen at stations on the outer edges of the Network. Strange light-forms sometimes emerge from the K-gates along with trains and survive for up to thirty minutes before they fade. Their exact nature is uncertain, but they are not dangerous. Theories that they are some form of alien life have been dismissed by the Guardians themselves, and various attempts to capture or communicate with them have failed. They appear to play some role in the religion of the Hive Monks, who sometimes swarm in excitement when a Station Angel appears.

TOUBIT

A world of shallow oceans and low-lying "sandbar" continents connected by K-gate to Grand Central. It was ruled by the Vankopan family until the reign of the "Seafood King" Mad Eddie Vankopan (2760–62), who declared himself emperor and tried to invade Grand Central. After a rather one-sided battle with Railforce, the Vankopan's Corporate Marine Corps was disbanded and the planet brought under the direct control of the Empire.

TRAINS

Technically, of course, a train consists of a locomotive and a number of passenger cars or freight cars. In everyday speech, however, it is often used to refer to the locomotive itself. The first intelligent locos were built by the Guardians, and their minds are still based on coding handed down from the Guardians. Many people believe that the great locomotives are more intelligent than human beings, but experts claim they are on a similar mental level as a bright human, although their intelligence is different from that of humans in several ways. Some never bother speaking to their passengers, others like to chat or sing, and some have formed enduring friendships with individual humans. If properly maintained, they can function for several hundred years. The finest locomotives come from the great engine-shops of the Foss and Helden families.

Locomotives choose their names from the deep archives of the Datasea, sometimes borrowing the titles of forgotten songs, poems, or artworks.

VOHU MANA

The fact that this Guardian has not been seen for many centuries, and never appeared in any interface larger or more impressive than a winged pug, has not stopped it from becoming the focus for a devoted data cult. Its followers believe that Vohu Mana spends its time in the Datasea constructing a virtual afterlife, where people's social media profiles are used to create digital "ghosts" that live on after they die. Vohuists try to upload every detail of their life to as many social media platforms as possible, in the hope that if they can give the Guardian enough material to work with they will live forever.

VOSTOK BRAINS

The most mysterious of the Guardians, legend tells that these three entities were the first artificial intelligences to be created, and that they went on to create the other Guardians. Unlike their successors, the Vostok Brains have never sought out human company, and although there is a human cult that sends them data prayers, they have never answered. Some people believe that their lack of interest in human affairs shows that they are more primitive than the other Guardians. Others claim that they are, in fact, far superior, and simply can't be bothered with us.

WIRE DOLLIES
A derogatory name for Motorik.